CATCH MY SMOKE

DEEANN

KEISHA ELLE

Copyright © 2019

Published by Urban Chapters Publications

www.urbanchapterspublications.com
ALL RIGHTS RESERVED
Any unauthorized reprint or use of the material is prohibited. No part of this book may be reproduced or transmitted in any form or by any means, electronic, or mechanical, including photocopying, recording, or by any information storage without express permission by the publisher. This is an original work of fiction. Name, characters, places and incident are either products of the author's imagination or are used fictitiously and any resemblance to actual persons, living or dead is entirely coincidental.
**Contains explicit languages and adult themes
suitable for ages 16+**

TEXT UCP TO 22828 TO SUBSCRIBE TO OUR MAILING LIST
If you would like to join our team, submit the first 3-4 chapters of your completed manuscript to
Submissions@UrbanChapterspublications.com

CONNECT WITH DEEANN

Website: http://www.iamdeeann.com
Facebook Author Page: http://bit.ly/DeeAnnFacebook
Reading group: http://bit.ly/DeeAnnsReadersDen
Twitter: http://bit.ly/DeeAnnTwitter
Instagram: http://bit.ly/DeeAnnIG
Email: iam.authordeeann@gmail.com

CONNECT WITH KEISHA ELLE

Website: www.keishaelle.com
Facebook Author Page: www.facebook.com/AuthorKeishaElle
Facebook Reading Group: www.facebook.com/groups/kickinitwithkeisha
Twitter: www.twitter.com/keisha_elle
Instagram: www.instagram.com/keisha_writes
Email: keisha.elle@yahoo.com

This book is dedicated to my brother, DJ. You're one of my biggest supporters and motivators, and you don't understand how I truly appreciate you. You give me strength, love, and motivation when I feel like quitting. You see more in me than I do myself, and I know that's why you continue to push me to be who you know I can be.

I love you so much, and I thank you for all you do. All the conversations we have about our future success...all those things will come to us VERY soon. We have to keep pushing and motivating one another to see the greatness we are destined for.

"Life is so easy. Life is so good. All good things come to me."

This book is dedicated to my daughter, Kiyan. You were my 'surprise' baby, but having you in my life has been such a blessing. Dealing with a child with challenges may be hard for some, but I wouldn't trade you for the world! You are unique in your own way.

You taught me about patience, overcoming obstacles, and how to keep shining when others try to dim my light. It's a beautiful thing when an eleven-year-old can do that for her mother.

Baby girl, you are and always will be my motivation. I thank God for you and your siblings every time I open my eyes. It's a privilege being your mother, and I can't wait to see what the future holds for you. I love you!

ACKNOWLEDGMENTS

DEEANN

First, I want to thank God for this gift. If it wasn't for Him, I wouldn't be where I am today, and I can't praise Him enough for it.

Secondly, I would like to thank my family. My husband, son, mother, siblings, nephews, and niece. I love and appreciate all of you so much. I'm grateful to have such an amazing support system, and just know I wouldn't be capable of moving forward if it wasn't for y'all.

UCP and Jah, I thank you all so much for the continuous support and drive. I'm so thankful to work alongside such a dope group of individuals. Family is the word that comes to mind whenever I think of y'all. We're so much more than meets the eye!

To my readers, old and new, thank you all for rocking with me. I pray you all continue rocking with me with future releases to come, and I pray I exceed expectations. Not only for y'all, but myself as well. As you read, I hope y'all enjoy this book more than Keisha and I enjoyed writing it, and boy…did we enjoy it!

ACKNOWLEDGMENTS

KEISHA ELLE

I want to take the time out to thank the talented authors that make up Urban Chapters Publications. UCP is more than just a group of amazingly supportive authors, we're a family! Thank you for the words of encouragement while DeeAnn and I worked hard to get this book done. It feels good to know that I'm a part of something much bigger than writing. I've developed friendships that will last even after I retire my pen. For that, I am grateful.

Thank you to my family for allowing me the space to write. My mother, husband, and kids have sacrificed a lot while I pursue my passion. I appreciate it more than they will ever know. I just hope that I continue making them proud.

Lastly, I want to thank the readers. With so many authors to choose from, I appreciate the fact that this book was given a chance. I hope that you enjoy this book as much as DeeAnn and I enjoyed writing it.

Now to the story...

PROLOGUE: CEASAR

Back in the day...

"Pay attention, nigga," I scolded Drako. "Can you get pussy off your brain for one minute and focus on the task at hand? Damn! That bitch ain't nobody." Drako took his dark eyes off the light-skinned cutie and glared at me as if he was offended.

"A'ight. A'ight. I'm focused."

"Good. Here's what we're gonna do."

I had his undivided attention as I laid out my plan. Earlier in the day, Mohammad, a slick-talking Arab cat who owned Bali's Corner Store, kicked me out for some stupid shit. He told me not to bring my Black ass back in his store because I refused to pay for the cheap strawberry Faygo in my hand. It was half empty when I walked in the store, which proved my point when I told him I didn't steal it. Besides, I had enough change in my pocket to buy a dozen Faygos if I wanted to. Instead of listening to my truth, he grabbed his cordless phone and dialed three digits that had me running with lightning-like swiftness. Five hours later, I still hadn't got over that shit. Mohammad fucked with the wrong muthafucka.

"You tryna rob Bali's?" Drako questioned, leaning in toward me. The sun had begun to set, making it difficult to see his full expression.

"Damn right! He accused me of stealing. I'ma show that nigga how it feels to be stole from."

Drako quickly surveyed our surroundings. We were nestled in between two abandoned buildings, but had a bird's eyes view of the front of the store. As Drako's eyes found their way back to Bali's and the same chick leaning against its brick exterior, he mouthed the words, "I'm wit it."

Not too many people would just go with the flow, but Drako was a rare breed. We met in the first foster home I was placed in three years prior. I'd been deemed a problem child, and none of my so-called family were willing to step up to the plate and help my ass. My mother couldn't do it alone. Drugs and alcohol consumed her life, making it damn near impossible to raise two kids. Wanting more than what she could offer, I turned to the streets and stirred up a whole lot of trouble in the process.

I was always down to make a quick buck. Petty crime was my thing. I stole to support my little sister, Kyan, and myself. I was thirteen-years-old when I ran up in the wrong nigga's apartment and started a cycle that would change my life forever. Unbeknownst to me, the mark was a retired cop, and I was sent straight to juvenile detention. After doing 366 days, I was sent back to my mother. That didn't last long. My probation officer showed up unexpectedly and after seeing the condition of our dingy project apartment and my mother passed out on the concrete steps, a call was made to Child Protective Services. Kyan and I were removed and placed into foster care.

Thankfully, Kyan and I were placed together. Big Momma was an older woman who kept way too many kids than she needed to. In addition to me and Kyan, there were five other kids calling the cramped, shotgun house a home. I was placed in a room with Drako and another kid who spent so much time running away that he was rarely even there.

Drako and I quickly became friends. Well, more like brothers. I was the knucklehead of the two, and Drako was the voice of reason. He would try to talk me out of all my dumb ass schemes to get money, but he always had my back. This was especially true when I stole two of Big Momma's rings and tried to pawn them. The fake ID I had didn't look anything like me, and the pawn shop worker was on it. He turned me away, forcing me to develop a plan B.

Drako was right in my ear, telling me to chill, but I wouldn't listen. He was a year younger than me, making me his superior. Judging by looks, you would have thought Drako was older than me. At thirteen, Drako had the height of an average-sized man, but the weight of one of the Olson Twins. That's exaggerating, but what he did have was a bird's chest and chicken legs. His skin was the color of milk chocolate, but smooth. He was lucky enough to not endure the teenage acne that I was plagued with. My much darker complexion had just began clearing up, thanks to prescription strength medication. Together, we were a force to be reckoned with.

I found a fiend begging for money in a nearby parking lot. I called him over, told him my plan, and agreed to split whatever money I received with him if he would pawn Big Momma's rings. I learned a valuable lesson that day. He went into the pawn shop, pawned the rings, and caught the Holy Ghost as his long legs sprinted in the opposite direction. Needless to say, I was out both the rings and the cash. He played my stupid ass for a fool.

Instead of telling me 'I told you so', Drako chased the man down. I don't know where his endurance came from, but as the fiend slowed his pace, Drako increased his. Tired and out of breath, I stopped halfway down the block. Just as I looked up from kneeling to catch my breath, I saw Drako take ol' boy down with a firm right hook. Adrenaline coursed through me as I found my strength and pressed on. Catching up with my boy, we beat the nigga so bad, he all but begged us to take the money. As Drako finished him off with a swift kick to the midsection, I confiscated my money from his pocket, along with a small baggie of some white rocks.

"What's that?" Drako asked, watching me stuff the baggie in my pocket.

I knew what it was. It was the same shit my momma smoked. The same shit she sold her pussy for. The same shit that had her looking like Skeletor. The same shit that had the smart getting rich, and the dumb addicted. Drako might have been a ward of the state, but he was naïve to the street life. Big Momma already considered me a bad influence. There was no need to add to that assumption and put him up on game.

"It's nothing."

Brushing off his question, I strolled back toward our house with Ceasar trailing close behind. We went about our day as normal. Everything was cool until Big Momma went to put on her rings. Of all the days to switch it up, she had to choose that day.

"Drake-Anthony!" she yelled, calling my nigga by his government name. "Have you seen my rings?"

Just as cool as can be, Drako appeared in her doorway and shook his head 'no'. I stood in his shadow, knowing my name would be called next. Anytime there was a problem, we were the first two questioned. According to Big Momma, she could always see the truth in Drako's eyes. Mine, on the other hand, were just like my mouth – filled with lies.

"Carl!"

I gritted my teeth, hating the way my daddy's name slipped off her tongue. Everybody and their mama called me Ceasar. Even the probation officers and CPS workers; hell, everyone respected my wishes. Everyone except Big Momma. She followed her own rules.

"Ma'am."

"Come here, boy!"

I brushed past Drako and entered her cramped quarters. Big Momma was a hoarder, still holding her 70's themed furniture captive. I swallowed the lump forming in my throat. The name suited her well. Big Momma was a tall woman with a thick frame and wide hips. I guess I wasn't moving fast enough. One of her large, rough hands grabbed me around the collar of my t-shirt and pulled me close.

"You don't take your sweet ass time when I'm talking to you, boy. What the hell is wrong with you?"

I didn't say shit. Big Momma put a fear in me that no woman had ever been able to do. She was like a man in a woman's body. Big Momma was no joke.

"You hear me talking to you, boy?"

"Yes, ma'am."

"Answer me then! Have you seen my rings?"

"No, ma'am."

She released her grip and peered at me through the small slits that had become her eyes. Cocking her head to the side, she eyed me suspiciously.

"Empty your pockets."

My eyes widened in surprise. My pockets. *Oh, no!* I wasn't emptying those.

"Now!" she barked.

I tried to push the money down and pull my pockets out halfway. Big Momma snatched me up, stuffing her big hand in each one. The seams busted under the pressure, releasing both the money and the drugs.

"What the hell?! Boy, where did you get all that money?"

"Wha-wha-what money?" I stuttered.

It was dumb, I know. I was caught red-handed, yet I refused to admit the obvious. There was no telling what she'd do if I told the truth.

"It's mine." Drako's voice rang out behind me. "He was holding it for me. I've been saving my allowance."

Big Momma looked from me to Drako, and back to me. She eased her hand on one of her huge hips and huffed. She saw right through his bullshit.

"Drake-Anthony! Boy, I ain't gave you all that money for no damn allowance. You get five dollars a week, and the way you been hitting up that candy store, I know you ain't got no damn money!"

I took a few steps back when her eyes returned to the fourteen bills with Andrew Jackson's face. Her gaze remained on the pile much longer than I expected. She opened her mouth to say something, but her voice was absent. I flinched when Big Momma took a step in my direction. I knew I couldn't take her, but I swear to God if she thought she was going to beat on me, she had another thing coming.

I balled my fists at my side as her hand came toward me. Instead of snatching me up, she reached down and fished the exposed baggie from the pile. *Shit!*

"What in the hell? I know this ain't—you doing drugs in my house, boy?"

"No, ma'am."

"What the fuck is this then?" She shook the bag in front of my face, as if it would restore my memory. It didn't work. I had my story and I was sticking to it.

"I don't know."

"Oh, you don't? Well...you're about to know!"

She began rummaging through her drawers until she produced a thick, leather belt. She swung it in my direction and missed. Catching her slipping, I lunged toward her and hit her with a two-piece. If the woman who gave me life didn't put her hands on me, I'd be damned if another broad did. I ain't proud of it, but that was the first time I put my hands on a woman. I was removed from the home later that night and placed in a different foster home.

Drako and I kept in touch. It wasn't hard. I was only moved about a mile away, keeping us at the same school. He kept me updated on my sister, Kyan, and I gained a brother from another mother. Real talk. Drako and I were as close as if we shared the same blood. He was the one person I could count on for anything. I had his back, and he had mine.

"A'ight. Cool."

I squinted my eyes and saw Kyan emerging from the store. She said something to her girl perched up against the building. Seconds later, they were on the sidewalk, distancing themselves from the store. When they were halfway down the block, I whistled to get their attention.

Kyan nervously glanced around, but quickly crossed the street and walked over to me. Her friend took her sweet ass time, but eventually made it to where we stood.

"I thought I was meeting you at the bus stop," Kyan huffed. "What happened?" She stepped past me and wrapped her arms around Drako.

"Change of plans," I countered. "What's up, Joie?" I didn't particularly care for the girl, but I didn't want to be rude. She never did anything to me personally, but the way she dismissed every nigga that stepped in her direction made me think she was a high maintenance broad.

"Hey, Ceas," she said with a half-smile.

Drako cleared his throat. I opened my mouth to speak, but Kyan made the introduction first.

"He's so rude, ain't he? Joie, this is my brother, Drako. Drako, this is my girl, Joie."

My dude hit her with a nod, and her olive cheeks blushed in response. That was a first. Joie gave every nigga I knew the side eye, including me. I wasn't looking her way or nothing, but still. When did she get all shy and shit? Females were so unpredictable. I broke up their little staring match and got down to business.

"So…Kyan, what did you find out?"

"Mohammad's in there. He's alone. You better hurry up, though. I heard him on the phone talking about closing early. Something about his wife's birthday."

The news was even better than I expected. I sent Kyan in the store to case the place. Mohammad didn't particularly care for Blacks, but his perverted ass had a thing for young meat. He was more relaxed in their presence and didn't follow them around like he did to the men.

"A'ight. Good lookin' out."

I reached in my pocket and handed had her a ten-dollar bill. She stared at my hand as if it were a pile of shit. Her hand stayed outstretched as her eyes met mine.

"Damn, girl." I took another ten from my stack and placed it in her hand.

"That's better. Joie, are you ready?"

The girls slipped off in the direction of the bus stop. Drako watched intently as they crossed the street. Kyan was like his sister, so

I knew he wasn't looking at her. Joie, on the other hand, had his full attention.

"She ain't in your league," I stated, patting his shoulder.

"What's that supposed to mean?" His tone was soft, but stern.

"It means that she ain't shit. If you ain't pushing a fly ass whip or got paper out the ass, she ain't checking for you." I wasn't trying to be rude, but my nigga needed to know the truth. Joie was nice to look at, but her mind was somewhere else.

"That's because she ain't never met a nigga like me," Drako said proudly. "She's gonna be mine one day. Just watch."

"Yeah…a'ight, nigga."

"I'm serious. That girl's bad. I gotta have her."

"You ain't gotta have shit but this right here." I reached into my waistband and handed him one of the two guns I had stashed. "Get that bitch outta your mind. It's game time. Let's do this shit."

Bali's Corner Store sat between an empty lot and a church. Traffic was usually heavy toward the beginning of the month, when people got their food stamps. Being that it was nearing the end, most people were already out. During the time Drako and I stood across the street, Kyan was the only person who entered the store. Pulling two ski masks from my pocket, I handed one to Drako. It was time to get shit popping.

The sun disappeared completely as we made our way across the street. With a quick head nod, Drako threw on his mask and entered first. I followed behind him with my gun outstretched in front of me.

"You know what fuckin' time it is!" I roared with confidence. "Getcho' hands up!"

Mohammad was caught off guard, but still raised his hands to comply with my demand. "What do you want?" he asked in a shaky voice.

"Open the register," Drako commanded, maneuvering his way around the counter.

Mohammad lowered one of his hands and pressed a button, freeing the contents of the machine.

"Get down on the fuckin' ground!" I barked. I could see the fear in

Mohammad's face, but I wasn't fazed...not one muthafuckin' bit. He shouldn't have lied on my name.

Quickly, Mohammad lowered himself facedown. He was careful to keep his hands where I could see them. With my gun relaxed at my side, I waited impatiently while Drako counted our earnings.

"Fifty-five dollars?!" Drako yelled in disbelief. "You've got to be kiddin' me. I know you got more than this. Where's the rest?"

"That's all I have. I swear."

My breathing increased and my chest heaved up and down in frustration. I didn't risk another possible stint in juvie for fifty-five fuckin' dollars.

Pointing my gun toward Mohammad's head, I cocked it back. "You have five seconds to give me what we came here for, or I'm blowing your fuckin' brains out. One...two...three..."

"Okay. Okay. Please don't shoot!" Mohammad whined. "I'm begging you. It-it-it's in the back."

"That's more like it. Lock that damn door," I instructed Drako. He did as he was told, hastily locking the door and making his way back to where we were. Keeping my gun aimed at Mohammad's head, I mouthed, "A'ight. Getcho' punk ass up."

Slowly, Mohammad rose, not taking his eyes off my gun. Sweat danced around the hairline of his short, dark hair and eventually trickled down the side of his face. Seeing him vulnerable and scared for his life gave me a rush that I had never felt before. It served him right. Just because he had a store in a Black neighborhood didn't give him a pass to talk to us any kind of way.

I loved the control the shiny metal gave me. Mohammad didn't have those same loose lips that he did when I wasn't strapped. My burner revealed the true pussy that he was. Mohammad was all talk and no muthafuckin' bite. None at all! I didn't respect a nigga like that.

"Lead the way," I instructed. "And don't try no funny shit either."

With his hands still raised, he led us into the back room. It housed various boxes and supplies required to keep the store functioning. Off to the side was a wooden door that Mohammad stopped in front of.

"I need to put my hands down to go in and access the safe."

"Okay. Go on," I urged.

He opened the door and I followed him in. Drako stood behind, watching out for me. The room was dark, but the safe was visible with the small amount of light that managed to shine behind us. I watched intently as Mohammad turned the dial various ways before it eventually opened. My interest was piqued. I had never hit a lick with a safe involved. I couldn't wait to see what Drako and I were about to walk away with.

Clearing his throat, Mohammad reached inside. Instead of producing cash, Mohammad turned around with a small pistol in his hand. My survival instinct kicked in. Without thinking, I acted quickly and pulled the trigger before Mohammad had an opportunity to pull his. Mohammad's chest exploded in front of me, spraying the front of my shirt with blood and flesh.

"Yo...what the fuck?!" Drako yelled in surprise.

I was still in shock when Mohammad's lifeless body fell to the ground. "I panicked," I spat, realizing what I had done.

"Panicked? You just shot somebody. You were supposed to use the gun to scare him, not actually shoot him. What the fuck are we gonna do now?"

I knew what I was going to do. I was going to get the money and run. Drako could stay behind if he wanted to, but I was about to be out.

Using my sleeve to trace the wall, I felt for a light switch. It was now officially a crime scene and I didn't want to leave behind any fingerprints. As the light brightened the room, I got a good look at the safe filled with stacks of bills. *Jackpot!* Hundreds of Benjamin Franklins stared back at me. I was so caught up in trying to stuff as much as I could down my shirt that I didn't notice Drako enter the room behind me.

"Nigga?!" he shouted in amazement.

"Come on now, man. You should be over here helping me. I can't get all this money on my own."

"Fuck all that. Look at this."

I stepped over Mohammad's body and walked further into the room. My mouth fell open once I realized what Drako and I had stumbled across. Three large pallets were pushed against the wall, holding perfectly stacked bricks of cocaine almost as tall as me. The money was sweet and all, but the drugs were worth so much more. Turning to my dude, a sinister smile formed on my lips. We hit the right muthafuckin' spot!

That day forever changed our lives. It was the day I bodied my first victim, and also the day Drako and I entered the drug game. Mohammad's death inadvertently put us on. It didn't take long for us to create a name for ourselves. We hit the streets running and never looked back. The city of Birmingham was ours!

1

NORIEN

Present day...

"Shit," I moaned, using my hands to guide April's head up and down. "Just like that, bitch. Just like that."

April was the type of hoe that liked being called a bitch. She liked it, and I loved it. Hell, she was a bitch. A nasty, sloppy, keep it soaking wet, put the dick and the balls in her mouth at the same damn time type of bitch. I swear that girl didn't have a gag reflex. She was my weakness, and the sole reason my phone was sitting beside me turned *all* the way off. I knew my girl, Joie, was probably calling, but the nut April had rising up my dick was more important.

Grabbing a handful of her hair, I jerked her head back, forcing her to stare at my one-eyed monster. A thick gob of spit fell from her chin and landed on her bare titties. She eyed me hungrily, waiting for her cue to continue. I thrust my dick forward and she took me all in again.

"Damn, girl!"

She was on a mission. Her mouth slid up and down my shaft like a vacuum, sucking me into pure bliss. My ass cheeks tightened up under me as she worked her mouth like only she could. Her head bobbed to its own rhythm, without stopping. A high soprano note escaped my lips and rang off the four walls of her modest, two-bedroom apartment.

"You like that?" she asked, pausing momentarily to jack me with her hand.

"Hell yeah! Don't stop." I pushed my dick toward her awaiting mouth. "Come on! I'm almost there."

She tickled the tip with her tongue, only to stop again. "Do you love me, Norien?"

That was her only downfall. She talked too damn much. *Just suck my dick*. Is that too much to ask? "Yeah, I love you," I lied. "Now, come on."

"You promise?"

Without answering, I forced my dick deep into her throat. We were past the time for questions. My nut ascended toward the tip and I was ready to release. With an attitude, April continued.

"Aww, shit." I pushed her head back and jacked my own dick with a vengeance. "Open your mouth."

My shit squirted out like a waterfall, giving her a creamy facial. Just like the hoe she was, she wiped my kids off her face with her fingers and stuck them in her mouth. She sucked each one clean before swallowing in one gulp. A sly smirk crept upon my lips. Like I said, April was a nasty bitch.

She rose from between my legs and sauntered her pretty ass into her bathroom. Seconds later, she emerged fully dressed and threw a damp hand towel in my direction. I cleaned myself up, stuffed my dick back in my pants, and zipped the zipper like it was nothing. Powering on my phone, I stood and waited to see if I had any missed calls. I'd busted my nut…now, it was time to go.

I had two voice messages from Joie and a text from Ceasar. Pressing the message icon on my phone, I tried to address Ceasar's message first, but Joie's call came through, interrupting my train of thought. Glancing in April's direction, I let the phone ring a few times before finally answering.

"What's up, baby?"

"Where are you?" she asked with an irritated sigh.

"On the block," I hissed. I hated being questioned about my whereabouts. "Why, what's up?"

"Did you forget?"

I thought about her question for a second. *Damn!* I did forget. "Aww shit, baby. I'm on my way! Be outside. I'll be there in twenty minutes."

"No need. Seven's on her way."

I forgot all about picking my girl up from the salon. I dropped her off before heading Ceasar's way and fucking with him. Right before I got to his crib, he sent me a text changing our meeting time. I had a few hours to kill, so I called up April and made plans with her. It wasn't like she had anything to do. She didn't work, go to school–nothing. Her life consisted of taking care of her three-year-old son, Damien, and getting on her knees anytime I called.

For as long as I'd known her, her looks were enough to get her by. Her hazel eyes and fat ass caught my attention first, but it was that mouth of hers that had me hooked. I ain't talking about the way she speaks either, if you get my drift. For four years, we kicked it off and on. Whenever I needed her, she was only a phone call away. That day, I bought her an outfit and some shoes at The Galleria. She showed me her gratitude by getting on her knees. That shit was about to have me in the doghouse with my girl.

"Okay. Cool. I'm sorry, baby. I promise, it won't happen again. I'll make it up to you tonight. What do you wanna do?"

April wrapped her arms around me, forcing me to divide my attention. She puckered her lips up and strained in my direction. I kissed her softly before promising Joie that I would be home later on that night. I ended the call after April lifted my shirt and trailed kisses up my chest.

"I take it we won't be seeing you tonight," she whined, removing her lips from my body.

"You know how it is. I gotta keep wifey happy."

"Don't I know. She always finds a way to ruin our plans. Everything is always about Joie," she complained.

I never kept my relationship a secret. April knew all about Joie, but Joie didn't know about April.

Joie and I had been kicking it for years. I met her through a chick named Kyan. Actually, I was trying to get with Kyan but when I saw her friend, I switched it up. Joie played me to the left at first, but I broke her down with my contagious smile and thoughtful gifts. Honestly, I was just trying to fuck. Once I got my first taste, I didn't stop. The way her pussy gripped my dick did something to me. She was my baby. I genuinely had love for the girl, even though I fucked around with other broads more often than I fucked with her. I was never a 'one woman' type of nigga. I liked variety.

April fell under the 'variety' category. She was easy. I fucked her the same night we met. For most niggas, that's a turn off but for me, it was the opposite. I knew I could have April anytime I wanted to. Even if she had a man, I still had first dibs on every hole in her body.

"What time are you picking Damien up?" I asked, opening the front door.

"In about an hour. I'ma take him to the park for a little while. Maybe take him to get some ice cream or something."

"He'll like that." I stepped out the door, but peeked my head back inside before closing the door. "Hey."

"What?"

"Tell my son I love him, okay. I'll call him tonight. Make sure he's up."

"I always do."

I can admit my own faults. I know I'm foul. Sometimes, shit just happens, though. I slipped up and raw-dogged April one too many times. Now, I was a father. My son was a spitting image of me; brown-skinned, wide eyes with a head full of curly black hair. The resemblance was so undeniable that a DNA test was never needed. Damien was a secret I didn't intend for Joie to find out about. For years, my secret had been safe. April was a good lil' side bitch; playing her position like a professional side chick.

Hopping in my ride, I read Ceasar's text. He wanted me to meet him at some soul food spot downtown. It wasn't far from April's crib, and I arrived there in no time at all.

I noticed a Black Denali parked off to the side. It was Ceasar and his goons waiting for my arrival. I didn't have to see his face to know it was him. That nigga was known to hit the streets in some fly ass whip with a car full of his entourage. Word on the street was that he never traveled alone. I guess when you hit the big time, that's how it was.

Parking my Camaro in the space next to his, I waited patiently for one of Ceasar's doors to open. When it did, a big nigga with arms the size of two of mine combined stepped out. He towered over my 6'1 frame. I slid into the backseat and tried to remain calm. As the big nigga slid in after me, I realized that things had just gotten serious.

"I heard you wanted to talk," Ceasar began, rubbing his big hand across his goatee.

My mouth went dry. I didn't know what to say. This wasn't the same Ceasar that I met in the Jefferson Youth Detention Center. Nah...this was a grown ass man. A boss. Someone in the position I hoped to be in one day. We hadn't seen each other in over ten years; however, when I learned that he was running things, I put the word out that I wanted to set up a meeting.

"That's right," I managed to say. "Long time no see."

"It's been a while," Ceasar acknowledged. "But I know you ain't here for no reunion. What's the deal?"

I expected his tone to be a bit friendlier. For damn near a full year, we watched each other's backs and stood our ground when muthafuckas tried to test us. I didn't let nobody fuck with him, and he didn't let anybody fuck with me. Sitting across from him now, he was all about business.

"That's actually why I'm here. For a deal."

That big nigga next to me smirked and gazed out the tinted window. Usually, I would have said something. I was far from a punk, but being that I was outnumbered, I let that shit slide. In addition to the three of us in the back seat, two more niggas occupied the driver and passenger seats as well. If something was to pop off, things wouldn't be good for me.

"I'm listening," Ceasar said smoothly.

The backseat was redesigned to allow two bench-style seats to face either other. Ceasar sat across from me while the big nigga invaded my personal space. I was hoping for a one-on-one meeting. Everyone didn't need to hear me practically beg my long-lost friend to help me get my money up. Things weren't looking so good my way. I was tired of dealing with chump change. I wasn't heavy in the street, but my faithful regulars kept me afloat. The problem was, my supplier was unreliable. As soon as I got a shipment in, it was gone. My supply didn't always support the demand. The bills for supporting Joie, April, and my son ate away any profit I made. Sometimes, I had to wait a whole week just for my supplier to pick up his phone. I was losing both money and clientele. I cut that nigga off, and now I was trying to start over. The only problem was, my funds were limited.

"I heard you're doing big things out here," I began, studying Ceasar's face carefully. He brought his wrist up to eye level and peered at his Rolex. Was I wasting his time? Fearing our meeting might be cut short, I put everything out there and hoped for the best. "Look, I'ma be honest with you. I'm hurting right now. I need help getting back on. I got deals lined up with no product to deliver. I was dealing with Roscoe, but that nigga ain't reliable. He won't even answer his phone."

"He ain't gonna answer," Ceasar responded with a mischievous grin.

"Why not?" I asked curiously. "Is he out of town or something?"

"Nah, something more permanent," he smirked. "Last time I checked, you can't talk from the grave. That is, unless you have some super human super power type shit."

Big ums next to me busted out with the ugliest laugh I'd ever heard from a man. It sounded more like a wounded dog that needed to be put out of its misery. Taking my eyes off him, I returned them to Ceasar, who joined in the laughter.

"Damn. That explains a lot. I thought he was just avoiding me because he was dry. Now I know…well, I know the truth."

I couldn't tell if Ceasar was paying attention to me or not. He was focused in on the fat blunt dangling between his fingers. I hadn't noticed it before, but as he brought it to his lips and lit that bitch, the distinct smell of some good kush commanded all my senses. He took a few tokes and handed it to me.

I hit it, feeling that things were going my way. Ceasar's facial expression softened, but the words falling from his lips were stern and direct.

"I ain't seen you in God knows how long. You think it's cool to approach me asking for a handout? This ain't juvie, Nor. You ain't the same muthafucka, and I damn sure ain't either. We don't give fronts around here."

We? Who the hell was 'we'? Did the big muthafucka next to me hold more rank than I thought?

"I hear you. I wouldn't come to you like this unless I really needed it. Joie's on my ass about the bills and I can't seem to keep my head above water. I need help, man. I need a come up, and quick." I took a long draw from the blunt and passed it to the big dude. Staring back at Ceasar, I continued. "I just need enough to get right. That's it. It ain't a handout. I'ma pay you back. I promise."

Bypassing everything I said, he repositioned himself in his seat and asked about my girl.

"Joie, huh? Damn, that's crazy. You fuckin' wit her fine ass? How long's that been going on?"

"You know her? We been kickin' it for a while now.

"Yeah, I know her." He took the blunt from the big dude's outstretched hands. I wondered how he knew my girl and, after hitting the blunt again, he fed my curiosity. "She used to be tight with my sister, Kyan."

My eyes widened in surprise. It was a small fuckin' world! Kyan was one of April's good friends. They were really close, almost like sisters. In all the time I had known Kyan, she never disclosed that Ceasar was her brother. If she had, I would have tried to get on a long time ago.

"Oh, okay. I know Kyan," I admitted, although I didn't elaborate.

"Yeah?" Ceasar asked through gritted teeth. "How well do you know her?" His tone insinuated that something was going on. I killed that assumption real quick.

"It ain't nothing like that. She's cool with this chick I know, that's all."

"That's all it better be," Ceasar said, simmering down. "Look…this is what I'll do. I'll talk it over with Drako and get his take on it. If he agrees, I'll be in touch. If not, you already know the answer. Gimme a few days."

Drako? He must've been a part of the 'we' Ceasar mentioned earlier. Big dude was just a sidekick after all.

If that's how it had to be, so be it. The only thing I could do at that point was hope that Ceasar could get Drako to agree to my request. It wasn't a definite 'no', and that was a good thing. There was hope. Everything rested with a nigga I had never met. Sighing loudly, I turned to Biggie so I could exit the ride.

Big dude stepped out first, and I was right behind him. Once both feet were firmly planted on the ground, Ceasar's voice caused me to turn around.

"Next time I send for you, don't make me wait all day. Time is money. Remember that."

The door wasn't even fully shut when the SUV backed out of the parking space and peeled off. I climbed back in my car and rolled out too. I had plans to go home to Joie, but learning that Kyan was Ceasar's sister changed shit up. I was now headed back to the same place I just left. I needed to get in Kyan's ear, and April was going to help me do it.

2

JOIE

"You straight?" Seven asked as I opened her passenger door. I slid into the seat and sighed loudly in frustration.

"I guess. Thanks for picking me up."

"Don't mention it. You know I got you. Are you going home?"

"Yeah."

"A'ight, cool. I got a stop to make first. Is that okay?"

After nodding my response, Seven pulled off into traffic. Being that she was my savior at the moment, I couldn't object to anything she had to do. She had already gone out of her way to pick me up, but that was just Seven. She was a true friend in every sense of the word.

We'd been cool since I moved back to Alabama from Tennessee. I moved to Memphis during my junior year of high school, but returned to my roots once I graduated. My mother and stepfather didn't work out, so she returned to the place that she could always call home.

Seven was the first person I ran into–literally. While moving a few boxes into my mother's new apartment, we collided when she stepped out of her door and into the hallway. I fell to the ground as the boxes in my hands landed on top of me. An angelic face with spikey, fire engine red hair stood over me. She helped me to my feet, apologizing in the process.

"I'm sorry about that. I didn't see you," she offered with a half-smile.

"It's okay. I should have been paying attention. I've made so many trips in and out that front door that I just wanted to hurry up and finish. I'm tired!"

"Oh, so you're the one moving next door. I wondered who the unlucky tenants would be."

"Unlucky?" I asked, raising an eyebrow. "Is there something wrong with that apartment?"

She chuckled, showing a mouthful of straight teeth lined with metal. "I shouldn't have said it like that. The apartment's straight. People just don't stay long. Everybody who moves in stays a couple months and leaves. That's how it's been for years."

"Well, only time will tell." I sighed. "I guess my mother chose the right place. She doesn't stay anywhere too long anyway. She gets bored quick." I turned away from her intense gaze. She was undeniably beautiful and as someone still trying to find themselves in the 'looks' department, I felt intimated. "It sucks for me, though," I added, staring at the worn carpet under my feet. "As soon as we get settled, we move. It's hard to get comfortable and make friends."

"Don't worry! That's gonna change today. My name is Seven."

"Like the number?"

"Yeah," she smiled. "You have to know my mother to understand. She's into numbers – big time. She's a walking calculator. She'll forget almost anything you tell her, but if you say a number, it'll be ingrained in her memory! Her favorite is seven, hence the name."

"That's what's up! It's unique. I'm Joie. There's no special story behind my name. My mother's name is Zoe and my father's name is Joseph. I just got a combination of the two."

"I like that. It's different. I never met a 'Joie' before."

"Well, now you have."

From that day on, we were inseparable. Seven years in, and our bond was strong enough to be considered family. I was the first person she broke the news to about her pregnancy. I held her hand when she gave birth to my godson, Deuce. I was her maid of honor when she married her husband three months after meeting him. I was also there, bailing her out of jail after she caught him cheating with the next-door neighbor. They divorced shortly after that, but not before Seven picked up an assault charge and was ordered to stay at least a hundred feet away from them both.

I sat back in my seat as Seven drove around downtown Birmingham. She turned on the radio and sung along to a few of the songs. I, on the other hand, was in my feelings. I was growing tired of being forgotten by someone who was supposed to be my man. Norien never made me a priority. The shit was getting old, and quick.

Our relationship started quick. I was with Kyan when we ran into him at a party neither one of us were old enough to attend. We exchanged numbers and eventually started messing around. At the time, my priorities were fucked up. Norien always seemed to have money in his pocket and, for some reason, he was attracted to me. I was a teenage girl battling self-esteem issues. People told me all the time that I was pretty, but in my mind, I didn't see it. With so many beautiful women around me, I felt as though I wasn't on their level. Being with Norien helped me overcome that.

After moving away and returning, Norien and I picked up right where we left off. Although I lived with my mother, Norien's apartment became my second home. At the time, it felt good to say that I had a man providing for me. Seeing the drama with Seven and her ex-husband made me thankful that I didn't have serious issues like infidelity plaguing my relationship. I was lucky in that sense, but my relationship was far from perfect. As time went on, those problems spiraled out of control, threatening to end my relationship once and for all.

"What's the deal?" Seven asked, catching me off guard. "You're sitting over there with your arms crossed. What did Norien do now?"

Seven knew me well. She was the person I confided everything in, including my personal business. She was well aware of my relationship struggles and all the shit Norien put me through. She gave it to me straight which, at times, had me feeling like a fool.

"I'm just tired, Seven. Norien keeps doing the same shit over and over. He was supposed to pick me up today, but he didn't show. It's always an excuse with him. Why is it so hard for him to keep his word?"

"Let me guess...he forgot." When I didn't respond, she continued, taking my silence as confirmation. "A man is only gonna do what you allow him to do, Joie. I keep telling you the same shit. You deserve better. I mean, really? What's he doing for you?"

"He does a lot," I mumbled.

"Like what? Fucking you every now and then? Girl, he's not even home half the time to do that. Open your damn eyes."

"He takes care of me," I defended. "He pays the bills, he—"

"Must have some good dick," she finished for me. It wasn't what I was going to say, but she did have a point. "Ain't no way in hell I would put up with the shit you put up with. He leaves you home alone every day while he's out doing him. You keep using the same excuse 'he pays the bills'. Fuck them bills! That's not a relationship. He ain't doing nothing you can't do on your own."

"Whatever," I sighed.

"No, it's not 'whatever'. That nigga acts like he's bigger than what he really is. He ain't out here pushing no major weight. Stop using that lame excuse. You're smarter than that. Think about it. You're so worried about the bills, but is he putting any *real* money in your pocket? No, he's not."

"He gives me money."

"What? A couple dollars? Joie, that nigga spends way too much time in the streets for the chump change he throws at you. What's he really out there doing? If he was hustling as hard as he claimed he was, you would have a whole hell of a lot more than what you have. I think he's spending his time and money on something else. I know you don't wanna hear it, but I'ma go ahead and say it...I think the nigga's cheating on you."

"You're crazy! He wouldn't do that. Norien loves me."

"Do you hear yourself? You sound just as stupid as the hoes on the *Maury Show*. You know, the broads that claim they're one hundred percent sure the man they drag on national TV is their child's father. Then they run off the stage like some dummies when the truth comes out. Trust...I've been around Norien enough to know that he doesn't love anyone but himself."

Instantly, I regretted opening up to Seven. Her intent was good, but her delivery needed work. She wasn't offering me any type of compassion or taking my feelings into consideration. My man was far from perfect, but that didn't mean he was out slinging his dick.

"Let's just change the subject. I know what my man is and isn't out here doing. I don't need anybody trying to convince me otherwise."

Turning her nose up, she flipped her light turquoise tresses off her shoulder and rolled her eyes. Her newly acquired color held my attention, but it didn't change the way I felt. I wasn't trying to have problems with my best friend.

"Fine," she murmured, rolling down her window. "You'll learn one day. Don't say I didn't try to warn you."

Her words repeated in my head as I turned away from the strong wind slapping me in the face. Norien wasn't cheating on me...I knew for a fact. His pockets didn't support that theory. He was out on the block, hustling for our future...just like he said he was. Our problems had nothing to do with infidelity. Norien worked so hard that, at times, I felt that I was in a relationship by myself. Making money took precedence over everything in his life, including me. That was what I wanted to change. I wanted us to spend more time together, but Norien wasn't willing to meet me halfway. He felt that his absence was justified. I could either accept it or move on. For years, I accepted it, but complained to the one person I could confide in: Seven.

Silently, I rode shotgun, absorbing the familiar scenery. I assumed Seven was driving to her mother's house to get Deuce, but when she made a sharp turn and ventured down a two-lane street, I knew I was wrong. She pulled up in front of Jamal's apartment building and turned off the engine.

"Have you lost your damn mind?" I quizzed. "What the hell are we doing here?"

"We 'bout to fuck this nigga up!" she said with a straight but intimidating face. "Are you rolling or what?"

"You 'bout to do what? Seven, are you crazy? You know Jamal got that restraining order on you. I love you and all, but I ain't trying to go to jail."

"Girl, calm down!" Her face softened as she laughed at my uneasiness. "Ain't nobody thinking about Jamal. He's old news. I wish him nothing but pain, misery, and an incurable disease. Besides, that order of protection expired months ago. Tia just moved into this building. You remember my cousin, right?"

"Yeah," I nodded.

"She left her baby's bag over Aunt Joyce's house. Since I had to pick you up, I told her I'd bring it by."

"Oh, okay."

Reaching over her seat, she retrieved a colorful diaper bag with large, overlapping circles. "I'm just going in to drop this off. You coming in or staying in the car?"

"I'll just wait right here."

"A'ight. I won't be long."

Seven eased her slender body out of the car. She was what people referred to as 'slim thick'; skinny, with just enough 'extra' in all the right places. She made my small frame appear as though I hadn't gone through puberty yet. I mean, I had enough titties to fill a B-cup. My ass wasn't big, but it wasn't small either. It was average and suited my body well.

Seven walked up the concrete steps and disappeared inside the main door. The large, rectangular building had a brick exterior and aged appearance. The street was part of a revitalization project that took place a few years earlier. The entire block was re-landscaped to add a more modern feel. The outside didn't look like shit, but all four apartments inside each of the quad-style buildings on the block had been gutted, remodeled, and updated with newer appliances and amenities.

I surveyed the quiet street before pulling my phone from my Michael Kors tote. The round, gold medallion with the letters MK inside held my gaze. Seven teased me about it when I showed her Norien's latest gift to me. She said it was a knockoff and mentioned something about the engraving on the logo. I brushed it off at the time as jealousy, but looking at it at that moment had me wondering if she was right. Using my phone's internet browser, I googled 'knockoff Michael Kors'. Several articles displayed with pictures identifying discrepancies. When I clicked on the first picture, my phone lit up in an array of different colors, identifying an incoming call. I quickly answered when MOM flashed across the screen.

"Hey, Momma. How you doin'?"

"Oh, I'm alright baby. I can't complain. The good Lord opened my eyes this morning. I'm blessed."

That was my mother for you. She found a way to incorporate her faith into everything. Even if you didn't want to hear the Word, she was going to tell you.

"That's good," I said, changing my position. The back of my thighs were sweating against Seven's leather seats. My attempt to be cute and rock a black cotton romper was a fail at that moment.

"So, how are you? I haven't heard from you in a few days. Why haven't you called me?"

"I was going to. I really was. Things just kept coming up."

"Umm hmm." My mother huffed. I could imagine how she looked with her nose turned up on the other end. "Are those *things* more important than your mother?"

"Of course not! Don't be like that. We're talking now. What's going on?"

My mother didn't waste any time. She immediately dove in, telling me about the latest conflict with her sister, Zora. They were too similar for their own good and their personalities often clashed. Usually, I would check a bitch quick for coming at my mother sideways, but Aunt Zora got a pass. She didn't mean no harm. She was just passionate about everything she said – just like my mother.

"Momma, she probably didn't mean it like that," I interjected, breaking up her verbal rant. "You know how she is."

"I don't give a damn! I work hard for what little shit I got. It ain't much, but it's mine and I'm blessed to have it. For her to just come in here and turn her nose up ain't right. That bitch thinks she's so much better than me. I'm tired of it."

Recently, my mother moved into *another* new place. It was in one of the city's poorest neighborhoods, yet she was proud of it. She was able to afford the five-hundred square foot space on her janitor's salary while still being able to keep a few dollars in her pocket. I was proud of her. Aunt Zora was too; she just had a funny way of showing it.

"Why do you care what she thinks? You got what you could afford. Don't let that bother you. Her place ain't no better."

"Who you telling? Last time I went over her house, a few of her friends left with me. She got some nerve. How you gonna talk about somebody when your place is infested with roaches?"

"Exactly. Take whatever she says with a grain of salt and keep it moving."

Out of the corner of my eye, I noticed the front door to the apartment building open. Two men exited as though they were on a mission. A lump formed in my throat when recognition hit me. It was Ceasar and Drako. I hadn't seen them in forever, but there was no doubt in my mind that it was them.

Ceasar still had his low fade and the stumble that struggled to grow during his teenage years had blossomed into a full goatee. His scrawny frame had filled out nicely – just like Drako. *My God!* That man was fine. I had a thing for dreads. Drako's neat locs hung down his back.

"Joie? Joie? Do you hear me? Are you still there?" my mother asked, partly gaining my attention.

"Uh, yeah," I mumbled, following the men with my eyes. "I'm sorry. What did you say?"

They walked together toward the side of the building before Seven finally emerged from the door. She said something in their direction, causing Ceasar to look back. They briefly exchanged words before Seven found her way back to the car.

"Momma, let me call you back."

I hung up without giving her a chance to object. Seven started the car and drove off without saying a word.

"What was that about?" I questioned, probing her for answers.

"What? I gave Tia her bag and came out. That's all. What are you talking about?"

"Don't act stupid with me. What did you say to Ceasar?"

Seven's foot slammed on the brakes, propelling me forward. My quick thinking had my hands out in front of me, stopping me from hitting the dashboard.

"You know Ceasar?" she asked with wide eyes.

"Umm...yeah," I responded sarcastically.

"*How* do you know him?"

"We met a long time ago," I exaggerated. "I know his sister."

"Oh," she mumbled, rolling her eyes. "I can't stand that bitch. But, that's not important. You and Ceasar...did y'all ever mess around?"

Her question had me offended. "No! Hell no! Never! I've never looked at him like that. Why would you ask me that question? What's really going on?"

With a girlish smile, she eased off the brake and continued on. "Nothing. I just said 'hi'...that's all."

"Yeah, right," I mumbled. Seven was lying through her teeth, but why?

3

DRAKO

"Y'ALL SO FUCKIN' obvious," I chuckled, shaking my head at Ceasar. He tried to put on a front in public with Seven, but I knew the real.

"Fuck you, Drako. It ain't yo' business what I do with my dick."

"You right, bruh. Don't say shit to me when you catch HIV from a bitch."

"Nigga, you will, too. You fuck just as many bitches as I do, if not more. My situation is different because I been fuckin' with Seven for a minute. You been slangin' dick everywhere," he clowned me, laughing.

"Fuck 'em and duck 'em. Toot it and boot it. Fuck and leave. That's all I know, homie."

Ceasar's ass was in love with Seven. I knew my brother. If he wasn't, she wouldn't have been around as long as she had. We had different views when it came to women. Ceas wanted to find the perfect woman to settle down with. Me, I was all about the pussy and money. Naïvely, I let a bitch fuck me over – once. It only took one time for me to learn my lesson. She played me for a fool when all I did was love her. I chalked it up to being young and dumb. After that, I vowed to never let another bitch outside my inner circle get that close to me again.

"You'll never find anyone with that attitude. You run women away with how you disrespect them. I know Willow hurt you, but not every female is her."

I kissed my teeth when he brought Willow up. I hated hearing that bitch's name and he knew it. Clearing my throat, I let it slide.

"If they can't handle my mouth, then that sounds like a personal problem to me. I talk to everybody the same."

He opened his mouth to speak, but I held my finger up when my phone rang. Smirking, I was pleased to see it was my favorite mouth piece, Taneka, calling. She was one of the loyal bitches who sucked and fucked me on command. She was cool as hell, too, but I rarely kicked it with her. She cooked for me a time or two. Other than that, it was strictly fucking.

"What's up, Nek?"

"Hey, baby. I miss you, big daddy. When you comin' to see me? I got this pussy wet and waiting for you," she moaned, and I could hear pots rattling in the background. Instantly, I bricked. I wanted to go, but money called.

"Keep it wet for me. I'll swing through later."

"Later? Why can't you come now, Drako?"

"Because, I'm out handling business."

"So, business is more important than me?"

Was she serious? What kind of question was that? "Look, I don't know who the fuck you think you're rappin' to, but you need to chill the fuck out. Business has always been more important than you and any other bitch, ma. Next time, say yes sir and do what the fuck I said. Now, you about to sit over there with a dry pussy. I'll be in touch."

Hanging up, I threw the phone in my lap and sparked up some green. I pulled hard, holding it in and passing it to Ceas. He glared at me and shook his head. I shrugged and pushed the blunt further in his face. He snatched it from my fingertips.

"Rude muthafucka," he grumbled. "See what I mean? Why you talk to females like that?"

"Because, they're only good for three things, and they all involve holes. If you know what I'm sayin'."

"You wild, Drake."

"A'ight, Carl," I shot back, chuckling. "Why you over here on my dick? What you doin' with Seven, bruh? Why you still tryin' to keep that a secret? I already know what's up."

"Man, it's hard to explain. Sev and I go a few years back. We had a run-in in the past, but it's never been more than what it is now. I'm gon' keep it one hundred and say I'm feelin' the fuck outta her. I know I'm not ready for a commitment, though. Plus, Kyan doesn't like her, and I know the feeling is mutual. I ain't tryin' to deal with all that added stress. Not yet."

"It doesn't stop you from getting the pussy, though," I chuckled. "You talk all that shit, but you foul just like me, nigga."

Ceas waved me off as we pulled up to the first house to collect our money and check on our supply. Wednesday's were the days we did our rounds and showed our faces to everyone who worked for us. It was mandatory that all niggas were present at each house when we got there. If anything came up short, we had everyone there to interrogate, or kill. I only gave them one chance to tell what they knew and if their story didn't add up, it was lights out.

The first three houses were our big money makers. We always started with them. Our first in charge man, Jake, had shit running smoothly. At first, I doubted him and gave him a hard time. A Black and Mexican nigga with the name Jake screamed pussy to me, but he showed me otherwise. Throughout his training days, I gave him hell and he got through the shit with his head held high. He brought in more sales than half the team alone, and his money was always accurate. When he bodied a nigga trying to set Ceas up, he earned his position. Since then, he'd only gotten better and quickly moved up in rank.

"I'm gon' need more pills over this way, Drako. The shit is potent as fuck. Got these fiends goin' loco, homes," he exclaimed, blowing smoke through his nose. "They went through the usual supply in half the time. I think I need to double up."

"That's what's up. I'll hit you with a new order tomorrow. Be expectin' it Friday. You got enough to hold you over until then?"

"Nah, but I can get some from Silas."

"Cool."

Before we left, I went to take a piss. As I washed my hands, I decided to put my dreads in a bun. It was heating up outside, and I didn't feel like dealing with them on my neck. I had been growing them for eight years, and they were down my back. They complemented my full, shaven-down beard and goatee. Women went crazy over my toffee skin, full, black-tinted lips, and slated brown eyes. I knew I looked good as fuck. It was easy to keep my appearance up with minimal effort.

Ceas was leaned up against the car talking to Jake when I emerged. I headed toward them when I heard someone yell my name. I knew that voice anywhere. Turning around, I jogged down the sidewalk to where Wilma stood. I embraced Willow's mother and kissed her cheek. Looking at her from head to toe, I nodded in approval. She looked good. She had definitely been taking care of herself.

Wilma and I formed a mother-son relationship while I was with her daughter. It stuck even after the hoe did me wrong. Wilma warned me about Willow and her wicked ways, but at the time, I was so in love that it fell upon deaf ears. She told me I was too good for her daughter and I needed to find someone who deserved a man like me. I didn't believe her, but she had been right on the money.

"Hey, Ma. You look good."

"Thanks, baby. I've been holding up. I saved most of the money you gave me. It's lasted me for a while," she replied, smiling. "How have you been, Drake? You haven't called me in months."

"I know. I'm sorry about that, but you know how it is when I'm deep in shit."

"Mmhm. You're still dealin' that mess?"

"I'm never gon' stop." I gave her the same answer I did every time she brought it up. She didn't like what I did, but it wasn't her life to live.

"We'll see. When the right woman comes along, you'll remove yourself from all this negativity. That's all it is." She scoffed and changed the subject. "Have you seen that no good daughter of mine?

She changed her number and hasn't called to check on me in God knows how long. I'd like to know if she's okay."

"You would know if I've seen her, Ma. You would have received a call to claim her body."

Wilma rolled her eyes and shook her head. Like with anyone else, I kept it real with her too. I didn't hold my tongue. She knew I wanted Willow dead, and that was why she went into hiding in the first place. Refusing to show her face saved her life. If she was smart, she would continue to do so.

I gave Wilma a couple stacks to last her the next few weeks and promised to stop by to see her soon. Ceas and I dipped to go check on the others when I got a call for a delivery. I didn't have what they needed on me. It was too short of a notice. Niggas knew to place orders at least two days in advance, but they were desperate. Not the one to miss out on any cash, I called up Kyan to see if she could go handle things for me.

"Drakoooo!" she exclaimed dramatically when she answered the phone. "What's up, big bro?"

"Why the fuck you be so loud, Ky? That shit ain't called for."

"Whatever, nig. It's my mouth. Now, what you need? I know you're callin' for something. I never get a call just to see how I'm doin'."

"Because I see yo' ass all the time, girl. Bratty ass. Check it, though. I need you to deliver a pizza for me," I spoke in code since I was on my personal phone. "It needs to be there in the next hour. I'll send you the details."

"Cool, but you owe me! There's this MCM bag I've been eyeing. That's yo' price. Plus, some of the commission."

"I swear Ceas got yo' ass spoiled as fuck. A'ight. I got you, sis."

"Bet. I'll text when it's done."

Ending the call, I pulled out my burner phone and texted her the information. Kyan was as thorough as any real nigga. She was one of the realest on the team when we needed her. Ceas and I trained her well. Ceas wasn't with it at first. His black ass raised hell when she stepped to him about joining our operation, but I told him to listen to her case. She explained how she could be an asset to the team. After we gave her a test, she passed with flying colors. Even Ceas was impressed. We had no choice but to put her on.

"Aye, I need to holla at you about somethin'," Ceas stated, leaning forward to turn the music down. I gave him an 'I'm listening' face and he continued, "A nigga I know from way back when set up a meetin' with me the other day. He's askin' to get put on. He was gettin' work from Roscoe, and I let him know he wouldn't receive shit else from him."

"You know I trust ya' judgment, bruh. If he got the money, cool. We gon' tax his ass, though. I don't know the nigga, and I don't put shit past anyone. How his ass pop up out the blue like that?"

"How the fuck am I supposed to know, Drako? Muthafuckas pop up all the time. I'll hit him up for a meeting with both of us. You can feel him out for yourself."

"I'm wit it."

I turned the music back up to dead the conversation. We continued to cruise through the city and collect our shit. I was tired as fuck, and couldn't wait to relax and settle down. I needed something other than weed to get me right. There was only one thing that could help me: pussy.

4

KYAN

Drako owed me big time! My girlfriend, Nova, and I were on our way out to eat, but his request changed those plans. I ordered her some takeout before getting dressed in all-black and pulling my long, silky brown hair in a tight bun on top of my head. Anytime I handled business, I wore black. Black was my favorite color, and something about it made me feel powerful. Ceasar and Drako clowned me for it, but I was me with no regrets.

I pulled my black turtleneck over my head and down over my breasts. They were large, much more than I wanted. I thought about getting a breast reduction, but Nova loved them. Studying my tall, slim frame, I admired the way black looked against my glowing chestnut skin. My bun made my facial features pop: high cheekbones, succulent heart-shaped lips, narrow nose, and pretty brown eyes. Even when I didn't try, I looked good. I had a natural beauty. Coating my lips with a thin layer of gloss, I smiled.

Pushing for time, I kissed Nova goodbye and quickly ran outside to my Tesla. Of course, she was black too. She was a gift from Ceasar after I bodied my first victim. Because of that, I considered her my prized possession. I didn't drive her much, unless I had a quick job to do. Checking my glove compartment, I made sure my gun was still in place. After confirming what I already knew, I backed out of my parking space, watched the gate to my apartment community open, and sped down the road.

Bumping Queen's EP, I sang along to the songs as I drove to pick up the supply. My adrenaline pumped as I thought about what was about to take place. I loved getting my hands dirty. I wasn't a typical female, and I never had been. When I was in foster care, I first discovered my boyish ways and interest in girls. I didn't take it serious at first. I kept telling myself that I was simply curious. One day, Ceas and Drako dared me to kiss my friend. Not being the one to turn down a challenge, I did, and I loved it. She tasted so sweet, and I wondered if every female tasted as good as her.

After that, I didn't show interest in girls again until after I had sex with a man. It was...an experience. It hurt like hell when I got my cherry popped. The next time was better, but there was something missing. It took me having sex with him a third time for me to realize exactly what the problem was. It wasn't him, it was me. I just wasn't into it. I didn't feel the same fireworks I felt when I kissed my friend. To test my theory, I had sex with a girl, and it was mind-blowing! Soon after, I came out. No one seemed to be surprised.

I considered myself to be a stem. I was somewhere in between a stud and fem. Just because I was a lesbian didn't mean I wanted to be a nigga. I just preferred pussy over dick. Being around Nova brought out the fem in me. We loved to do each other's makeup, get bundles, and have our nails and toes done. We weren't just lovers, we were the best of friends as well.

In the presence of Ceas and Drako, the stud in me came out. I had been around them all my life, and they had me rough as hell. Anything they could do, I could do better. I loved being a part of the action. It gave me a rush, and I lived for that shit.

Pulling up to the spot, I hopped out the car and strutted to the door. All the niggas knew who I was and what I was about. Still, it didn't stop them from complimenting how fine I was, like I didn't know. The bitch who birthed me had some damn good genes. Ceas and I were both fine as hell.

Busting in the house, I gave everyone a head nod and went straight to the back. The supply was right where Drako said it would be, making things that much easier for me. I retrieved what I needed, jogged out the house, and pressed the gas all the way to the dock for the exchange. I pulled up four minutes after the arranged meeting time, and the nigga's face told me exactly how he felt.

"You're late," he spat.

He had the audacity to grill me like I wasn't the bitch who had what he wanted. "And? I'm here now."

"It doesn't work like that. My time is valuable. Ain't nobody got time to wait while you sit at home puttin' on makeup and shit. I got shit to fuckin' do."

"Well…go do it."

"I will. After you compensate me for wasting my time."

"Your time?" I laughed in his face. "You're on my time, bitch. Remember that."

"Man, fuck you. Why Drako send a bitch to handle his business anyway? This shit's crazy. I know he better drop the price big time for this shit."

"Let's get one thing clear," I began, closing the gap between us. "You call me a bitch one more time and I'ma show you that my balls are bigger than yours. Disrespect costs, muthafucka. The way your pockets are lookin', you can't afford the payment. Stop actin' like you got a pussy between ya legs and get out ya feelings. Now…where's the cash? You're wastin' my muthafuckin' time now."

"I ain't givin' you a muthafuckin' thing," he spat, turning up his nose.

"Cool."

Not being the one to go back and forth, I turned to walk away. It was his loss, not mine. I was good regardless.

Continuing toward my car, my sixth sense kicked in. I heard his light footsteps creeping toward me. Listening intently to each step, I was able to determine when he was within arm's reach. His attempt to be secretive blew up in his face when I spun around just as he reached for the bag. He managed to tug the strap off my shoulder, but that's about it.

"You niggas will never learn, will you?" I announced, whipping out my custom made Nine. His ass couldn't exhale fully before I sent one to his dome. I watched his body slump to the ground, shaking my head. Why did muthafuckas like to try me?

Tossing the bag in my backseat, I called our clean-up crew and searched the guy's pockets. I got the money he owed me, plus more. Just for the hell of it, I slapped his cheek and spit in his face. Drako owed me more than a fuckin' purse. *Muthafucka sent me out here to an attempted robbery*, I thought. What type of customers did he fuck with?

I waited thirty minutes for clean-up to arrive, only adding to my list of things I wanted from Drako. Knowing him, I knew I would get everything I asked for. Being the only girl had its perks, even though when I was younger, I prayed for a sister. I wanted someone that I could relate to. There were other girls in and out of the foster home I lived in, but I didn't like those sneaky bitches. They tried me, and I showed them just what I was about. Big Momma threatened to send me back numerous times, but Ceas would always raise hell. He was young, but Big Momma knew he wasn't just talk. Whatever he said he would do, he did.

When Ceas went to another home, Big Momma started giving me more freedom. I was allowed to go places with Drako instead of being stuck in the house all day. She thought he was responsible and with Ceas gone, she trusted that he would watch over me. Technically, we were the same age, but since Drako was a few months older than me and a boy, she felt comfortable leaving me in his care. Little did she know, we would link up with Ceas and get into shit we had no business getting into.

I learned quick that I liked being in the action. I developed a slick tongue that would cuss a muthafucka out in a heartbeat. When my words weren't enough, I let my fists do the talking. My hands were just as vicious as my mouth. If I got some heat between my fingers, it was over. I never hesitated pulling a trigger. With two brothers watching over me, I turned into a force to be reckoned with. Knowing I was always down, Ceas and Drako started to spoil me. It got worse when the money started flowing in faster than it could be counted. Any and everything I asked for, I got. Because of that, I turned into a spoiled brat...and I was proud of it!

I realized I was hungry when my stomach began to growl. Watching the clean-up crew at work, I called and ordered Chinese to be delivered to my apartment. The estimated delivery time was approximately an hour, which gave me enough time to get home, shower, and unwind.

Drako called just as I pulled off. I told him to meet me at my place. He tried to press me for information, but I didn't want to explain anything over the phone. He agreed and said he would be there with Ceas shortly. Turning on Sirius, I found a station that had me nodding my head to the beat. I turned the volume up and danced in my seat as the bass shook the car. When the next song played and I knew all the words, it was over. I rapped my heart out like I was on somebody's stage. A string of familiar songs followed before my Tesla returned to the same parking spot it previously departed. Still in 'concert mode', I listened to three more songs before finally getting out of the car.

"Nova!" I called out when I walked through the door. I threw the bag down on the couch and navigated the apartment to find her.

I found her in our bedroom. Licking my thick lips, I leaned against the door frame and watched as she got dressed. Music played in the background, which was why she didn't hear me come in. Thoughts of what I wanted to do to her filled my head. Everything about her was sexy to me; from her hair that was always laid to her soft feet, which I rubbed every night. I was proud to call Nova mine. It took everything in me not to remove the pants she carefully slid up her thighs and bend her over our bed.

It was funny how we met. She was fucking around with Ceasar when he brought her over. One look in her direction and my panties were moist. When I saw her, I had to have her. I didn't care that she had been with my brother. I wanted her! Ceasar become occupied on a call and I made my move. I smooth-talked her into the bathroom and broke her lesbian cherry. From that moment on, she was mine.

I loved Nova. She was a great woman with goals and ambitions. During the day, she went to school and at night, she worked at Target. She was loyal. She knew the things I did, and she still held me down. I kept that life separate from her. I wasn't as deep into it as Ceas and Drako, but that didn't mean it was safe.

"Oh shit, Ky! You scared me," she mumbled, pulling her shirt over her head. Before she could get it down, I inhaled one of her hard nipples in my mouth. She gasped and giggled, trying to wiggle out my arms. I held her tight until her giggles turned into moans.

"What we doin' tonight?" I asked, breaking the hold my lips had over her nipple.

"I don't know, but I know what I wanna do right now." She pointed to her unbuttoned pants.

"Is that right? I got you, baby," I stated with a smile. "Later."

Ignoring the disappointment in her face, I softly bit her nipple, kissed her lips, and walked away. I didn't want to start something I couldn't finish. A 'quickie' wasn't gonna do. Pleasing my girl was an all-night event and with my brothers on their way, sex with Nova had to wait. Instead, I hopped in the shower and let the warm water wash off any evidence of the day's events.

When I turned off the water, I heard Ceasar and Drako's loud mouths. They arrived earlier than I expected, but it was no big deal. Wrapping my body in a thick towel, I peeked my head into the living room to speak and disappeared into my room to get dressed. The smell of Chinese traveled through the apartment. My mouth was watering by the time I returned to the living room.

"Who ate my food?" I whined, jumping up and down. Throwing the empty container on the floor, I sighed in frustration. I was hungry!

"Who do you think?" Nova giggled. "I told him it was yours, but he ate it anyway."

"Don't explain shit, Nova. Her ass will be all right. I ordered you some more, fat girl," Drako spat.

I knew then that he was the culprit. "Well, just add that to the list of shit you owe me."

"List? One thing ain't a list, Ky."

"You should have thought about that before you sent me to do your dirty work." Taping Nova's shoulder, she stood, allowing me to have her seat. Pulling her arm, she fell into my lap.

"That nigga was on one," I continued. "I pulled up on homie, and he started talking some rah rah shit about me being late. He kept goin' on and on about some nonsense, and I had to put him in his place. You now me...I don't deal with disrespect, so I was just gon' leave. Do you know that muthafucka tried to rob me?! Nigga thought he was sneaky, so I had to handle him. I dropped his ass before he even saw it coming. So yeah, nigga. It's a list. Once again, I dropped another body...*for you*. I got your shit back and I almost broke a fuckin' nail. You owe me!"

Drako looked at Ceasar, who fell over in laughter. He knew I meant business, and so did Drako. Sitting back, I smirked and rubbed my fingertips together. I mouthed 'you owe me,' and nudged Nova to get up when the doorbell rang. Drako remained quiet as I walked toward the door. When my gaze spotted the bag on the edge of the couch, I reached for it and threw it in Drako's lap.

"Everything's still in there," I smirked, answering the door for the delivery man.

I made Drako come up off two twenties to pay for my food. He complained about paying for the first order, but still gave me the money anyway. The delivery man smiled when he realized his tip was more than the actual order.

Drako's focus remained on the bag as I retrieved my food and sat down. He opened it and inspected the contents while Nova eased down next to me. She rested her head on my shoulder and watched as I scooped up a fork full of fried rice.

"Baby, you want some?" I offered.

Of course, she did. Nodding her head 'yes', she smiled. I let her have the first bite and sent her into the kitchen for a plate. I licked my lips at the sight of her walking away. I loved seeing her ass bounce with each step she took. Apparently, I wasn't the only one.

"Don't be lookin' at my girl, Ceas. That's all me," I joked.

"Been there, done that. Ain't nobody lookin' at that girl."

He waved me off, but I knew his ass was butt hurt. Anytime the opportunity arose for me to throw my girl in his face, I did. Ceas liked to play tough, but knowing his little sister took his bitch had him sick. He said he didn't care because she was nothing but a fuck, but I knew it was more than that. None of the hoes he fucked with after Nova came close to her level…especially that bitch, Seven. She was a major downgrade. The whole city ran through that slut bucket, and I was glad to know she was no longer in the picture. If only Ceasar could find someone to get him out his feelings. It would take a special kind of woman to do that. Nova was in a league of her own.

They stayed and rapped with me for a while. I liked it when the four of us hung out. There was never a dull moment being around the people I loved most. We talked about bullshit until Drako turned serious. He apologized for the way things went down and promised never to put me in a situation like that again. I told him it was cool. The situation was fucked up, but not once did I feel threatened. I had the situation under control from jump.

"It ain't cool," Drako advised. "That nigga's lucky you already put him out of his misery. My punishment would have been ten times worse. How much you get off his ass, anyway?"

"Nothing," I lied.

"Yeah, right. I know you, Ky. Let's just split it 50/50 and call it a day."

Drako could see through any lie I told. I admitted to the cash I came up on and agreed with his request to split the money. Nova returned with her plate and slid comfortably onto my lap. Even if I gave Drako every penny I took, he would have given it all back to me in the form of an expensive gift.

I zoned out of Ceas and Drako's conversation when Nova commanded my attention. She kissed me behind my ear and ran her hand up and down my back. When Ceas stepped in the bathroom, she got bold and started rubbing my pussy through my clothes. She acted like Drako wasn't even in the room. Ceas wasn't gone long but when he returned, my pussy was soaked. Yearning to feel Nova's tongue massaging my clit, I let my brothers know what time it was. They had to go.

5

CEASAR

I HADN'T MADE it a full mile before my phone rang in the center console. Kyan's number appeared on the screen.

"What's up?" I answered. "What? You forgot somethin'?"

"Yeah," she giggled. "Nova, stop. My brother's on the phone."

"What the fuck y'all got going on?"

"Nothin'! Mind ya business."

"Shit...that's what I'm tryin' to do. You called me, remember? What's goin' on?"

"I forgot to tell you...my girl hit me up earlier. Her dude wants to talk to you. I think you might know him. Have you ever heard of a nigga named Norien?"

I shook my head and glanced over at Drako. He was all up in my conversation anyway, trying to figure out what was going on. Norien's antics were quickly pissing me off. I'd already had a one-on-one with the dude. There was no need for his bitch to go through my sister to get at me. That told me what kind of nigga I was dealing with. Women didn't need to be put in the middle of business. He was supposed to come to me as a man, which I thought he did.

"Yeah, I know the cat. We already talked. I was gonna let Drako feel him out, then go from there. Now, I don't know if I wanna do business with that pussy at all."

"He's cool people," Kyan vouched. "He's a little off, but something's wrong with everybody, right?"

"No. Ain't shit wrong with me."

"Yeah, okay Ceas. If you say so."

Drako hung on to every word as I spoke. Anything that affected me usually affected him. He should have known that I would fill him in once the call was over, but he eyed me cautiously anyway.

"What?" he asked.

I held up my index finger, momentarily silencing him. "Aye, why didn't you tell me you reconnected with Joie?"

I smiled slyly at Drako as his eyes widened in surprise. That was the only piece of pussy he was never able to conquer. As much as he teased me about Seven, it was only right for me to give him a dose of his own medicine.

"What are you talking about? I ain't seen that girl in years."

"That's Norien's girl, right?"

"No! Where did you hear that from? She moved away, remember? He's with April. Well, sort of. You know how niggas are. They claim you only when it's beneficial for them."

"I guess," I sighed. "I could've sworn that nigga mentioned Joie's name. Maybe I was hearing shit." Steering the car onto the next block, I inquired further into her relationship with Norien. "How you know that nigga anyway? You fucked him or something?"

"Please!" she huffed. "Dick don't do shit for me unless it's strapped on a female. I like pussy...Nova's pussy."

"You can have that wack shit," I shot back, still feeling the sting of my sister taking one of my side bitches. It wasn't like she was my main, but still.

"Don't be mad cuz I eat her pussy better than you. I got that pussy trained to cum on command. That ain't w

ack, big bro. She just needed some guidance. It ain't like a nigga ever taught her shit."

"Fuck you, Kyan."

"I love you, too! Bye." She made a kissing noise before hanging up in my ear.

"Must be talkin' about Nova," Drako chuckled, leaning back in his seat. "I know you ain't still mad over that shit. That's old news, my nigga."

"I ain't thinking about that bitch. She wouldn't know good dick if it slapped her in the face."

"That's what you shoulda been doing."

"What?"

"Beatin' that bitch's face with yo meat, that's what. You got something Kyan don't. Ain't no way in hell somebody without a dick shoulda been able to swoop in and fuck up what y'all had going on." He looked at me and smirked. "Unless of course, you wasn't hittin' it right."

"You crazy, you know that? My stroke game's A1." Shaking off his comment, I focused on the road. We were nearing the highway, and I needed to merge over. "That ain't even what she called for. Norien's broad reached out to Kyan. That's some ol' bitch shit."

"For what?"

"What do you think? He's tryna get on."

"But didn't you already—"

"Yeah," I cut him off. "I already rapped with dude. That's what I don't understand. I told him I would get back to him. He's an impatient muthafucka."

"That shit's gonna cost him. We don't need him. He needs us. We move on our time, and not a second before. Call that nigga up. Time is money, and I got plenty of it today."

Norien answered his phone on the first ring. He agreed to meet us at Pappadeaux's within the hour. The restaurant was Drako's idea. He claimed to be hungry, even though any of the hoes he dealt with would have dropped everything just to fix him a hot meal. My boy was a ladies man. He could cuss a bitch out to her face and the same bitch would still wash his dirty draws. Hoes claimed they wanted respect, but when Drako didn't give it to them, they continued to stick around.

Inside the restaurant, we ordered our food and waited for its arrival. I asked Drako if he wanted to wait for Norien, but he gave me the side-eye and placed his order anyway. We were halfway done with our seafood platters when Norien finally arrived. He was late. Drako noticed it, too. He glanced at his watch before diving into his crab cake. I scooted my chair over to give Norien some room. Drako glanced up in Norien's direction, but didn't stop eating.

"What's up, fellas?" Norien asked, reviewing the menu placed in front of him. "Hmm. Let's see…what looks good? What did y'all get?"

Drako didn't say a word. He used his hand to pick up a piece of shrimp from his plate, pulled the tail off, and threw it in his mouth. One thing about Drako was that he kept it real. If he didn't like you, you knew it. Norien was dumber than he looked. He didn't pick up on it and continued his line of questioning.

"What's that you got over there?" he asked Drako.

"What does it look like?" Drako responded dryly. His intense stare shot daggers through Norien. Maybe it wasn't a good idea to have them meet after all.

"I don't know. That's why I'm askin'. Ceasar, what's up with your boy? This is a good time, ain't it?"

I opened my mouth to speak, but Drako beat me to it. "It would have been if you were here twenty minutes ago. I don't wait for nobody. Ceas, you can entertain this clown if you want to, I ain't got shit else to say. Once I'm done eatin', we out."

Where the hell was he going? I drove. I wasn't going anywhere until my thirty-dollar meal was ingested. Nobody told Drako to gobble his shit down like it was his last meal. He had a problem with Norien, which was cool, but that didn't have shit to do with me.

"You can chill with that shit. I ain't leavin' till I'm done."

"On second thought," Norien hesitated, setting his menu down in front of him. "I'm not really hungry. I ain't tryin' to run up your bill more than it already is. Let's just discuss what we're here for and I'll be on my way."

"Wait a minute," I paused, tossing my fork down on my plate. "You really thought I was paying for you?"

"Yeah, you invited me."

"This nigga's crazy," Drako spoke in between bites. "You a grown ass man."

"So, that wasn't the plan?"

Norien looked as though he was genuinely confused. He had life fucked up. Why would I pay for him? And at Pappadeaux's? Man, crazy didn't describe his thought process. I wouldn't even pay for a bitch unless I was guaranteed to smash. Why would I come out my pocket and pay for him? This meeting was going left, and fast.

"Let's just get this shit over with," I stated, giving Norien my full attention. "I got what you're lookin' for, but ain't gon' be no fronts. The price is firm. I'm runnin' a business, not a charity."

"You already know how my finances are set up. I ain't got it like that right now, Ceasar. I'm fucked up. I spent my last just to get here."

Finishing his meal, Drako took his napkin and wiped his mouth clean. Throwing it on top of his plate, he scooted his chair back and stood. "Ceas, you ready?"

Damn. Drako dismissed Norien like he wasn't even there. I felt kind of bad when Norien looked to me with confusion laced on his face. Drako was all for meeting up. Now, he didn't have shit to say.

"How much are you talking about?" I asked, clearing my throat.

"Ceas? You really about to do this?" Drako barked. "He just told you he ain't got no money. Fuck that! We out."

"Come on, Ceas," Norien whined, referring to me by the name only my close friends and family used. I didn't appreciate that shit at all. We knew of each other, but we weren't close. "All the shit we used to get into back in the day. I had your back just like you had mine. That gotta count for something."

I rarely let a muthafucka get me in my feelings. Norien and I did have history. He wasn't a natural born leader like myself, but his quick thinking kept me straight with the ladies. I was wild during my teenage years. It was nothing for me to fuck a bitch, then turn around and fuck her friend without even cleaning my dick. What can I say?

Bitches loved me. After dicking down one broad, her homegirl hit me up. She heard about how I put it down and wanted to see what I was about. Needless to say, I smashed…and added her to the rotation of hoes I fucked on the regular. Fast forward a few weeks and the broad caught her homegirl at the crib. It was Norien who ran interference. He had recently been released from the detention center and temporarily placed in the same foster home that I was in. He stepped up and claimed the scared girl on the couch as his own. I appreciated that shit. Thanks to Norien, I continued to fuck them both until I got turned out by my first piece of 'grown' pussy.

"Our price is thirty a kilo," I advised, drastically upping the price from our usual twenty-two five. Drako eased back in his seat with a smile on his face. He liked those numbers. He wasn't in such a hurry to leave after all. "I can't just give it to you, though. That ain't how it works. I need at least ten stacks before we even hand over the product. We can discuss options for the remainder, but I need cash money in my hand first."

"Ten thousand? That's kinda steep. Man…is there any way you can come down on the price a little bit?"

"I wouldn't even be having this conversation with anyone else. Those are the terms. If you need a couple days, I understand. Hit me up. Just don't have me waitin' forever. The offer expires whenever I say it does. A'ight, Drako…now, we can roll."

We stood in unison. Norien remained seated, but his low voice commanded our attention.

"I'll have it tomorrow. What time you wanna meet?"

Drako and I glanced at each other. That was quickest come-up I'd ever seen. Norien went from complaining about not having shit to a little more than thirty-three percent of our asking price. Something wasn't right about that. Being the nigga that Drako was, he spoke up.

"One thing I hate is a lyin' muthafucka. You better be glad Ceas made the deal. I wouldn't have negotiated shit. We'll be thru tomorrow at noon. You got a week to come up with the rest, no excuses." He turned to leave, but stopped and turned back around.

"Matter-of-fact, make it three days. We got a Houdini on our hands… pulling racks out of thin air."

I laughed as I followed Drako out. We hopped in my Mustang and I dropped him off at home. Calling Seven, I made plans to kick it at her crib. After all was said and done, I was ready to bust and chill. With her, I could do both.

SEVEN

"Come on, baby. Let's go to bed," I informed my five-year-old son, Deuce. After reading over Ceas' text, it was time to put lil' man to bed. I had been waiting for his text all day, and I couldn't wait to see him.

"But, Mommy," he whined. "I'm not sleepy."

"I know, Deuce, but you have school tomorrow. It's thirty minutes past your bedtime, anyway. I let you stay up long enough."

"Yes, ma'am."

I took him to use the bathroom and brush his teeth before tucking him in. We finished our nightly ritual with me reading him one of his favorite bedtime stories. Deuce loved books. When I was pregnant, I read to him all the time. I heard that it helped develop a child's early language learning. So far, it had worked. Deuce was already reading second-grade level books. Even though he was more than capable of reading the book to me, I smiled as I read the words. We practiced the same routine every night he stayed home. I enjoyed our one-on-one time together.

Deuce fell asleep before the story ended. Sitting back in the chair, I closed the book and watched him sleep. I loved my son so much. He was my everything, literally. He was conceived from a one-night stand that I never planned on having. That particular night, I went to the club with Joie and some friends. I got sloppy drunk and let my guard down. I woke up the next morning lying next to some naked, fine, dark chocolate Nigerian man. Two months later, I found out I was pregnant. I was terrified. The Nigerian man and I didn't exchange numbers or any contact information, so I couldn't reach out and tell him. It was embarrassing, but I didn't even know the man's real name. He told me to call him D, and that's all I knew. At the time, it wasn't a big deal. The sex was good, and he got me right, but I never expected to see him again.

For three weeks, I contemplated on whether I wanted to keep the baby or not. I was a few weeks shy of my twentieth birthday, so I felt life had just begun for me. My life was moving fast and although I'm not proud of it, I got around. A kid wasn't in my plan. To be honest, a child could only do one of two things: ruin or save me. My initial thought was that having him would be a big mistake. How could I bring a child into the world when I didn't even know his father? I knew what it was like to have an absentee parent. I didn't want that my for child.

I was set on an abortion, but Deuce was destined to be in my life. The first time I felt him move, I knew I had to keep him. It became real at that point. I had a life growing inside me. I would never forgive myself if I harmed him in any kind of way.

My pregnancy strained relationships with people I thought were my friends and family. Even my mother showed her true colors. We were close growing up, but when she learned about Deuce, our mother-daughter bond took a turn for the worse.

The people I called friends started falling off, one by one. They had their own lives to live, but in my time of need, I expected to have the people closest to me by my side. That didn't happen. It hurt, but I couldn't let it kill my spirit. Deuce was coming whether he had a village or not.

Honestly, the only person who didn't fold on me was Joie. She'd been there for me every step of the way. Over time, she became my bestest friend, ride or die, sister, confidant, and Deuce's godmother. I didn't know what we would do without her.

Snapping back to reality, I kissed Deuce's midnight skin and went to shower. I let the water heat up and studied my bare body in the tall mirror. I'd always loved myself. I was confident with a little splash of conceitedness. Toasted vanilla skin, long, thick legs, succulent lips, and deep-set eyes...I was the shit! My light, sea blue wig made me look exotic. I hardly wore a lick a makeup because of my natural beauty and blemish-free skin. I think that's what attracted Ceas to me in the first place. When we first met at the club, I was with a few co-workers and I was plain old me; nothing spectacular. We had just gotten off from work, so I was still in my work clothes, looking rough. Still, he thought I was pretty enough to approach, and we'd been kicking it on the low ever since.

Ceas held a special place in my heart. He was the first man who showed true interest in me and not what I had to offer. I could admit, I was wild growing up, but having Deuce slowed me down. I knew *of* him, but Ceas and I didn't officially meet until I was twenty-two. By that time, Deuce was two-years-old. Not expecting anything serious out of our situation, I kept Deuce away from him. It wasn't anything personal. I just didn't want to bring a man into his life only to have him go ghost if things didn't work out. Ceas surprised me, though. He initiated the meeting with Deuce. He wanted to know everything about me, and that included my son. We took it slow at first but after a few months, the way Ceas interacted with my son had me sold! He started helping me with Deuce as much as he could. I appreciated it more than he knew. The more he helped and the more we got to know one another, the harder I fell. I wasn't the type to express my feelings and neither was he, but I was happy. Waking up knowing that I had someone who kept a smile on my face was the best feeling in the world.

For us, it worked. We'd been fucking on the low for three years. We knew people would object to us being together, so we chose to keep everybody out of our business. Now that I was getting older and thinking more, I wanted us to be more...much more! If he got down on one knee and proposed marriage, I would accept in a heartbeat. I was in love with Ceas, but I worried he didn't feel the same way. We had gotten comfortable. I mean, why fix what's not broke, right? Although that may have been true, I wanted Ceas to know how I felt. Whenever I got the courage to open up and tell him, something would happen. I took it as a bad sign and continued to keep my true feelings for him buried. I just prayed that he felt the same way.

"Shit, Ceas!" I screamed as he ripped my shower curtain back and the cool air shocked my soaking wet body. I had just stepped in the shower and didn't hear him come in. Using his key, he was able to sneak up on me.

"Scary ass," he chuckled, removing his clothes and getting in with me. "Ah, shit, Sev! Why you got this water so fuckin' hot?"

"Because it's what *I* like. No one told you to get in and get right under the water. That's on you."

"Tryin' to burn my damn skin off. How the hell can y'all women stand this shit?"

Giggling, I stepped closer to him, running my hand down his muscular, dark mahogany chest. It had been a few days since I'd last seen him, and I missed him like crazy. I guess the feeling was mutual. Licking my lips, I got a glimpse of his hard, curved dick. Ceas wasn't lacking in that area. He was very blessed. He shared that blessing with me any time I wanted.

"I see someone missed me," I teased, licking his chin.

Roughly, he gripped my face and shoved his tongue into my mouth. I savored the taste of weed and mint on his tongue and lips. I hungrily kissed him, allowing my feelings to radiate from my body. He bit my bottom lip, causing me to cream. I felt my nectar mixed with the water streaming down my inner thigh and legs. Ceas never failed to make my pussy run like a faucet. He trailed his kisses from my lips to my neck, and then to my breasts. I stroked his dick while he attacked my erect, aching nipples. His massive, calloused hand massaged one breast while he pleased the other with his fingers.

"Suck yo' dick, Seven," Ceas demanded in a sexy, husky voice.

Happily, I obliged. I kneeled to where I was eye to eye with his black monster. Ceas was a good eight or nine inches with a left curve that knew all my spots. Smiling, I kissed and sucked his dark mushroom head before lifting his dick and sucking his balls. He loved when I got porn star nasty and the way I felt, he would get that all night. He tensed up when I licked the spot between his balls and ass. I teased him with my tongue until I found my way back to the head.

"Fuck, baby. Swallow that shit."

I rested my throat and stuck my tongue out as far as it would go. When I felt his oozing tip hit the back of my throat, I curved my tongue around his throbbing shaft and closed my mouth. I couldn't help but moan at how good he tasted. I could suck on Ceas all day. With one hand around my throat and the other placed at the back of my head, he thrusted himself in and out of my mouth until his warm, tasteless nut was slithering down my throat. Pulling back, I spit it back on his dick and massaged it.

"You so fuckin' nasty," he moaned, peering down at me.

"You love it," I purred.

"Damn right! Come here. Let me wash you up."

He helped me stand up. Never taking his eyes off me, he lathered my loofah in his favorite body wash: Peach Mango. For some reason, he loved the scent on me. It was a heavenly smell, and Ceas kept my cabinet stocked. I didn't mind. It was one less thing I had to spend money on. As long as it made him happy, I had no complaints.

I enjoyed the feel of his hands and the loofah roaming my body. Ceas' touch was intense. The way he touched my body made me think we shared the same feelings for one another. He was gentle, but rough. The mixture of the two had me on the brink of an orgasm, and he hadn't even inserted a finger or dick into my body. His touch alone was powerful enough to send me to the edge and back.

Once he was satisfied, he stuck me under the shower head. With eyes full of pure lust; he watched as the water washed away the soap. Leaning back, I balanced myself on the wall and opened my legs, giving him the perfect view of my waxed pussy. If we weren't in the shower, he would be able to see my juices sliding down the crack of my ass. Taking my middle finger, I slowly slid it across my clit and into my opening. Ceas' dick jumped, making me even wetter. Without a second thought, he removed my finger, stuck it in his mouth, and replaced my finger with his dick.

"CEASAR!" I screamed, welcoming the painful pleasure.

No matter how many times we had sex, I had to adjust to his size. With two long, deep strokes, my pussy sucked him in. I wrapped my legs around him to help him get his balance. My back was pressed against the shower wall with my hands resting on his shoulder. I matched his thrusts with bounces of my own. He loved when I fucked him back. It made him put in work.

"Bounce on yo' dick, Sev. Fuck! This pussy good, girl."

"Ooo, I'm about to cum, Ceas!"

"Spit it out. I'm right behind you," he barked.

Seconds later, I came so hard I was sure I woke Deuce up with how loud I screamed. My orgasm was that intense. Ceas quickly pulled out, careful not to drop me, and sent his kids down the drain with the water on the brink of turning cold. We caught our breath, washed up, and got out.

After putting on clothes, we found our way to my kitchen. Opening the refrigerator, I pulled out some leftovers from earlier that day. Ceas took a seat at the table and began scrolling through his phone. Pausing for a moment, I listened carefully to see if I heard Deuce. Stepping toward the doorway, I confirmed no one was there. Satisfied, I removed a glass plate from the cabinet.

"How was yo' day?" Ceas asked, glancing up from his phone to see what I was putting on his plate. Anytime he came over, I made sure there was a meal waiting for him. He wasn't a little dude, and Ceas loved to eat. I didn't mind fucking and feeding him, especially when he was the one who supplied the food and everything else in the house.

About a year in, Ceas put Deuce and me up in a nice ass house. It wasn't anything super big or fancy, but it provided more than enough space for two people. Before that, I stayed in a small, two-bedroom apartment. I loved my little apartment. It was the first 'big girl' thing I did on my own, besides getting my car. Ceas constantly complained about how small it was, how noisy my neighbors were, and how

Deuce needed more room. That didn't matter to me, but I did agree that the kids running across the floor above me was nerve-racking. Besides, Deuce was getting bigger. His small room was only big enough to hold his toddler bed and a dresser. It was what I could afford, though. I was far from rich and didn't have the money for something bigger. I was fine with my apartment until I could do better for myself. That day came sooner than I expected. Out of the blue, Ceas picked me and Deuce up and brought us to the place I now call home. It was fully furnished with a stocked kitchen. I cried like a baby when he said it was mine. He even put the deed in my name. He told me to save all my checks from my job and he'd handle the rest. Taking his advice, I started two savings accounts; one for me, and one for my son. If Ceas walked out of our lives today, I'd be hurt, but I damn sure wouldn't be broke.

"It was chill," I responded, passing him his plate. He immediately dove in. "How was yours?"

"Busy, as usual. Aye, this food good as fuck, Sev."

"You know I throw down in the kitchen and everything else. I'm a woman of all trades," I boasted, smiling.

"I don't know about all trades, but some." He threw shade, slopping up his food like somebody was going to come and take it.

"Damn, slow down."

"You know how I do," he chuckled, pausing momentarily to chew. "I been waiting on this all day. A nigga was hungry."

"I see."

I sat down across from him and watched as he ate. The way he devoured the meal, it didn't take long. When he was finished, he pushed his plate forward and sighed.

"Thank you, baby. I needed that."

"My pleasure. Do you want some more?"

"Nah, I'm full and sleepy. You ready to go to bed?"

"Yeah. Deuce and I need to get up early in the morning."

"For what?"

"We're having breakfast with my parents before I take Deuce to school. They made me feel bad because they haven't seen him this week. I don't wanna go, but-"

"You know you don't have to go if you don't want to, right? I know how you feel about them, and I don't want y'all gettin' into it."

My relationship with my parents was complicated. I loved them dearly, but we always bumped heads. Growing up, my mother was strict as hell. She raised me alone and kept me on a tight leash. She didn't want me doing shit, which caused me to rebel. I did everything she didn't want me to do and more. It caused such a strain on our relationship that I moved out before I turned eighteen. Eventually, we reconnected. I was all my mother had and I didn't want to go through life with animosity against the person who brought me into the world. I got through a year and a half at our local community college with her support. It was hard, but I managed. Halfway through my second year, I became pregnant with Deuce. That's when shit really hit the fan. She was quick to verbalize her disappointment, which severed our relationship once and for all. I loved her, but I didn't like her.

Shortly after Deuce was born, my father reentered my life. He had been gone for damn near twenty years and finally decided to reappear. I don't know what he said to my mother, but she took him back and they carried on like no time had passed. I was skeptical about his return, but the way he treated me forced me to remove any ill-feelings I had toward him. He turned out to be a great father, and an even better grandfather. Both he and Joie watched Deuce while I finished my associate degree. He was there cheering me on when I graduated and even brought me a bouquet of roses on my first day as an administrative assistant. Not only did he love me, but he genuinely loved my son, too. Eventually, he softened my mother's hardened heart and got her to accept my son. Although me and her didn't get along, she began treating my son like he was her own. Because of that, I swallowed my pride and willingly let her be a part of Deuce's life. It wasn't about me. It was about what was best for my son. The more people that loved him, the better. The only reason I tried to work on my relationship with my mother was for my son's sake.

"I know, but I feel it's only right I give Deuce a chance to know his grandparents. Just because we bump heads doesn't mean they will. Plus, I know they would never do anything to hurt him. They love him just as much as I do."

"You know what's best, baby girl. If you believe it, everything'll work out."

"I hope so."

Placing his plate in the sink, Ceas picked me up and threw me over his shoulder. He walked to my bedroom, slapping my ass the entire way. Throwing me down on the bed, he pinned my arms above my head and grinded against me. I felt his hard-on through his boxers and giggled.

"I don't know if I can go another round," I whined as he kissed my neck.

"Let me just slide the head in. I'll be gentle."

I opened my legs wider and he smirked. Fooling around with his ass, we fucked all night. I woke up sore the next morning, but happy as hell; I always did waking up next to him. Too bad the feeling didn't last long. Before Deuce opened his eyes, Ceas was gone. I had never let my son see a man laying in my bed.

7

NORIEN

Drako was the type of nigga I didn't fuck with. I didn't like the dude, and I wasn't the type of muthafucka to pretend like I did. The way he twisted his face every time I came around rubbed me the wrong fucking way. Not being one to bite my tongue, I called him out on it.

"What is it with you? Huh?" I questioned, handing over the cash to pay my debt. I didn't need three full days after all. I was able to flip that shit and have Ceasar and Drako paid off in two. "What's the deal?"

"Chill with that noise," he demanded, turning his nose up. Still watching me, he called out to Kyan sitting pretty on a stool behind him. Handing her the black backpack I passed to him, he spoke. "Aye, Ky…count this for me."

Without hesitation, Kyan jumped up from her seat and took the bag. From one of the cabinet drawers, she produced a money counter and went to work. No one said a word while we waited for Kyan to confirm what I already knew. It was all there. I wasn't trying to cheat no damn body.

I would have rather dealt with Ceasar. The only thing was… Ceasar was a no-show to the meeting *he* scheduled. After texting him that I had his money, he responded back with a location and time. I showed up on time, only to be greeted by Drako and Kyan. Kyan wasn't the problem. She'd always been cool people. It was Drako that I had an issue with. I don't know what it was with that nigga. He had a problem with me from day one. I didn't do shit to the muthafucka.

"Twenty," Kyan spoke confidently. "It's twenty thousand."

"Count that shit again," Drako barked.

"For what?" I complained. "You heard what she said. I ain't gotta cheat you. Man, listen…it's twenty stacks…just like she said."

When Drako walked up to me, I defensively balled my fists up at my side. It was a natural reaction that seemed to piss Drako off even more.

"Relax those hands, nigga. Your pussy ass ain't gonna do shit." Through gritted teeth, he continued. "If I tell Kyan to do something, she's gonna do it. I don't give a fuck if she counted it ten times. I don't trust a nigga I don't know."

"If Ceas was here, I wouldn't be going through this shit," I muttered loud enough for him to hear.

"Well, he ain't. Things are done one way around here: my way. If you don't like it, don't come back." Smirking, he added, "But muthafuckas always come back. Now, kill that fuckin' noise."

After nodding Kyan's way, she straightened the rows of cash again. I remained quiet while she counted the money for a second time. Once again, the number came out the same…twenty-thousand dollars in a mixture of various bills. I hand counted that shit myself. If I could have kept a few dollars for my own pocket, I would have. That's how I knew it was right. Everyone in the small room knew what it was. Drako just wanted to be difficult.

"Satisfied now?" I asked, feeling vindicated. For some reason, I felt that Drako wanted the number to be off. Disappointment spread across his face when it was confirmed that every penny was present.

"I ain't never satisfied. You'll learn."

"Nah," I sneered. "Ain't shit I'm gon' learn from you." If he thought I was intimidated by his intense gaze, he thought wrong. Drako was just another nigga in the street. He might have been better off than me, but he was still a nigga, nonetheless. I didn't owe him shit. "A'ight, Kyan," I spoke, waving as she lit the end of a freshly rolled blunt.

"You outta here, Norien? You ain't smokin' first?"

"Hell nah, he ain't smokin'," Drako interjected. "I don't know where that nigga's mouth been. He ain't puttin' his lips on my shit."

"You're crazy, Drako!" Kyan laughed at his comment, like it wasn't disrespectful as fuck. "Why you say that shit in front of him? Dude, he's standing right here."

"Like I give a fuck."

Drako reached for the blunt being passed in his direction. As he inhaled deeply, the tip of the blunt lit up a bright orange color before slowly fading away. Drako held the smoke in his chest for a while before blowing it out in a forceful stream in my direction.

The nigga wanted to show out. I let him have his fun and talk his shit. It was cool for the time being. In the end, I would have the last laugh. As long as I stayed cool with Ceasar, it didn't matter how Drako felt about me. I was good.

"I'm out," I announced to Kyan. "Let Ceasar know I'll be in touch."

I exited the shotgun house that we'd met up at. Having Drako talk to me like I was some random bitch had me hot. I put up with a lot of things, but a bitch nigga with an attitude wasn't one of them. Drako was going to learn the hard way what type of nigga he was dealing with.

The rest of the day had been smooth and drama-free. Joie had a major attitude, which prompted me to leave our apartment within fifteen minutes of arriving. I wasn't with the bullshit. If she wanted to be mad because I was out making money, then so be it. If I couldn't get peace of mind at home, there was no reason for me to be there.

Things with Joie were complicated. I loved her and all, but not enough to stop my eyes from roaming. I kept her at home so I could stay in the streets doing me. I used the fact that I was working to cover up all the other shit I was doing. I fucked hoes out the ass, but I still came home to her. Well, sometimes. If I was knee-deep in some pussy, home was the last thing on my mind. All she could do was deal with it. I wasn't changing for her or no one else.

Our longevity proved that she would always be in my corner. My girl wasn't going nowhere. I'd been around her long enough to know that she was in love with a nigga. Even when she was mad, I knew with confidence that she would eventually come around. I had that effect on females, especially her. I was able to step in and mold Joie just the way I wanted. Without me, she didn't have shit. That made her need me and because of that, I could do anything I wanted.

I started off by removing her friends from her life. I didn't need those 'new age' independent bitches putting ideas in my girl's head. I made up shit to have Joie question their loyalty. When that didn't work, I lied and told her that they tried to push up on me. When it all boiled down, it was my word against theirs. She believed me and cut those bitches off.

Seven was the only hoe I let Joie kick it with. When I say hoe, I meant that shit literally. Years before she had her son, Seven got around. I never fucked the bitch, but I knew niggas that had. They called her 'The Head Master' and for good reason. I was standing a few feet away when she pulled my nigga's dick out his pants and sucked him off in front of my crew. That nigga's toes were curling in his shoes. As bad as I wanted to be next, sirens in the distance had us all running in opposite directions. The next time I saw Seven, she was with Joie. Everything about her was different, even the way she carried herself. I guess her 'hoe' days were behind her.

The only reason I let Seven stay in Joie's life was because their bond was too strong for me to break. They acted like family, and Seven stayed in her place. She wasn't all up in my business like the other broads. When she came around, she spoke. That was good enough for me. Besides, Joie was entitled to have one friend and one friend only. Other than that, I was all she needed.

April started blowing up my phone. I figured Kyan told her that we'd seen each other, and April knew I was out-and-about without Joie tagging along. If I wasn't with April, she assumed I was with Joie. She thought she was my only side piece, and I let her go with that assumption. If I stayed away from her too long, April got in her feelings and assumed the worst. Deciding to catch up with her later to bust one, I drove around solo until I reached the West End. The family and few friends that I had still considered the crime-ridden neighborhood home. Shit, I did too. Although I no longer lived in the hood, I would always and forever be a 'hood' nigga.

Acknowledging the familiar faces, I knew with a head nod, I cruised down the uneven streets. A few people waved and called out my name, but I didn't stop. If it wasn't about money, it wasn't worth my time.

"Yo, Nor!" Scooby called out, waving his arms. "Nor!"

I wasn't the type to stop and kick it with a coke head, but Scooby was an exception. Technically, he was family – my father's oldest living brother. He was a 'functional' fiend, working as a maintenance man for the projects in which he lived. For the right price, he would fix anything inside an apartment without reporting it to the agency. His payment was always white, and in powder form. There was no shame in his game when he posted up on the side of the project buildings and snorted his shit until he was high as a fucking kite. Then, he would resume working until his high started to fade, only to stop and repeat the process over. Scooby had issues, but he was still a stand-up guy.

"What's up, Old Man?" I asked, slowing down at the curb. I rolled down the passenger's side window and spoke directly to his face. "How you been?"

"Nephew!" he responded, slowly walking toward my car. He let his raggedy ten-speed fall to the ground. "I thought that was you. You know me. I'm making it." Reaching his hand toward the door handle, he asked, "Do you mind?"

"Nah, get in."

As he eased in, I got a good look at his frame. My eyes had been deceiving me. Scooby looked the same from afar, but up close, the difference was obvious. His sunken in face had more wrinkles than a little bit.

"Damn, Unc. What the fuck happened to you?"

"Life. Shit, lemme get a Newport."

"Come on now, Unc. You know I don't smoke that shit. Talk to me. What's going on?"

"I've been having a string of bad luck lately. Your auntie passed away last month. I took some time off to take care of her arrangements and when I went back to work, they fired my ass. Said something about I missed too many days. I been at that same job almost twenty-four years and never had a problem with being late or missing days. After everything I did for them." Shaking his head, he let out a loud, exasperated sigh. "I sat back while everyone around me was promoted, except my Black ass. They waited til' I was down on my luck to let me go. That shit wasn't right, and they know it."

"Yeah, that's fucked up. Can't you sue or something?"

"I wish I could, but I doubt it. Everything was verbal. My stupid ass didn't get nothing in writing. I ain't got proof of shit. It's their word against mine. You already know how that goes."

I didn't need Scooby to elaborate further. A single Black man was practically mute against a large government corporation. Even if he had proof, his word wouldn't mean shit. It was unfortunate, but Scooby was lucky to have kept his job as long as he did. The niggas I knew didn't stay employed long.

"Damn, how you makin' it?" I asked as my curiosity got the best of me. Scooby wasn't a dumb muthafucka. Surely, he could find a way out of his situation. The work he did with his hands was pure talent. He could fix just about anything or assemble a device without looking at the directions. His craft wasn't overshadowed by his regular drug use.

"By the grace of God, I been doing odd jobs here and there, but nobody really wants to hire an old man like me. It feeds my habit, but that's about it. I don't have much left for anything else. I can't seem to get nothing solid going."

"Where you been sleepin' at, Unc?"

"I still got my place. I don't know for how long. They've already started the eviction process. It's only a matter of time before the little shit I do have is sat on the curb. Something gotta come through, and fast, nephew."

"It will," I stated, losing interest in the conversation.

My focus was on the drug deal playing out in front of me. A street nigga like myself could sense action before it even started. The late model car that pulled up a few car lengths in front of me attempted to be discreet, but I peeped how it all went down. I knew exactly what it meant when the driver lowered the passenger's side window and the paranoid customer glanced around before leaning in. After the exchange was made, the man power-walked toward the brick building he came from and disappeared. The driver took his time pulling off. It was a fatal mistake.

A black Tahoe raced by me. The windows weren't tinted, allowing me to see all three occupants. Both windows on the passenger's side of the SUV were lowered and the tips of automatic rifles were pushed out. What sounded like fireworks stung my ears as bullets sprayed the unsuspecting car.

I sat frozen at the sight. The driver of the SUV was bold, but the gunmen were even bolder. They carried out their mission in broad daylight without the cover of a mask or disguise.

Seconds felt like minutes as Scooby and I watched in silence. Once the job was complete, the SUV drove off and the meddling neighbors took over. Several doors opened to see the aftermath, but everyone was smart enough to stay inside.

"Aye, Unc...go see if that nigga dead?"

"What? You saw the same shit I did. That nigga's dead. He ain't gettin' up."

"Exactly. Go see what that nigga got."

"I ain't going over there, nephew. What if he really ain't dead?"

"Man up, Unc. You sound like a bitch. Do you hear yourself? You know what...it doesn't even matter."

I got out the car and jogged over to investigate. The man was slumped over on the steering wheel facing the opposite direction. *Good*, I thought, quickly surveying the scene. At least I didn't have to look the muthafucka in the face.

The shattered window allowed me to reach in and grab the black bag sitting on his lap. I wanted to check his pockets, but that was too much of a hassle. Besides, fingerprints and DNA weren't anything I wanted to leave behind. Taking what was readily available, I snatched the bag and ran.

Scooby was still sitting in my car when I returned. Seeing his scary ass become elated when he saw the bag in my hand had me turning up my nose. The least he could have done was get out the car and watch my back. Shit, I did everything else.

"What you got?" Scooby asked, rubbing his hands together.

"Nothin' for you. Get the fuck outta my car."

"Damn, nephew! Don't be like that. Lemme see."

I looked inside the bag first. There were two eight-balls and a few grams of weed. The contents were disappointing, but the potential wasn't lost. I may not have come up on a lick, but I stumbled upon something much more valuable.

Tossing Scooby his drug of choice, he caught the cocaine as it flew toward his face. "What's this for?"

"For you helpin' me."

"But I didn't do anything."

"You will," I advised. "I want you to tell all your little friends that I'm the go to nigga from now on. You hear me? This is my block now. I'll be through tomorrow."

Scooby nodded and opened the door when he heard sirens in the distance. Once he pushed the door closed, I stepped on the gas and got the hell out of the vicinity.

8

JOIE

I DIALED Seven's number twice, but she sent me to voicemail. I felt some kind of way about being blatantly ignored, but my girl had a life, too. She couldn't stop everything just for me – even if I wanted her to.

Norien was MIA, leaving me alone in our apartment. I watched old reruns of *Martin* until I was tired of seeing his face. His usually funny jokes had me staring at the television in confusion. I didn't laugh or even crack a smile. It was then that I realized that I needed some fresh air. Something was definitely wrong with me. If Martin couldn't make me laugh, I wasn't in the right state of mind.

After putting on clothes, I opened the front door, not anticipating that the wind would push my hair behind my shoulders. "Whoa," I exclaimed, getting more of a breeze than I expected. I contemplated taking my Black ass right back in my bed, but I was tired of being cooped up. It was either stay home and be bored or get out and do something. Without a second thought, I chose the latter. Easing my feet into a pair of slides, I closed and locked the door behind me.

There was a small convenience store was within walking distance. Norien had the car, so I was on my own. It gave me a chance to think about all the shit going wrong in my life. When was I going to stop being so stupid and get my life together?

"Damn!" I heard someone call out with conviction behind me. "Aye!"

I didn't stop to see who it was. I wasn't a dog. Having a nigga call out to me like I was one didn't do anything for me. Niggas thought that just because they opened their mouth with a lame ass line, a chick was supposed to turn around. I wasn't that kind of girl. I didn't need male attention to boost my ego. If a nigga wanted me, he needed to come correct.

'Fuck you then, bitch' was the response to my dismissal. Hearing those disrespectful words caused me to stop. I whipped around, ready to give whoever it was a piece of my mind, only to see a nigga old enough to be my daddy riding off on a bike. A fucking bike! He had some damn nerve.

Picking up a rock, I threw it in his direction. Years of playing softball at the Rec Center payed off when it hit him on the side of the head. All I heard was *'Awe shit'* before he lost his balance and his whole body fell over. He tried to get up but with his legs still intertwined with the metal, it was a difficult task. Our eyes locked, and the pitiful expression on his face had me laughing uncontrollably. It served him right! You don't disrespect a female just because she's not interested.

"You fuckin' bitch," he barked, struggling to stand up. "Just you fuckin' wait! You ain't gonna be laughing when I get over there!"

As funny as the situation was, he was still a man out for revenge. He found his way to his feet and rubbed the area of his temple where the rock hit. When he saw the bright red blood staring back at him, he forcefully spun his bike around and cussed at me some more. I saw the devil in that man's face when he started in my direction.

That's when I put my track skills to use. I bobbed and weaved several cars, running straight into oncoming traffic. Cars slammed on their brakes so they wouldn't hit me and honked their horns to get my attention. I apologized in my mind because Lord knows I wasn't dumb enough to stop. I might have talked a good game, but an ass-whoopin' wasn't something I wanted. Maybe I should have thought twice before letting my emotions get the best of me. Because I didn't, I was literally running for my life.

"You can't run forever," he scolded, sounded closer than I imagined. "I'ma get your ass, bitch. Just wait and see."

I gained a sizeable lead when I entered an empty school parking lot. The chained gate had enough leeway for me to squeeze my small frame through. Once inside, I looked over my shoulder and noticed the man trying to get through with the bike. It was a lost cause. He was twice my size, and too damn big to slide through the tight space – especially hauling a big ass bike. I continued running, knowing there were two exits leading me off school grounds. I began to relax knowing that once I made it to the back of the building, I could make a left and enter a residential neighborhood. A right would lead me toward a busy street, making it harder for the crazy man to catch me. Either way, I was good. As long as he stayed held up at the gate, freedom was just beyond the high school's football field.

When I heard a loud gunshot behind me, my heart stopped. The nigga had a gun and was crazy enough to use it! My feet froze against the pavement as if I had been struck. Curiously, I turned around. The chain had been blown off the gate and the man was back on his bike, swiftly pedaling in my direction. He held his hand out and fired another shot, this time toward me. At that moment, my life was in danger. It was time to get the hell out of dodge.

I didn't even wait for the exit. Turning the corner and sneaking out of his view, I scaled the fence, cutting my hands in the process. I broke two of the natural nails that I struggled to grow, but I didn't have time to worry about the pain. I had to keep it moving.

Trees and bushes became my friend as I used them to shield my presence. The man was stuck on the school's property, scanning the field to see where I had disappeared to. When he rode his bike toward the football field and stopped to inspect the bleachers, I ran the opposite way, praying like hell that one of his bullets wouldn't stop my escape.

"Hey!" he yelled, watching me cross the street. "Get back over here! I ain't done with you yet!"

If he thought I was going to stop, he was the dumbest man alive. I ran until I couldn't run no more. My adrenaline kept me moving, even when my legs were ready to give out. Only when I knew I was out of harm's way did I allow myself to stop and catch my breath.

I was further away from home than I wanted to be. Dreading the walk back, I studied my surroundings and saw a sign for a small neighborhood store. Needing to refuel, I walked toward the building, cautiously glancing around. The psycho out to get me was probably long gone, but I didn't want to let my guard down.

With only a few dollars to my name, my selections were limited. I settled on a bag of chips and a fountain drink before making my way to the counter. Pulling out my wallet, I counted out the exact change as the chime of the door opening caught my attention.

"Kyan?" I quizzed, narrowing my eyes.

It had been awhile, but there was no doubt in my mind it was her. She looked different, more grown up, but still as pretty as ever. I, on the other hand, looked rough as hell, but that didn't stop me from speaking.

"Umm...hey."

Her greeting was dry. I wondered if the chick next to her with an obvious attitude had something to do with it. Before I moved away, Kyan was my best friend. I knew we would eventually run into each other again, but I thought our encounter would play out differently.

"It's been a minute. How've you been?" I continued, wondering if I should step forward for a hug. The way Kyan bypassed me and navigated through the store made that feeling quickly disappear.

"I'm good," she called over her shoulder. "Just making it as usual. You take care."

I didn't question her further. It was obvious that she didn't have much to say to me. I didn't know what I had done but somewhere along the line, my friendship with Kyan had dwindled down to nothing. Was it because I had been back in Birmingham for some time and never reached out? It wasn't intentional. I linked up with Seven and my life moved in a different direction. Was she mad at me for that?

After paying for my things, I turned to walk out, but my conscience prevented my legs from moving. I had to know what was up with Kyan. Even if we agreed to not be friends, there was no reason why we couldn't at least be cordial. I hadn't done anything to her.

Kyan was whispering something into her friend's ear when I walked up on them. The girl giggled, but stopped abruptly when I approached.

"You need something?" she asked, resting her elbow on Kyan's shoulder.

Ignoring her, I turned my attention to Kyan. "What's up? I thought you would be happy to see me. Why are you being like this? What did I do to you?"

"Wait? You know this chick?" The girl looked from Kyan to me, and then back to Kyan. "Why didn't you tell me?"

"Huh? Do I know you?" I asked, feeding off her wordplay. The girl didn't look familiar at all. Why would Kyan need to tell her that we knew each other?

"No," she blurted out with a sly grin. "It was just a question."

Her explanation didn't make sense to me, especially after she rolled her eyes and grilled Kyan with an attitude. I don't know what the girl's problem was, but it was obvious that there was one.

"What do you want, Joie?" Kyan quizzed.

"Damn, it's like that? What did I ever do to you?"

"Nothing," she shrugged.

Turning away from me, she began scanning the contents of the aisle. Standing there awkwardly, my feet refused to move. I didn't understand what all the animosity was for. We lost touch, so what? That didn't mean I didn't care about her.

"Ooo, I want some of these," Kyan's friend mentioned, bending down to pick up a bag of candy. "You want some, Ky?"

"Nah, I don't want shit. I'm good."

"Really? You're the one who wanted to stop. How you just gonna let her ruin your mood like that?"

I huffed in surprise. How was I ruining her mood? All I tried to do was get an answer out of her. Kyan sure had changed a lot over the years. I never thought that she would have a problem with me, of all people.

"It's all good, April. Get what you want so we can go. Oh, don't forget to get Damien something too."

"You're right. I'll get him some Skittles. You know how that boy loves candy…just like his daddy."

The mention of Skittles had me thinking about Norien. Even though I couldn't stand the fruity candy, Norien loved it. He kept a few packs in our apartment at all times. Knowing I wouldn't touch it, the candy was always available when he wanted some.

"Don't just stand there," Kyan mouthed in irritation. "If you got something to say, say it."

Honestly, I didn't know what to say. The person standing before me was a stranger. The fun-loving chick that I had grown to love was long gone. Her name may have been the same, but she wasn't the same person I used to know.

"I ain't got nothing to say," I finally stated. I realized, at that point, it was a lost cause. I couldn't force Kyan to feel something that wasn't there. "Y'all have a good day."

"Oh, we will," April responded with a hint of sarcasm.

Something about that girl was off, but I wasn't sticking around long enough to find out. I shook my head as I turned to walk away. I regretted going into the store in the first place. If I hadn't, I wouldn't know Kyan had an issue with me. At least then my mind wouldn't be filled with so much confusion.

When I was a few steps away from exiting the door, Kyan's question had me retracing my steps.

"How long you been fuckin' with that nigga, Nor?"

"Who?" I asked, not familiar with the shortened version on my man's name.

"You know who I'm talkin' about. Norien."

"Wait, how did you know that?"

"I know a lot more than you think I do," Kyan revealed.

"Don't we all," April giggled. "How's he doin', anyway? I haven't seen him around the block in a few days."

"Why don't you ask him yourself?" I challenged, feeling as though the girl was trying to be funny. Why would she ask me how my man was doing? Norien and anything he had going on had nothing to do with her.

"You know what," April began, biting down on her bottom lip. "I just might do that."

I didn't have time to respond. The door chimed, identifying someone had either entered or left. Out of the corner of my eye, I saw him. Everything in me froze.

"Jackpot! There you are, bitch!" My nightmare reappeared, dragging his raggedy bike in the store with him. He let it fall beside his feet as he retrieved his gun from under his clothes. "I told you I was gonna get that ass."

Sweat began forming on the side of my face. There was nowhere to run for cover. He had the aisle blocked. A satisfied grin spread across his face. Not ready to accept my fate, I turned to Kyan for help. Glancing over my torn attire, jacked up nails, and disheveled hair, she cleared her throat loudly.

"If you don't put that shit away, nigga," Kyan spat, crossing her arms in front of her. "You ain't scaring nobody, Tyson. Get the fuck on somewhere."

"Nah...this bitch got something coming. Look what she fuckin' did to me?" With his free hand, Tyson pointed toward the dry blood staining the side of his face.

Kyan shook her head and smirked. "And? Man up, nigga. You probably deserved it. Go on now. If I have to say it again, we're gonna have a problem."

To my surprise, Tyson returned his gun to its previous position and walked with his bike out of the store. Kyan's words held enough weight for that nigga to reconsider fucking me up. He left without saying another word to me, or anyone else for that matter.

"Thank you," I noted, exhaling a sigh of relief. "I really appreciate it."

"A little word of advice," she began, disregarding my apology. "Don't let that mouth or those hands write a check yo' ass can't cash. I saw what you did to that nigga's head. Things have changed, girl. Niggas don't just walk away no more. Personally, I would have fucked you up and pulled the trigger. Remember that! Next time, you're on your own."

Kyan walked away, leaving me standing there looking stupid. Her words reminded me of a female Ceasar. Who was this girl? More importantly, what had she done to my former friend?

9

DRAKO

Leaning back in my recliner, I toked on the potent joint laced between my index and middle fingers. I studied it carefully, admiring how I perfected my roll. I felt the high instantly, so I knew it was some good shit. Ceas and I never delivered weak product. Our shit was the best around, and we had plenty of customers and money to vouch for that. It was so good that we often took flights to deliver what we had.

That day, we flew out to San Antonio to deliver to a regular customer. He ordered from us every month, making the trip more than worth it. Herring was a White man who owned an illegal nightclub underground. He supplied his customers with the drugs he ordered from us. He faithfully paid close to a quarter of a million dollars for what he needed. Even still, he always threw in a little extra for our inconvenience. Herring had been a loyal customer for years, so we didn't mind traveling for money.

I had a few errands to run before we were scheduled to leave out. Fighting the urge to cover myself with my blanket, I forced myself out of bed and got dressed. Strolling down the hallway, I saw the door to one of my spare bedroom was open and something caught my eye. I stopped mid-stride and backtracked. It was an old sweater of Willow's laying on the bed. I thought I had gotten rid of any remnants of her, but I remembered I'd kept that sweater because she had it on when we first met. *Deceitful bitch*, I thought. Storming into the room, I grabbed the sweater and took it outside, where I set it on fire. I watched as it burned with a one-sided smirk.

"If only it was you, bitch," I mumbled under my breath.

I hardly ever talked about Willow. She scarred me, and that shit was dangerous. Not just for her, but for any other woman who tried coming into my life. That was why I only used women for what they were good for. Dick was the only thing a woman could ever get from me, and it damn sure wasn't for their pleasure. After Willow did me wrong, I became selfish. She fucked it up for every woman after her.

I met Willow six years prior at a neighborhood party. Everyone was talking and mingling except for me. I chose to sit on the porch and observe the scenery. There were too many people around for me not to be on my shit. My past made it hard for me to trust a muthafucka, so it was habit that I had eyes on everyone at all times.

Ceas and I passed a blunt back and forth, nodding our heads to the music when Willow caught my attention. I'd never seen her around the way before. She stood out among everyone in the crowd. I watched her sway her thick hips to several songs before she looked my way. Our eyes locked and she blushed. Right then, I knew I could rap to her.

Willow was a beautiful woman. Her smile was the first thing I noticed about her. It was big enough to brighten anyone's day. Deep dimples indented her cheeks when she smiled, and I loved that shit. It was sexy as fuck. She had short, curled black hair with skin the color of a Tootsie Roll. The curves she had should have been illegal. I could picture her ass rippling as I fucked her from the back, and I knew I had to make that magic happen.

"I'll be back," I said to Ceas. I swaggered down the steps with low eyes. I nodded at the people who spoke as I made my way to where she stood. All her friends jumped around and giggled as I approached. I chuckled at how child-like they acted. My presence seemed to always affect woman. I didn't do anything special. I was just being me.

"Excuse me, baby girl. What's yo' name?" I asked, looking her in her almond-tinted eyes.

"Willow. You're Drako, right?" she giggled.

"You know who I am. Everyone out here does, so don't front. Come holla at me."

We spent the remainder of the party kicking it and getting to know each other. After a few drinks and joints, we were both lit. I fucked Willow on the first night and immediately got hooked. Her pussy was like a fuckin' secret potion I became addicted to, along with everything else about her. Shit was good with us for about two years, until I noticed she started acting different. The way she moved became sketchy and her actions changed. It was as if she stopped caring. For the life of me, I couldn't understand why. I was feeling her, big time. Not ready to let go of what we spent so much time building, I made our relationship my priority. I went the extra mile to show her I loved her, and that I would do anything to keep her happy. Her response was always negative or half-hearted. The love just wasn't there anymore on her part.

To find out what was up, I started being smart and clocking her moves. One day, I told her I would be late coming home when I really was sitting across the street at the neighbor's house. I watched the house like a hawk for anything out of the ordinary. It was after midnight when a car pulled in my driveway. A man got out and Willow waited at the door for him dressed in only a robe. The short, satin number left little to the imagination. When the man reached the door and Willow leaned up to hug him, the robe fell open and proved what I already suspected. She didn't have shit on underneath it. The anger I felt had my veins pulsating. The bitch was cheating on me, and in my own damn house.

Anything Willow asked for, she got. She had the best of everything; cars, clothes, jewelry. Money was no object when it came to her. All I asked in return was for her to respect three things: my house, her body, and me. She fucked all that up in one night. I took twenty minutes to smoke and cool off. As mad as I was, the clean-up crew was about to have two bodies on their hands. Instead of acting out of anger, I took my time and thought about other possibilities. When I realized that there were none, I casually strolled across the street to my house.

Quiet as a mouse, I eased inside through the garage door and shut the door behind me. The sound of low music playing came from our bedroom. My pistol was in my hand as I tiptoed down the hallway. The door was cracked, so I peeked inside. What I saw made me lose it. Willow was on her knees sucking some nigga's dick as he counted *my* money. I knew it was mine because the safe occupying the corner next to Willow was open and empty. I fucked up when I got too comfortable and allowed her access to everything in my life. I felt I could trust her, but sadly, that bitch proved me wrong.

Kicking the door off the hinges, Willow ducked, and it barely missed her head. The nigga went to his waist to retrieve his gun, but he was too slow. He was dead before he could do a full turn.

"AAAHHH! DRAKE!" Willow screamed.

My pistol was trained on her with my finger on the trigger. My mind told me to kill her, but my heart wouldn't let me. I allowed her to walk away before I lost it. That was the biggest mistake I ever made. People who played with my emotions didn't live long. Willow was lucky in that sense, but the bitch was on borrowed time. I had something for her. The next time I laid eyes on her, she would be meeting her fuckboy in hell.

After our relationship ended, I changed. Willow fucked up any chance for any female to receive any form of love from me. Like Biggie said, 'Fuck bitches, get money'.

In all honesty, she was lucky that I showed her love in the first place. There were only three people I gave a damn about in life: Ceas, Kyan, and my grandmother, Nita. Everyone else was dispensable. My top three couldn't be replaced.

My grandmother raised me after my mother passed from a brain aneurysm when I was three. I didn't remember my mother, only the pictures and stories my grandmother told me. She passed away a few years later, leaving me to fall into the hands of the legal system. No one knew who my bitch ass father was, and no other family member wanted to take me in. I was placed in Big Momma's care, and she housed me until I was seventeen and moved out.

Moving in with Big Momma was a blessing in disguise. Meeting Ceasar and Kyan saved my life. After my grandmother passed, my thoughts turned dark. The older I got, the more I felt there was no purpose for me to live. Many nights, I sat on top of Big Momma's roof contemplating on whether I wanted to jump or not. Even Ceas didn't know about those dark nights or thoughts I had. No one did, and the shit haunted me every now and then. Thinking about Willow caused all those suppressed feelings to resurface. It only added to the list of reasons why I desperately wanted to blow her fuckin' wig back.

Snapping from my thoughts, I stomped the small fire out and swaggered back inside to get dressed. I put on all-black and tied my dreads into a low ponytail. Patting my pockets to ensure I had everything, I jogged out to my truck and left with a blunt hanging from my lips. I was backing out the driveway when my phone buzzed against my thigh.

"Ceas, what's good, nigga?"

"Not shit. Fuckin' with Seven before I roll out. I got something to run by you."

"It ain't about that weak ass nigga, is it?" I huffed, gripping the steering wheel tighter.

"Nah. You said his shit was good, right?"

"Yeah, but that doesn't mean a fuckin' thing to me, bruh. That nigga ain't right."

"I hear you."

Ceas brushing off my comment pissed me off. He knew how I was when I felt a way about a muthafucka.

"Don't get dropped, Ceas. I know you hear me, but listen to what the fuck I'm sayin'. I don't get gut feelings for no reason."

"Stop complainin', Drake. You whinin' just like that singin' muthafucka," he clowned me, laughing hard as hell. I heard Seven muffle a low moan, followed by Ceas whispering something. Shaking my head, I hung up on him, only for him to call me right back.

"I ain't tryin' to hear what the fuck you and Seven over there doin'.

Hit me back when you finished fuckin' that girl. Don't be in the pussy so long that you miss the flight to San Antonio."

His bitch ass hung up in my face. Chuckling, I shook my head and fired up my blunt. I drove around and handled the list of things I had to do. My day was running smoothly until I got to my last house. There was too much commotion going on in the front, and it had me heated. Ceas and I liked for our shit to be low-key and ran in a certain order. The shit I witnessed was far from acceptable.

I sat back and finished off my blunt while recording what was going on. It was about to be lights out for all those muthafuckas, so I let their little party last a few moments more. I spotted a few of our workers smoking what I was sure was our product while entertaining a slew of ratchet bitches. Licking my lips, I exhaled slowly to calm my rising anger. My blunt was still lit, and I wasn't about to blow my high for dumb muthafuckas.

What pissed me off the most was that they weren't doing what the fuck we paid them to do. No one noticed me. We trained them to be on their shit at all times, but it was obvious they didn't take notes or even care for that matter. That was a waste of my time, and my time was fuckin' valuable. They should've been on my ass the second I turned onto the damn street.

Throwing my roach in the ashtray, I sent Ceas the video and waited for a reply. Like I knew he would, he called me.

"I hope you about to blast all those bitches," he spoke calmly into the phone.

"My name ain't Drako for nothin'. I've been sittin' here for a good ten minutes, and not one of them even turned my way. I'm about to light this bitch up. Anyone in the way better move or get blasted. Their choice."

"Handle that and by the time you're finished, I'll have some new niggas on the roster to take their place."

"Sayless."

"Aye, what you think about lettin' Seven tag along with us to visit Herring? You know business is always quick, so we can get into some shit later," Ceas suggested.

I'd been around Seven before and she was cool and chill as fuck. If she was any other bitch, I would have declined. I didn't like other people being in our shit, but Seven had been around for years. Plus, I knew Ceas' punk ass pillow talked with her. I did the same with Willow. Only difference was, Willow was a snake bitch and used all my shit against me.

"Yeah, I'm cool with it, only because we got different suites, nigga. I ain't tryin' to be a third wheel and hear y'all fuckin' all night."

"You gon' hear that regardless. Seven a damn singer in the bed."

Seven started going off on Ceas in the background. I laughed at their crazy antics and hung up. It was obvious that my nigga was in love.

Securing my pistol, I opened my truck door and leaned against the roof. I sent a head shot to the first worker I saw, and shit was on ten after that. Everyone was screaming and running in different directions. I successfully sent a head shot to five of the six workers with precise accuracy, leaving the one in charge of the house for last. He was sprinting down the street carrying some bitch. I followed behind them, driving with my door open.

POW!

I killed the woman on his shoulder before sending one straight through his legs. He fell to the ground, and the dead weight of the woman caused him to fall harder. I heard him yell out in pain as I threw my truck in park in the middle of the road and hopped out. He was trying to low crawl away from me, so I stomped on his open wound to stop him.

"Aaaggghhh!"

"Shut that shit up, nigga. Why the fuck you playin' with me? You stand tall instead of runnin' like a bitch when I come around," I barked, applying more pressure to his wound.

"Dra...Drako? I ain't know that was you," he stammered, lying straight through his teeth. "Wh...what's goin' on?"

I shot him in the arm for thinking I was stupid. After I got the answers I needed from him, I killed him with a bullet to the head.

After calling the clean-up crew, I made another call to shut the block down.

The shit took longer than I thought. Pressed for time, I headed straight to the strip to meet Ceas and Seven. When I pulled up, my mouth fell open when I noticed Joie standing next to Seven. Ceas stared at me with a smirk, and I knew that nigga had set everything up.

"Ol' sneaky muthafucka," I mumbled to myself.

This trip was about to be one to remember. I could feel it.

10

KYAN

"Why these muthafuckas always want to act a fool when Ceas and Drako ain't around?" I mumbled to myself.

Everyone knew when Ceas and Drako were out of town on business that Jake and I were in charge. It hadn't been a good thirty minutes that their jet took off, and shit was already popping off. Jake was attending other business, leaving me to deal with childish ass niggas who didn't take their lives seriously. It was the low-level niggas who got in the game to floss and who were money hungry. They were the types who could ruin everything, and it was my job to get rid of scum like that.

Applying a thin coat of lip gloss, I popped my lips and smiled at my reflection in my car mirror. Adrenaline rushed through my veins as I thought of the three bodies I was about to add to my body count. I had some built-up frustration from arguing with Nova, so I was itching to take it out on someone other than her.

When Nova and I argued, I balled my anger and frustration up tightly before burying it deep inside. I hated bad vibes in our home, so I did whatever I could to keep that energy away. It was hard because Nova didn't like to let things go. She could keep an argument going for days if I allowed her to. She knew better, though. She knew that was one thing I hated. Lately, she'd changed. Things were better than they ever been, and I prayed Nova didn't revert to her old ways.

Don't get me wrong; I loved Nova for who she was, and I was in no way trying to change her. She took it upon herself to work on things when she noticed how her actions pushed me away. We still had small petty arguments, but nothing big enough that we couldn't handle. A small disagreement about hanging out with some of her work friends rubbed me the wrong way. I wanted Nova to have a life outside of me, but because of my line of work, she had to be cautious. The place she wanted to go was notorious for gang activity and violence. If I was there to watch over her, it would be a different story. Since I was in charge of everything, I couldn't hang out and chill. I told Nova she couldn't go, and that started her attitude. Instead of spazzing out on her, I left. Now, the three men fucking up on the job were about to feel my wrath for both Nova and their own shady ways.

About a year ago, Nova and I split up from her pettiness and immaturity. I grew up around two mature, strong-willed men, so it naturally rubbed off on me. Ceas and Drako were hoes, but they didn't fuck with just any ratchet female. Well, maybe they did. I don't know, but they sure as hell didn't bring any hoe around me. The females they acknowledged in public had good ass jobs or careers. Even when Drako fucked with Willow, she had something going for herself. She worked in the registration department at the local hospital and still her own money. My brothers had standards. Being the youngest, I took in their likings and meshed them with mine. I developed standards, too. There was no doubt in my mind that I could have any female I wanted. I just didn't roll like that. I was a one-woman type of chick, which was something Nova found hard to believe.

Nova and I split up because of her jealousy. I met with a potential client for lunch, and that client just so happened to be a woman. I didn't inform Nova of the meeting because I never discussed much with her about what I did in the streets. It wasn't of her concern, but she felt that particular meeting was. Long story short, one of her envious ass friends saw me and snitched. To get back at me, Nova went on a date with one of her ex-boyfriends and I shut the muthafucka down. I killed that nigga and made Nova square up with me. It didn't matter that we were in a relationship and it was considered abuse. That bitch had to see me. Nova begged me not to fight her, but when I hit her with a nice, quick two-piece, she swung, and it was over. I beat her up, then broke up with her and ignored her for a whole month straight. I didn't utter one word to her or even look her way. I hated that fact that I had to fight someone I cared so much about. She hurt me to my core, and I wanted to express that. We didn't talk again until we ran into each other at a gas station. Her tears didn't move me, but her actions after that did. She proved to me that she wanted things to work, which was why we were together again.

Shaking off my ill feelings, I cocked my matte black glitter Nine and stepped out my vehicle. I swayed my head at the clack of my heels against the concrete. I took a slow and steady stride with a smirk turning the corners of my glossed lips. On the outside, I remained calm and cool. I never let a nigga see me sweat or see my true emotion. In no way did I want to seem vulnerable to anyone who wasn't close to me, and I mean inner circle close. Being in foster care made me like that.

I rolled my neck and opened the door to be met with the barrel of a gun. Now, the worker wanted to be on his shit. By that point, it was too late.

"I should be dead. Now, you are," I said, shooting worker one in the head.

His body fell to the ground with a loud thump, causing the other two workers to come around the corner with their guns raised. They didn't hear me shoot worker one because of my silencer. I was trying to catch all the muthafuckas by surprise.

"Kyan, what did you—"

I sent a bullet through worker two's throat, sucking my teeth as I watched him choke on his own blood. The anger and pressure I felt earlier was releasing with each death. There was only one worker left. With our guns pointed toward each other, my intense gaze dared him to shoot first. He opened his mouth to speak and I pulled my trigger.

Shooting him in the kneecap, he fell to the ground, crying out in agony.

"Oh, shut up," I taunted. "You sound like a bitch."

"Wh…wh…why? What did we do?" he stammered through gritted teeth.

Spit flew from his mouth, and his face turned red from the pain. I was amused. Watching a niggas squirm and stumble over their words was always satisfying to me.

Cocking my head to the side, I quizzed, "Are you supposed to be questionin' me?"

Silence.

"Oh, you can't talk? Now, you're ignorin' me?"

"No."

"No what?"

"No ma'am."

"Ah, that's better!" I exclaimed, smiling.

Slightly pulling up my skinny jeans, I straddled him and sat on his chest. It became uncomfortable for him, and he didn't know whether to focus on the pain in his knee or his breathing. I roughly grabbed his cheeks and shook his head back and forth forcefully.

"I heard y'all muthafuckas think this is a charity. Y'all be givin' out free shit like y'all pay for the shit. Tell me that ain't so?"

I stopped jerking his head long enough to look in his eyes and study the guilt in them. Before he could spit a lie from his dry, crusty lips, I snapped his neck, killing him instantly. Pleased with my work, I went through the house, collecting all the drugs and money. It took me an hour to get everything I needed before setting the house on fire. After the blaze had destroyed any possible DNA linking me to the crime, I used my burner phone to call the fire department. The place would be ashes by the time they arrived.

I sent Jake a text letting him know I handled everything and headed home. I took a detour to stop and get Nova some flowers. My head was in a different place after murking those three dudes. I was ready to talk and hear her out. She loved when I apologized with a beautiful bouquet followed by an all-night, mind-blowing sexcapade. I could admit that I was the cause of our argument, so it was only right that I was the one to apologize. I hated when Nova was upset with me.

Our place was close to her favorite flower shop. Scanning the selection, I grabbed what I needed and made my way to the front. There was a man ahead of me in line picking up an order. I was scrolling through my phone to pass time when something he said caught my attention.

"They're for my girlfriend, Willow."

I whipped my head up and cocked it to the side. I knew I heard him correctly. The Willow who broke my brother's heart was the only Willow I knew. The name wasn't common. Was he talking about her? If so, that was one hell of a coincidence.

"Uhm, excuse me," I said, tapping his shoulder. He turned around, looked me up and down, and licked his lips. I rolled my eyes as I kissed my teeth. "I eat pussy, nigga. Anywho, I heard you say Willow. Is this the one you're talking about?"

I showed him the picture I had of her. He looked back and forth between the picture and me with a raised brow. He observed the picture a few seconds longer before shaking his head no. Lying muthafucka.

"No, that's not my Willow."

"Oh, sorry."

He paid for the flowers and jetted out the shop without looking back. I placed Nova's flowers on the counter and glared at Chelsea, the florist.

"What did you do now, Kyan?" she asked with a smirk.

I was a regular at the shop and Chelsea knew me by name. She'd learned my choice of flowers meant different things. If things were bad with Nova, I bought red roses. If things were good, I bought sunflowers.

"I fucked up. I was picking with her and took it too far," I informed her, sliding extra money across the table. She peeked around before taking it and sliding it in her pocket. "Check it though, I need your help."

"What do you need?"

"I need whatever information you have on the man who just left out of here before me. Phone number, address, whatever you got."

"Let me see."

I waited patiently as Chelsea tapped away at the computer beside her and printed off a paper. She handed it to me with a pleased smirk. I read over it and bounced in excitement. It had everything I asked for.

"Yes! Thank you, Chelsea. You don't know how much you just helped me."

"Any time, girl. Go make up with Nova, and tell her I said hello."

I promised to do just that as I darted out the shop on my toes. Drako had been trying to get his hands on Willow for some time. I had, too. I couldn't wait to beat that bitch to a pulp. She deserved death and so much more.

As I drove home, I debated on calling Drako and telling him the good news.

"There's no way I can keep this to myself," I mumbled to myself as I tapped Drako's name on my phone. It rung several times before going to voicemail. I hung up, only for Drako to ring me back in seconds. Smacking my lips, I let it ring all the way through and waited for him to call back. If he couldn't answer the phone the first time, then neither could I.

"Hello?"

"Why the fuck you ain't answer when I called you back?" Drako rudely spat.

"Why the fuck you ain't answer when I called you the first time? Yeah, okay."

"Man, what you want, Ky?"

"Well…I called to give you some of the best news of your life, but since you want to have a funky ass attitude, I'm good."

I hung up on him and threw my phone in my passenger seat. Turning my music up, I jammed the ten minutes to my place while ignoring Drako's calls. He was relentless and when I finally parked in my spot and answered, he was fuming.

"Ky, thank God you my lil' sister or I would beat yo' ass like a real nigga. Why you like to play so fuckin' much, but get mad when niggas do that shit to you?"

"I'm not playin', Drako. You so damn rude all the time, so I said fuck it."

"You know how I am, so deal with the shit," he stated nonchalantly. I couldn't stand him sometimes. "Real shit, what you need to tell me?"

"I may have found Willow."

"Didn't I tell you to stop fuckin' playin', Kyan?"

Instead of acknowledging him, I sent him the information on the paper Chelsea gave me and explained what happened at the florist shop. Drako knew I wouldn't lie about something so serious. He was silent for a few seconds, and I had to yell to get his attention.

"You good, Bruh?"

"Yeah. We'll rap about this shit more when I get home. Good lookin' out, sis."

I ended the call and sighed. When Drako got quiet like he did, it wasn't good. I didn't know what he was thinking, and it made me second guess if telling him was a good idea or not. I sent Ceas a text to get his opinion before going inside to make things right with Nova.

11

CEASAR

SEVEN AND I couldn't catch a break. Every time we snuck off for some 'alone time', Drako was right there reminding me of the whole purpose of the trip. It was for business, but I wanted to mix a little pleasure in there too. My nigga made that difficult, though. He could have easily entertained Joie for a bit while I helped Seven with some vocal lessons. Every time my dick slid up in her tight walls, she sung my name in a high soprano. Just the thought of it made my dick hard, but Drako was blockin'.

"Where you think you goin'?" Drako asked, watching me open the door of our suite. Seven had already left and was outside the hotel waiting for me.

"Damn…can a nigga get some air?" I snapped. I hated being asked about my whereabouts. Drako knew that.

"Make it quick," he demanded. "We're leavin' in fifteen."

"Don't fuckin' rush me."

I grilled him as I left out the door. We didn't have to be at our spot for another hour. Drako claimed he didn't want to be late, but he never worried about that shit before. We moved on our time. That's how it had always been. The real issue was Joie. Drako didn't want to be alone with her. He talked all that shit, but was avoiding her at all costs. For his sake, I hoped Joie jumped on his dick when I left. Maybe that nigga would be out of his feelings and give Seven enough time to jump on mine.

Unfortunately, there wasn't an extra room to sneak off to. The hotel mistakenly double-booked our reservation, giving our second room to someone else. With the hotel booked for an event, our money bribe didn't go the way we wanted. Instead of immediately seeking an alternative, we all settled in the room and agreed to find another spot to lay our heads after our meeting with Herring.

It sounded good at the time, but after Seven took my hand and stuffed it under her skirt, my dick jumped in my pants. She wasn't wearing panties and my fingers were slick with her juices.

The bathroom wasn't an option. Drako would have busted in and called us on our shit. We needed to get away, and our ride was the first place that came to mind. I hadn't got down in a car in years, but the thrill of it all had me quickening my pace.

By the time we reached the car, three minutes had already passed. Opening the door, Seven slid into the passenger's seat while I stood by checking out the scene. No one was close enough to notice her unzipping my pants and caressing my dick with her hand. I did, though. The muscles in my upper thigh tensed when her tongue tickled the head and her warm mouth sucked me all the way in. I got into it, fucking her face while holding her head steady. The slurping noises she made took it to a different level. I could have busted right then and there, but I wanted some pussy first. I didn't like getting mine until Seven got hers.

"You ready for me?" I asked, glancing around once again. A couple entered the parking lot, but they walked in a different direction.

I thought Seven would have freed my dick from her mouth and got down on all fours, but she didn't. She kept sucking…and sucking…and sucking. My eyes rolled back in my head. *Damn.* Her mouth needed to be bonded and insured.

"Seven," I warned. "Come on now, you 'bout to make me cum. Let me get some of that pussy first."

She ignored me and continued sucking my dick like her life

depended on it. I leaned against the top of the car for support. That shit felt so good, a moan slipped from my lips. There I was, a big rough nigga turning into a bitch behind some of the best head of my life. I couldn't help it. Seven did things to me that no other woman had ever been able to do. I cared about her. It made anything we did sexually that much more special.

Seven started talking all freaky and shit, and I let my pants and boxers fall all the way to my ankles. She told me exactly where she wanted my kids, and I pumped harder to fulfill her request. Leave it to Drako to fuck up the experience. He appeared out of nowhere, sending the nut creeping up my shaft back down to my balls.

"Really, nigga?" he complained. "This what you out here doing? Put yo' shit up."

My dick was still hard when Seven retreated further into the car. She was embarrassed to have been caught slobbing on my dick, but I wasn't. Drako's the one who walked up on us.

"You said fifteen minutes," I responded coldly, giving him my back while securing my dick in my pants. "My phone ain't even went off yet." Out of curiosity, I glanced at my cell, noticing that I still had two and a half minutes left. *Inconsiderate muthafucka*, I thought.

"Money calls. All that other shit can wait."

Joie strolled up a few seconds later. She was breathing hard and bent over for a second to catch her breath. "Sorry, y'all. Drako didn't tell me he was leaving. I walked this whole damn lot trying to remember where we parked."

"That's fucked up, Drako," I spat. "You could have at least waited for the girl."

"For what? She ain't my guest. That's y'alls responsibility. Besides, they ain't going no way. You know how Herring is. He doesn't like new faces."

Drako had a good point. Herring was a paranoid muthafucka. He questioned any and everything around him. Sliding Seven the card for the room, I instructed her and Joie to stay put until we got back.

I took my position in the passenger's seat while the girls reentered the hotel. Drako knew better than to say shit to me. I was on one. The more I thought about it, the madder I became.

"That was some fuck boy shit you did," I told him, rolling down the window. "You could have fuckin' waited."

"Just like you could've told the fuckin' truth. Just say you wanted some ass. Why y'all sneakin' around anyway? Come on, now. That's kiddie shit."

"Nah, that's a nigga not wantin' everybody in his business. Joie was up there. Shit...y'all could've been getting it in just like I was. Maybe some pussy will do your ass some good."

"Fuck that! I don't want that bitch. Fuckin' with a nigga like Norien, her pussy probably got miles for days."

"How would you know? You ain't never been close enough to sniff, nigga. That's what the real problem is. You still on that bullshit."

"You must want to get out and walk," Drako mumbled.

"I ain't walkin' no muthafuckin' where. Don't get mad at me cuz you couldn't smash. That ain't my fault. I practically hand delivered you the pussy, nigga. Joie knew who was comin' on this trip. She didn't have a problem with it. Why do you?"

Turning up the music as loud as it would go, Drako ended our conversation. I couldn't understand why he had a problem. When I invited Seven to hang with me, Joie was right there. I extended the invitation to her as well and she tried to hide her smile when she found out I was rolling with Drako. I thought I was doing the nigga a favor. He felt some kind of way about the past, and I gave him time and opportunity to clear all that shit up. Instead of taking advantage of it, he chose to keep the chip on his shoulder.

Cool, I thought, texting Seven on my phone. I told her to keep it wet for me and I'd be there as soon as I could. She replied back with a picture that had my dick on mega rock. Turning off my phone, I pushed my sexual feelings to the back of my mind.

Something was off when we arrived at Herring's club. He was acting funny, even more paranoid than usual. The way he kept looking over his shoulder alarmed Drako as well. My dude called him out on it before handing over his order.

"Man, Herring, what the fuck is wrong with you?" Drako scoffed. "Why you keep lookin' back there? You expectin' somebody?"

"Nope. Nobody at all."

The sound of scuffling could be heard behind one of the doors. We were in the basement of a brick building that doubled as a pawn shop. Drako and I shared a knowing glance. Herring's ass was lying.

"Who's here?" Drako asked cautiously.

"Just us," Herring responded. He refused to make direct contact with his eyes. "Oh, and Duke. I brought my pit with me today."

"A pit, huh?" I smirked. "Mind if we check?"

"Yeah, I do. There's no need. Let's just get this over and done with."

Herring's reluctance confirmed my suspicion. Some shady shit was going on. Drako passed me the bag containing our product and stepped toward the door with his gun raised. I threw the strap over my shoulder as Herring's eyes followed Drako.

"There's nobody back there," he warned.

Ignoring him, Drako continued on. "You sure about that? Not even a pit?"

Raising his foot, Drako kicked in the door. It fell in and broke in half under the pressure.

"Tank! Salvador!" Herring called out. "Watch out!"

Gunshots rang out as Drako unloaded in the room. The familiar sound of bodies hitting the floor echoed in my ear. I heard two, but the way Drako kept shooting, there could have been more.

"You got a lot of explainin' to do," I announced coldly. When Herring turned around, he was face-to-face with the barrel of my gun. "Start talkin' or I'll start shootin'."

"Nobody was supposed to get hurt," he cried, resting his hands on his head. "It wasn't personal. I just needed the money."

"What money? What are you talkin' about?"

"Business ain't doin' too good. I'm losin' money, and lots of it. The FEDs are on my ass and my lawyers are taxing the hell out of me. I just thought—"

"You thought you'd get over on us," Drako finished for him. "That's bullshit, Herring. You was gonna have those two lil' niggas rob us?"

"I just needed to get my hands on something quick. Something to bring in some money."

"You had us fly all this way and you didn't have the money all along?" I pressed my lips together and exhaled loudly. "That's cold, Herring. I didn't expect that shit from you."

"We been doin' business way too long," Drako added. "Now, look what you did? You fucked up a good business relationship and got three niggas killed in the process."

His eyes practically bulged out of his head when he realized he was number three.

"No...please," he begged. "Don't—"

I pulled the trigger, silencing him for good. I was tired of hearing that muthafucka talk.

Texas was short-lived. Drako and I went back to the hotel and checked out that same night. We flew back home without any mention of what transpired. The situation was fucked up, and I was happy to be back on my own turf. Being in familiar territory allowed me to move around how I wanted to. It also gave me a chance to kick it with Seven without extra eyes following us around. Just because I wasn't ready to announce to the world that Seven had me on some monogamy type shit didn't mean there was anything wrong with what we were doing. Last time I checked, we could do whatever we wanted to. We were both grown.

I gave Seven a day to get settled in before hitting her line. I thought I was being considerate, but my action rubbed Seven the wrong way. She answered the phone with an attitude.

"What?"

"Damn...it's like that? What did I do?"

"You're really gonna act like you don't know? Ceas, don't play with me. Why didn't you come over last night? I was waiting for you and everything."

Here we go, I thought, rubbing my forehead. Women…they're so damn complicated. "Did I tell you I was comin' over?"

"No."

"How 'bout this…did you *ask* me to come over?"

Her voice softened as she answered honestly. "No."

"So, let me get this straight." Pushing the half-eaten box of Chinese out from under my face, I made myself comfortable on the couch. "I didn't tell you I was coming over. You didn't ask me to come over, but you're mad at me for not comin' over, right?"

She had the audacity to agree with me. "Right."

"You done lost your muthafuckin' mind. Do you hear yourself? Do you know how stupid that sounds?"

"It's not stupid, Ceas! You know how bad I wanted you in San Antonio. It ain't like I got a chance to do what I really wanted to. My pussy was on fire when I got back home. I'm surprised I didn't burn a hole in my thong. I just knew you were coming to put that shit out."

"Oh, is that right?" I chuckled. "So, you wanted this dick."

"Don't play with me, Ceas. You already know the answer to that. I was ready. I had my momma keep Deuce an extra night. My girl Malaysia stopped by and sewed my wig down and glued my edges so tough that when you pull that muthafucka and hit it from the back, that bitch ain't going nowhere. I soaked in the tub and used some of those cucumber bath bombs. I pulled out the good, thick, expensive lotion just to make sure my body was smooth when your hands touched all over me. I laid in the bed naked all night waiting on you… and you were a fuckin' no show!"

"So, what you doin' now?" I asked, rubbing my dick through my pants. Her words gave me one hell of a visual. My dude was standing at attention.

"About to put some clothes on. I gotta go pick up Deuce before he drives my momma crazy."

"Your momma can handle it for a while. I'm on my way. Make sure the door is unlocked, cuz I ain't knockin'. All that talkin' you was doing, you better be ready. We 'bout to see how secure that wig really is. Gimme thirty minutes."

I arrived in twenty. The door was unlocked, just like I requested. Seven had the blanket up to her neck and failed miserably at trying to play sleep. The rapid flutter of her eyelids and the not so subtle attempt at hiding her smile gave her away. Standing at the foot of the bed, I tugged at the blanket and saw nothing but flesh staring back at me. I snatched that bitch all the way off, removed my shoes, and pulled her ankles until her ass touched the edge of the bed.

"What are you doing?" Seven asked, forgetting that she was supposed to be sleep.

"What does it look like? I'm about to finish eatin' lunch."

Before she could object, I dropped down to my knees and devoured her pussy like a starving man. Her moans were music to my ears as I stiffened my tongue and darted in and out her hole. Enclosing my lips around her clit, I sucked hard and savored the taste.

"Ceas," Seven called out breathily, arching her back in the process. Her hands found the top of my head and held it firmly as she grinded her hips toward my face.

It was cool and all, but I was running the show. I didn't need a guide. I knew Seven's body inside and out. The way her juices slid out her pussy, entered the space where her ass cheeks connected, and wet the bed underneath her was proof that I was doing my job. I knew how to eat some pussy. Holding her hands down at her side, I let my elbows spread her legs wider and admired the view.

The sight was beautiful. No hair, sandy brown pussy lips, and a swollen clit playing peek-a-boo with me. She was so wet it looked like she had just taken a shower and the water created a puddle underneath her ass, but no…that was all me.

"Play with it," I demanded, freeing one of her hands.

Her index finger massaged her clit faster than a bullet. I jacked my dick watching her pleasure herself. I had my own solo XXX movie playing out in front of me, but I wanted to be a participant. When two of her fingers found her hole, I watched intently. Coated with her juices, those same two fingers found their way into her mouth. Precum leaked from my dick. My bitch was nasty.

"Turn that ass over," I requested, climbing onto the bed. She tooted it up for me, and my dick slid in without resistance.

Seven had me losing my damn mind as I fucked her raw for the first time. I claimed her pussy and took it every way I wanted – from the back, the side…I even picked her up and bounced her up and down on my dick while her titties boxed me in the face. Sweat dripped down my forehead, but the pussy was too damn good to stop. Even when Seven disclosed that she was cumming for the umpteenth time, I didn't let up. I laid her down and hit her missionary style while my fingers played with her clit. It took major dick control not to bust inside her, but I made her ride that wave out with my dick pounding her pussy with a vengeance. She had my name on repeat as my balls slapped against her ass cheeks. I fucked her so good, her eyes began to water. Only then was I satisfied. Giving in to the undeniable feeling of pleasure, I ejected my dick and squirted cum all over her stomach. Falling over beside her, I let out a long, sexually-relieved sigh.

"Next time you want some dick, what are you gonna do?" I quizzed, pushing her chin up to face me.

"Call you," she mumbled.

"That's right," I smiled, wiping away the tears stuck in the corner of her eyes. "And daddy will be right over to get you together."

SEVEN

WE'D BEEN BACK from the short-lived 'trip' for about a week, and 'mommy duties' were kicking my ass. No, let me rephrase that... Deuce had been kicking my ass! I didn't know if he was going through a little 'bad' stage, but whatever it was, I was beyond ready for it to be over. I'd never yelled and whooped him so much in his five years on Earth. I needed a break, and I mean a two-or-three-day break. Just Joie and me. A nice little girls' getaway didn't sound so bad. I wondered if she'd be down for it?

"Deuce, stop! You know better!" I screamed, popping his hand as he picked up the knife I was using to chop up my vegetables. He poked his trembling bottom lip out and glared up at me with wide, bright eyes with water droplets resting on the rim of them. He held his left hand over the back of his right, like it really hurt him.

"Go sit down until Ceas gets here."

Deuce nodded, dragging his feet to the living room with his head down. I shook my head and continued chopping up the peppers and mushrooms for the chicken fajitas. I could see Deuce from where I stood. Carefully, I studied over him and his demeanor. My eyes got misty as I thought about how I was raising a young, black boy alone. Well, not completely alone, but I was the only parent Deuce knew. With the way he'd been acting out, it scared me to think about his future. Would I be strong enough to guide him down the right path?

My phone buzzing on the counter next to me caused me to jump. I glanced at the ID and smiled brightly when I saw it was Joie. Using my knuckle, I tapped the green phone icon and then hit the speakerphone button.

"Hey, boo. What are you up to?" I asked, preparing the stove.

"Nothing. Alone. As always," she sighed heavily.

"Norien stayed out all night again?"

"He didn't even come home, Seven. He strolled in around eight o'clock this morning. He just extended the silent treatment I've been giving him and he ain't getting no sex for another week. I'm so over it."

"Why do you deal with it, Joie? You know you don't have to."

"It's not that easy when you love someone."

"Hmph. I wish Ceas would try some shit like that. I don't care how much I love him; some things are just off limits when you're in a relationship."

The words slipped out before I knew it. It felt so natural to say that I loved Ceas, but I'd never said it out loud to anyone before. I was hoping Joie didn't hear me, but when I heard her low gasp followed by a giggle, I groaned.

"So, you love him, Sev? When did you start keepin' all these secrets from me?" Joie pried, and I could sense of hurt in her tone. "I just found out about y'all. Now, you're confessing your love for him. Damn, I'm late. Why are you just now telling me this? I thought we were better than that, Sev."

"I'm sorry, Joie. I really am, but I was scared because I've loved Ceas for a long time. I was afraid if I admitted it out loud or to anyone else, then shit would go left between us," I explained, realizing I sounded childish. "I should have told you. It's not like we're officially together anyway."

"It's okay, I understand...now that I know how you feel. It's okay to be scared to love someone. I'm sure he loves you, too. I could see it from the way he looked at you when we were in San Antonio. Have you tried talking to him about it?"

"No. I know he cares about me, but love is on a different level. You never know with Ceas."

"Never know what?"

Ceas' baritone vibrated my eardrum. I looked up from the stove to see him standing behind me, leaning against the wall. He eyed me up and down before giving me a sexy wink. Blushing, I ended my call with Joie, promising to text her later.

"Nothing," I finally answered with a smile.

Turning back around, I got a better look at him and creamed in my panties at how good Ceas looked. He had a fresh cut and lineup, so he looked extra scrumptious. The way his neat mustache and goatee surrounded his thick, black-tinted lips made me want to sit right on them and rock back and forth. The flick of his tongue and tickle of his low, shaven beard would drive me insane.

Ceas was dressed in a simple red Nike tracksuit with a black shirt underneath. I loved the way red complimented his chocolateskin. It was like the color was made for him.

His smell was divine. It wasn't strong, but I could smell it over the food, and I couldn't stop myself from inhaling deeply. Wetting his lower lip and flicking his nose, Ceas gazed at me with a smirk.

"You gotta wait for Deuce to go to bed before you get this dick, Sev. Now, stop lookin' at me like that."

Rolling my eyes, I gave him a once over before getting back to cooking. It didn't take long for the food to finish. Ceas helped me set the table and got Deuce washed up before we were all seated to eat. Deuce talked most of the time, telling Ceasar about his day and other things he rambled about. I ate silently, watching their interaction. The love in Ceas' eyes as he talked to Deuce warmed my heart and made me wonder if that was the look he saw when he looked at me.

"I'm full," Deuce announced, and he'd hardly touched his food.

"You need to eat more than that, Deuce, or you won't get a snack."

Deuce didn't like my response, so he thought he could get away with throwing a fit. He kicked the air while slamming his hands on the table. I stood up so fast that my chair dropped in the process. I went to whoop him, but Ceas stopped me by clearing his throat and shaking his head for me to stop. Confused and frustrated, I crossed my arms, shifted my weight, and glared at him with a raised brow.

"Deuce," Ceas spoke in a stern tone. He only had to say his name once and Deuce gave him his undivided attention. Ceasar leaned over, cut a third of Deuce's fajita, and put the rest on his plate before saying, "Eat that and don't get up until it's gone. The next time you decide to act like a baby and not a big boy, I'ma send you right to bed. Understood?"

"Yes sir," Deuce said, picking up his food and taking a bite. My eyes widened in surprise at how effortlessly he obeyed Ceas when I would still be yelling at him.

Mouthing 'thank you' to Ceas, I sat back down and finished my food. Deuce cleaned his plate, shoving it in Ceas' face when he was done.

"Thank you. Now, apologize to your momma for the way you acted when she told you to eat."

"Sorry, Mommy," Deuce apologized.

"It's okay, baby. Go wash your hands and wait for us in the living room," I instructed.

I waited until Deuce was down the hall before thanking Ceas again. For some reason, it made me emotional. I couldn't stop the tears from falling. Ceas walked over and lifted me from my seat, placing me in his lap. He asked why I was crying, and the only thing I could think of was that I was tired and needed a break. I felt overwhelmed with everything in my life, and shit wasn't even that bad. My emotions were all over the place. I couldn't help it. I needed some 'me' time.

"Deuce has been acting out for like two weeks, and I'm overwhelmed. I need time to myself to breathe and relax. Unfortunately, that's something I'll never get," I sighed in frustration. "I thought that going to San Diego would have given me some relief, but Drako ruined it."

"Fuck that nigga. It ain't about him. You act like you ain't got me for shit like that, girl. I can handle Deuce while you step away for a bit. All you had to do was ask."

"I'm not talking about a few hours, Ceas. More like a few days... but I ain't trying to interfere with anything you got going on."

"And? Take you a few days. Matter of fact, where do you want to go? You and Joie can go wherever on my expense. I'll plan some shit out for Deuce and me to do while you're gone. This isn't an option either, Sev. I mean that. I can already see the wheels turnin' in yo' head. You said you needed a break. Let me give you one. I ain't tryin' to see you over here all emotional and shit."

I couldn't believe the words coming out of Ceas' mouth. I didn't expect him to offer me a break. I was only venting. Excitement filled my veins, and I bounced on his lap in delight. With a wide smile, I flicked my tongue across his bottom lip and smirked when he sucked hard and pulled my tongue into his mouth.

As bad as I wanted him, I needed to hear confirmation again. "Before I get too excited, are you sure about this? Deuce can be a handfu—"

"I ain't tryin' to hear that shit. You heard what I said. Just tell me where you wanna go. It's on me."

Squealing, I hopped off his lap and ran to get my phone.

"Joie, pack your shit!" I announced, practically jumping up and down. "We're going on a girls' trip! Before you start making excuses, you're going...and Ceas is paying!"

"I FEEL LIKE A TRUE ISLAND GIRL! I COULD BE A NATIVE!" I EXCLAIMED, shaking my long, Brazilian loose wave bundles for emphasis. "I mean, look at this shit. Look at the ocean! This view is amazing."

Ceas stayed true to his word and sent Joie and I on a trip wherever we wanted to go. Although I could have chosen a number of different tropical locations, I kept it simple and remained in the States. Miami was my destination of choice. Joie agreed to accompany me and off we went. I didn't expect to be on one of the many beaches in the city within a day of me mentioning it, but Ceas made it happen. The short notice didn't sit well with my job, but oh well! Who turns down a free trip to Miami?! Nobody I knew. In return for his generosity, I gave Ceas some extra good loving before I left.

"We're not even on an island, Sev," Joie said, laughing. "You do look good as hell, though."

"You do too, boo! We shuttin' all these hoes down."

It was true. Joie and I were a couple of bad bitches, and we'd been turning heads since we landed. Even minding our own business, lying on the beach in our skimpy swimsuits, we still managed to command the attention of anyone who walked by. Men, women, and even kids did double-takes in our direction. It was flattering, but I was used to it.

Joie wanted a simple one-piece, but I encouraged her to get something sexy. Miami was all about sexy, and I wanted us to fit the part. Joie wore an olive-colored one-piece with the sides cut out, and the dip on the front that went all the way down to her pierced belly button. It complemented her pale skin, which I was sure would be nice and toasted before we left. Her hair was in a messy bun on top of her head, and she wore a stylish pair of oversized shades. Joie thought she looked plain because she didn't have as many curves as other women, but that was a lie. My best friend looked damn good. She was a natural beauty.

I rocked a nice two-piece thong swimsuit that had an African pattern. My breasts were sitting up just right, and I knew my ass looked amazing. Before Deuce, I didn't have as many curves, and I took advantage of showing them off whenever I could. Ceas would kill me if he knew what I was wearing, so I decided against posting any of those pictures to my social media accounts until I got home.

Joie and I stretched our bodies out on lounge chairs, while talking and sipping on fruity drinks. There was so much to do in the city. Since we were on Ceas' expense, I convinced Joie to parasail and surf with me. Earlier that day, Joie took a walk on the wild side and faced her fears. She wore a genuine smile that remained even after she fell off her surfboard and into the open water. The look on her face as she struggled back onto her board was priceless. She claimed she was swimming away from Jaws, but she couldn't tell that lie to me. I was there to witness it. Her ass was just clumsy. She couldn't keep her balance. We had a blast anyway, and I knew the getaway was everything I needed.

Later that day, I started feeling like crap. Being out in the sun and drinking drained me, and I needed all the energy I could get for the fun night I had planned. I woke up with a killer headache, but I wasn't going to let that stop me. Checking the time, I saw that it was still early, and I could get some more shut eye. I got up to get something to relieve my headache. I peeked in Joie's room and giggled at how she was sprawled out on the bed. She was snoring loudly and everything. My girl was worn out!

When I walked back into the room, my phone was ringing on the bed. I smiled when I saw that it was Ceas FaceTiming me. Answering it, I expected to see his handsome face staring back at me. Instead, my son's smile greeted me.

"Deuce! Hey, baby. Mommy misses you."

"I miss you too, Mommy. Guess what?"

"What?"

"Uncle Drako said bad words in front of me," Deuce revealed, lifting a hand to hide his mouth.

"You wasn't supposed to tell," Drako griped in the background. "That was supposed to be our little secret."

"Ain't no secrets with kids, my nigga," Ceas chuckled. "They tell everything."

"I'm sorry, Uncle Drako," Deuce spoke with a frown. "I didn't know."

"I'll forgive you this time. But next time, you gotta keep things between you and me, okay?"

"Okay!" Deuce's eyes lit up when Drako extended his fist for a pound. Deuce mimicked the gesture, connecting his fist with Drako's.

"There wouldn't be nothing to tell if you would watch your mouth," I hissed with a hint of a smile.

Taking control of the phone, Drako made sure I saw his face.

"What do you want, anyway? Me and my niggas over here chillin'. You botherin' us."

"Yo niggas?"

"Yeah...Ceas and Deuce."

I heard Ceas' laugh before his sexy face appeared on my screen. "Don't pay that nigga no attention, Sev."

Damn, this man is fine, I thought, licking my bottom lip.

"You tryna do somethin' with that tongue," Ceas questioned with a smirk. "I can think of a few things."

"Stop talking like that in front of Deuce. You're almost as bad a Drako. Matter-of-fact, Keep him away from Deuce, Ceas. I don't need him setting any bad examples," I ordered, noticing I had his full attention.

"Chill out, girl. Drako ain't gonna do nothin' to that boy. They been chillin' together all day. What about you? You havin' fun? Damn sure looks like it." I knew I looked rough at that moment, so all I could do was give him the finger. "You know that pussy is all mine when you get back."

"Ceas! Where's Deuce? Did he hear you?"

"He's in the kitchen. Drake-Anthony just fixed him a plate."

Drako's voice rang out in the distance. "Fuck you sayin' my government name and shit for? I bet she doesn't know yo' name Carl, does she? Old ass fuckin' name."

I didn't want to laugh at Drako's words, but I couldn't hold it in. I had no idea Ceas' name was Carl. He didn't look like a Carl. Ceasar fit him well, but I would no longer call him that.

"Hey, Carl," I giggled, and Ceas mugged me.

"Don't make me hang up on you. Don't call me that shit."

"Why? It's your name. Right, Carl?"

I heard Drako chuckling in the background. Ceas took a deep breath and licked his lips before changing the subject.

"What are you doin' tonight?"

"Joie and I are goin' to one of the clubs. Depends on which one is poppin' the most."

"Be on your best behavior, Seven. Don't make me fly down there because you know I will," Ceas threatened.

"I know, Carl. I'm a big girl. I can handle myself."

Ceas gave me a look before nodding. I talked to him for five more minutes before he got off the phone. I popped my medicine and was back to sleep within minutes. My alarm going off woke me two hours later. Stretching, I woke Joie up and got in the shower.

An hour and a half later, we were all dolled up and ready to go. Joie and I posed in the full-length mirror that was in the sitting area of our suite. Pulling out my phone, I captured the moment with a selfie. Studying the picture, I smiled. It was definitely one I'd print off and frame. The smiles etched on our faces showed we were truly enjoying ourselves. Well, that and the fact that we'd consumed a few shots while getting dressed.

We took the elevator down to the lobby where an Uber waited for us outside. Ceas had rented us a car, but neither of us would be able to drive once we left the club. Uber was our best bet to get back safely, especially since the club was thirty minutes away.

"This club is packed," Joie said, looking at the line outside. It was almost a quarter-mile long, but it was moving at a steady pace.

"It'll be okay. Come on. If we don't like this one, we'll go to the next."

Taking her hand, I pulled her out and went to the back of the line. Once we were inside, I realized the twenty-minute wait was worth it. The club had three different levels with bars and dance floors on each one. The vibe was good and chill; not wild and ratchet like I would have thought. Joie and I headed straight to the bar, dancing through the crowd. It was hype, and I couldn't wait to join everyone.

I ordered us both a shot of Cîroc and a Long Island. We sat at the bar sipping our drinks, observing the scene. I wiggled my hips to the beat of the music as I felt all the liquor I'd consumed begin to take over. I finished off my Long Island and made my way to the dance floor with Joie following behind.

We danced together until a fine ass man grabbed my winding hips and pulled me into him. Feeling good, I wrapped one arm around his neck and gave him what I was sure was the best dance of his life.

Time flew by and before I knew it, it was going on three in the morning. I'd been twerking and grinding on Joie and whoever wanted to dance. Well, not whoever, but men who looked appetizing to my drunken eyes. I was headed to the dance floor once again with my newest partner of the night when a tight grip around my arm pulled me in the opposite direction. I tried to jerk away, but the grip got tighter. Whipping my head around, I sobered up quick when I saw a look of pure rage plastered all over Ceas' face.

What was he doing here?

"So, this is what you out here doin'? This is why you can't answer your damn phone? You gon' make me kill every muthafucka up in here that got close to you. I should snap yo' fuckin' neck, Seven. What the fuck did I tell you?" Ceasar growled lowly in my ear. "Bring yo' ass on."

Without giving me an option to protest, he dragged me to the exit. I looked around for Joie to see her stumbling behind Drako. She tripped over her feet numerous times, but Drako kept on walking. It wasn't until some random man attempted to help her that he showed some concern. Drako said something to the man before picking Joie up and carrying her out the club bridal style. I couldn't help but smile because my friend was tore the fuck up. Even with Ceas coming in and breaking everything up, we'd had so much fun. Unfortunately for me, it was time to face the repercussions.

Ceas didn't say one word to me the ride back to the hotel, not even when I asked where Deuce was. When we walked in the suite, I stormed to my room and tried to shut the door, but Ceasar almost knocked it off the damn hinges.

"Why the fuck you so hard-headed, Seven? Got me all out here worried and shit. I had to trace your phone just to find out where you were. I been callin' you all muthafuckin' night! Look at that little ass shit you got on. Got niggas all up on yo' ass and shit."

"It's not that deep. I was just dancing, Carl."

"Oh, so how would you feel if some bitch danced all on my dick and I was holding her hips like I do when I fuck you from the back? You wouldn't like that shit, would you?"

Closing my eyes, I tried to remove the image in my head of Ceas holding another woman that way. It pissed me off, but what could I say or do? Technically, he wasn't my nigga to claim. I wouldn't dare say that to him, though. The way I felt, I wasn't in the mood to do anything but sleep. I didn't have the energy to entertain Ceas or his angry shenanigans.

"Where's Deuce?" I asked again, changing the subject.

"Where the fuck I left him. He good, but I had to come get his damn momma together before she made me blow the entire club up."

"Where did you leave him?"

"He's with my sister."

"You left him with Kyan? Are you crazy?"

"No, you are. Out here showin' yo' ass. Got me ready to fuck a nigga up."

Ceasar walked up on me, shoving me against the wall while gripping my face. He leaned his face down so close that our lips touched, but we weren't kissing. Each time I tried, he moved back. He knew what he was doing, being so close to me with his intoxicating scent filling my nostrils. I wanted him so bad. I reached for his dick, but he slapped my hand away.

"Really, Carl?"

"You've been too hard-headed. You don't get any dick tonight. I'm out. Don't make me come back down here, Seven."

Ceasar kissed me so passionately that it made my knees weak. I wanted him in the worst way, but he meant what he said. He didn't give me any dick. He flew back home with Drako, leaving me with a moist, purring center.

After checking on my girl, I finally called it a night.

13

NORIEN

"Damn you're wet," I announced, pulling a fistful of Joie's hair. With my hands firmly gripping the sides of her waist, I pounded her pussy with no mercy. An exaggerated moan escaped her lips, boosting my ego. "Yeah, you missed this dick, didn't you?" I taunted. "I know I missed *my* pussy."

Joie kept me in the doghouse for eight long days. She gave me the cold shoulder and refused to let me sleep in the bed next to her – and it was *my* fucking bed! I thought she would give in after a day or two; just like the numerous times before. Somehow, I was always able to work my way back into her arms.

Time apart was just what we needed. A few nights, Joie didn't even stay home. I was worried at first, but an unlikely source helped ease my mind. April explained to me that when a woman is upset, it's best for me to give her space and let her figure things out. I did exactly that. I allowed Joie to pack an overnight bag, chill with her friend Seven for a few days, then come back to me as a renewed woman.

Losing my girl just wasn't an option. Whatever I needed to do to make things right, I was willing to do. Of course, it was only going to be temporary, but it was going to show that I was making an effort.

That's all that really mattered anyway. Once things died down, I would resort back to the same nigga I'd always been.

On day six, I walked up behind her and slid a hand in between her ass cheeks. When she slapped my hand away and pushed me in the opposite direction, I lost my footing and fell backward into the dresser.

"Damn, Joie. Was all that necessary? You act like I can't touch your ass."

"You can't," she asserted, crossing her arms in front of her lace bra. I shook off the sharp pain radiating from my left side and stood straight up. "Keep your hands to yourself."

Joie was sexy as hell when she was mad. Her body wasn't thick like I preferred, but she still looked good from the back. That's why I couldn't help myself. I wanted to feel the same warmth that the back of her matching thong felt.

"What is it with you? Huh? What's the deal?"

"You really don't know? That's a damn shame!"

"I don't know what you don't tell me. How can I make it right if I don't even know what it is?"

"It's you!" she yelled, startling me for a moment. I had never heard some much anger in her cracking voice. Joie became emotional right there in front of me. Her eyes began to water, and a single tear slid down each outer corner. "Why are we together? It's obvious you don't wanna be with me!"

She had lost her fucking mind. Leaving her was the last thing I wanted to do. "You crazy! Where's this shit coming from?"

"Your actions...that's where. A man who really cared about me wouldn't forget about me each time he dropped me off." She used air quotes to emphasize the word 'cared'. "You're out in the streets all night long. Sometimes, you don't even come home until the next morning. You go straight to sleep, get up, and do the same shit over again. I'm tired of it, Norien. I can't do this no more."

The next day was spent catering to her every need. I made it a point to make her feel like a priority. I sat and watched her dumb ass TV shows, posted a few pics of us together on social media, ran her bath water, and massaged her back in hopes of breaking down the wall she had up. All that lovey dovey shit I did, and my ass was still on the couch.

Day eight was more my speed. Instead of kicking it at the crib, I brought Joie along for the ride. She met a few of my homies from the block and followed me around to various locations. After a few hours, the heels I insisted she wore had her feet on fire. She started sitting in the car instead of trailing behind me. I used that to my advantage. My last stop of the day landed me right in April's neighborhood. Parking in front of her building, I told Joie I needed to holler at my boy for a minute. Nodding in agreement, she reclined her seat and propped her feet up on the dashboard. I kept the car running as I jogged up the stairs, knocked on April's door, and bent her over the arm of the couch. Her pussy was subpar at best, but I closed my eyes and imagined grinding all up in Joie's tight walls. When the feeling didn't match my imagination, I stopped and let April do what she was good at – slob on my shit. She sucked my dick like she got a rush from tasting her own pussy. The way her head bobbed back and forth combined with the gurgling sound from my dick hitting the back of her throat had me cumming in her mouth. April didn't stop. She continued sucking my sensitive head until my legs damn near gave out. April cleaned my dick off with a washcloth and tucked my man back in my pants. I broke her off with a few dollars for our son before rejoining my girl in the car.

"You were in there for a minute," Joie pointed out. "Is everything okay?"

"It is now," I responded with a wink. "I had to handle a few things. It's all good now."

Joie teased me most of the night. After showering, she allowed me to sleep in our bed, but I couldn't touch her. It wouldn't have been so bad if she wasn't naked up under our blanket. I wanted my girl in the worst way. Each time I tried to cop a feel, she pushed my hand back. Growing frustrated, I contemplated calling one of the hoes in my phone. Even April was an option. I'd already linked up with her earlier that day, but I had no problem reaching out again. 'No' wasn't in her vocabulary. I could fuck her any place, any way, and any time I wanted to. The warmth and tightness of her asshole was a close second to Joie's pussy.

Instead of giving into temptation, I stuck it out with Joie. When she eventually fell asleep, I rolled over and palmed her breasts with my hands. I massaged her nipples until they hardened between my fingers. Positioning myself behind her, we laid in the spooning position until my eyes got heavy. I dozed off with a tittie in each hand.

I woke before Joie. My dick was rock hard and oozing at the tip. Our blanket had somehow fallen on the floor. Joie's legs were slightly ajar, giving me a glimpse of her pussy. I had to have my girl. As my fingers spread her lower lips apart and I started massaging her clit, she moaned and opened her legs wider. *It's about damn time*, I thought, positioning myself on top of her. Her eyes fluttered and eventually opened. Without saying a word, she closed them and enjoyed the magic my fingers performed on her body. I kissed her lips before moving on to her neck. My downward journey had me flicking my tongue against her nipples and trailing small kisses down her stomach. I slurped at her belly button, kissed all the way around it, and stopped. That's as far south as I went. Only lames ate pussy.

Before she could object, I slid right on in. Holding her down by her inner thigh, I rhythmically thrusted in and out of her wet hole. She tried to act like she wasn't enjoying it, but soon her hips began to move to my beat. "That's right," I said under my breath. "Get this dick."

I continued to grind into Joie's sweet pussy until my body couldn't take it any more. I pulled my dick out and jacked it until my thick cum lined the opening to her pussy. She looked at me, stone-faced, like she hadn't experienced ten of the best minutes of her life. Well, five minutes was just some quick foreplay to get her wet, but I put in work those last five minutes. If she thought anything different, she was delusional.

"What?" I asked, easing off the bed. "You got something to say?"

"Not at all," she countered, scooting her way to the edge of the bed. She grilled me before racing off to the bathroom. As the door closed and locked behind her, I could have sworn I heard her voice mumble, 'I coulda got my own self off better than that'.

"What did you say?!" I yelled.

I was hot. Joie bruised my ego. I walked to the door and shook the knob violently, trying to gain access. I wanted Joie to say that shit to my face. Hearing her turn on the showerhead and blatantly ignore my question had me ready to break the damn door down. My ringing phone stopped that from happening. Money came before bullshit. Seeing Ceasar's number flash across the screen was always a good sign.

"Yo, Ceas…what's good?"

"Nigga, you tell me. You been blowin' up my phone like a fuckin' bitch. What the fuck's that about?"

"Business. Damn Ceas, you act like you ain't tryna make no money?"

"I'm on the line. Talk."

I made a nice piece of change off my first order with Ceas. To keep the money flowing, I reinvested everything into more product. In fact, I was a little over a quarter of the way through my second order when I called Ceas to re-up. At least, that's what I was going to tell him. The truth was, I found a nigga looking for the same thing I was selling. I was skeptical at first, but when my boy Red vouched for him, I knew he was cool. He went simply by the name J and was interested in some serious weight. His request was too big for me to accommodate so I reached out to Ceasar, hoping I could get another 'back in the day' favor. J agreed to pay only upon delivery. Since I represented myself as having the shit on deck, and added ten stacks onto the price of each kilo, I couldn't let Ceasar and J meet. The problem was, I didn't have five kilos sitting around, nor did I have the six-figure price tag that went along with it. Ceasar did, though. If he could front me what I needed, I could run him back the payment, plus ten percent interest within twenty-four hours. The rest was going in my pocket, right where it belonged.

"I need to place an order," I advised.

"A'ight…you know what to do. You blew my phone up for that

shit? What's wrong with you? You know who to contact if I ain't around."

"I know, I know," I agreed, grabbing my t-shirt off the floor. I wiped Joie's juices off my dick and tossed it toward an empty clothes basket. "I needed to talk to you directly, though. I didn't want to talk to Drako. You know how he is. He don't like me for whatever reason. I don't even know. Besides, what I need doesn't have anything to do with him. You're the only person who can help me. I'm really hoping you can. It's kinda, you know, complicated."

"Nigga!" he huffed, raising his voice in my ear. "Stop playin' with ya fuckin' words and spit that shit out. I ain't got all day."

"Okay, damn."

Ceas was beginning to act more and more like Drako. His patience was wearing thin, which was a characteristic he didn't portray back in the day. I mean, Ceasar was always a straight forward kind of guy, but he wasn't as hardcore and direct as he had become.

"This is the thing," I continued, searching the floor for my pants and boxers. I found them after kicking the blanket that fell off the bed. "Hold up. Let me put my clothes on real quick."

"Nigga, I don't want to hear about…"

I laid the phone down on the bed while Ceas protested. It didn't take long to step into the intertwined garments and pull them up to waist length. Ceas thought so. By the time I placed the phone back by my ear, he had hung up.

"Really, nigga," I said aloud. "That's some bullshit."

It didn't stop me from dialing his number again and waiting patiently on the line. It rung four times before I finally heard Ceasar's voice.

"You done with that bullshit yet?" he barked. "Don't you ever tell another man you ain't got no damn clothes on, especially me. I ain't with that homo shit. You better be lucky I even answered your fuckin' call. Now, what the fuck do you want?"

"I need you to look out for me," I spoke, ignoring his bullshit introduction. "I'm trying to make big moves, but I need your help to make that happen."

Ceasar gave me the opportunity to say what I needed to say. When I was done, he nonchalantly asked what I was smoking.

"What? I ain't smokin' nothin'," I shot back, offended. "At least not yet." His comment had me searching the ashtray for the half smoked blunt I put out before climbing in bed with Joie.

"Well nigga, you just stupid then. You really think I'm gonna front you that much weight? Get the fuck outta here. Who the fuck you supplyin'?"

"I ain't supplyin' nobody," I lied, lighting the tip of the blunt. "This is all for me. I told you. I'm makin' moves."

"You must think you're dealing with somebody new to this shit. I know how the game works. How the fuck can you pay me back that quick unless you're getting the money from somebody else? Come on now, Norien. I've been doing this shit too long."

"Look...I hear all that," I advised, sucking hard on the end of the blunt. I broke out in a coughing spell, but recovered enough to continue my conversation. "You'll get your money, plus some. All I need is twenty-four hours. Forty-eight tops."

"Now, you need two days? Nigga, did you hear anything I said! The answer is 'No'!"

"Ceas, I need this," I begged, trying to play on his emotions. "I'm trying to do something special for my girl," I lied. "It's a fucked-up feeling knowing your girl deserves so much but you can't give it to her. I mean, Joie stuck by me through it all."

"And what does that have to do with me?"

"Nothin'. I'm just sayin'."

"If you can't provide for your bitch, that sounds like a personal problem. Joie knows what kind of nigga she's fuckin' with. Either she's gonna stick around or find somethin' better. Neither one of those scenarios is a concern of mine. That's all on you."

He spoke as if he knew something I didn't. Taking another pull of my blunt, I let the THC work its magic. My plan wasn't working the way I expected it to. Instead of giving in, I kept right on going.

"You're right. It is my problem. I was just hoping you could help an old friend out. I've already proved to you that I'm good for it. I paid you back everything I owed. I ain't trying to cheat you, Ceas. You're gettin' an extra fifteen grand, with no strings attached. How can you turn that down?"

"That's a muthafuckin' insult. I can spend that in an hour."

"True, but how does thirty sound?" I asked, upping the percentage to twenty. It took away from my profit, but still left me with more than enough to play with.

"You don't give up, do you?" Ceasar noted. "You're just gonna keep on, aren't you?"

"You already know. This ain't no game. I'm serious about this shit."

His silence was music to my ears. It told me he was thinking about my proposition, and that was a good thing. It was hard for anyone to turn down that much money, especially when he didn't have to do anything for it.

"This is what I'll do," he began, clearing his throat. "Meet me at the same location in an hour. I'll give you three, but I better have my money in hand by this time tomorrow. Once I'm paid in full, you'll get the rest."

"Bet! I'll make that work. I'm getting dressed now."

"Didn't I tell you I don't wanna hear nothing about your clothes, nigga? That's too much fuckin' information. Keep that shit to yourself."

"It slipped, sorry. I'll be there shortly. Oh, and Ceas…can we keep this between us? Drako don't need to know about anything we got going on."

"Anything dealin' with my operation is Drako's business. Just be there. If I have to wait more than thirty seconds, I'm out."

In true Ceasar fashion, he had the last word, hanging the phone up in my ear when he was finished. Joie emerged from the bathroom wearing only a towel. My man quickly stiffened up, but I couldn't give in to temptation. Her pussy could wait.

"Where are you going?" Joie asked as I slipped the same socks I had on the previous day back on my feet. I grabbed a t-shirt from my drawer before answering her.

"Out for a minute. I'll be right back, though. I should only be a couple of hours."

"Can I go?"

"Nah, not this time. We can ride out when I get back. Just you and me. A'ight?"

"Whatever."

There went the attitude again. That was one of the main reasons why I fucked with April so tough. She didn't do all the back talk and shit like Joie did. She appreciated the time I gave her and didn't get mad about all the unnecessary shit. Sure, she wanted more time with me, but she knew what it was. Joie was my girl, but if she didn't get her act together, that was going to change real quick.

"You know what…" I caught myself before I said something I would regret.

Leaving my statement lingering in the air, I slipped my feet into my shoes and grabbed my keys off the nightstand. Arguing with her was pointless. Nothing would be accomplished.

It took me less than forty-five minutes to make it to Ceasar. That included me stopping to put some food in my stomach and gas in my tank. I parked in front of the same duplex I'd previously had and waited for Ceasar to arrive. Thirty minutes later, a dark, late model Tahoe pulled up. Ceasar rolled down the back window, letting me know it was him.

"Get in," he demanded. "And hurry up."

I left my car parked on the street and did as I was told. The smell of some bomb ass green was in the air. It was strong enough to give me a contact high once I climbed inside. Drako held the blunt. He gave me the death stare as he blew out a stream of smoke in my direction.

"Yo, Tango," Drako called out to the driver. "Drive this muthafucka around the block. I'll let you know when to park." The driver acknowledged the request with a head nod and closed the partition. It gave Drako the opportunity to continue without an extra set of ears listening. "I see you still asking for handouts."

"Not at all," I replied, hoping that Ceasar would come to my defense. Instead of doing that, he took the blunt Drako handed him and inhaled. "I rapped to Ceas about a little situation I had and he's gettin' me together. Ain't that right, Ceas?"

"Don't bring him into this shit," Drako barked. "Nigga, I'm talkin' to you right now." Drako turned to Ceasar as he smirked, but kept going in. "What makes you think you so fuckin' special? You think a muthafucka owes you something? We don't *give* nobody shit. I heard all about the deal you and Ceas worked out, but let me shut this shit down right now. It won't happen again. You hear me? I don't give a fuck how many times you blow my nigga's phone up. Unless you come with cash in hand, y'all ain't got shit to talk about. Here."

He threw a black duffle bag onto my lap. I made the mistake of unzipping the bag to review the contents. Everything was there, but two pair of eyes grilled me coldly.

"Really, Norien? After all that, you think I'ma cheat you?" Ceasar snapped. "Come on, now. What kind of nigga do you think I am? I'm a man of my word."

"It ain't that, I-"

"Tango!" Drako called out. "Stop this bitch. I'm tired of lookin' at this ungrateful muthafucka."

Ungrateful, I thought, scrunching my face up in confusion. How did I give off that impression? I was more than appreciative. Drako cut me off before I could let Ceasar know just how much. The SUV came to a screeching halt and all eyes turned to me.

"Get the fuck out," Drako insisted. The blunt returned to his fingers without being passed in my direction. "What? You can't hear now? Do you need some help?"

"Can you at least take me back to my car?"

Drako turned to Ceasar and huffed. "Hell nah! Nigga walk! It'll do you some fuckin' good. Maybe that fresh air will get that pussy smell off ya body."

Ceasar busted out in laughter. Embarrassed, I opened the door and mentally prepared myself for my walk of shame. I cursed under my breath for not hopping in the shower after digging into Joie's guts. *At least I'm getting pussy*, I thought, allowing my feet to hit the asphalt.

Drako's anger could be summed up in two words – blue balls. That nigga needed to get laid, and quick.

"One more thing," Ceasar added, trying hard to keep a straight face. "Don't forget about what we talked about. I want the money tomorrow. No excuses."

"It better not be," Drako interjected. "Excuses are for dead muthafuckas." He lifted his shirt, allowing me to see what he was holding on his waist. "Even then, we're still gonna get our money. I don't give a fuck if it's ya momma, ya daddy, ya cousin, ya bitch…somebody's gonna pay up. Now, close that muthafuckin' door!"

I hated Drako with a passion. That hatred increased each step I took toward my ride. He was nasty muthafucka, just for the hell of it. He needed to take that built up frustration and dive in something wet and warm. If he wasn't such an asshole, I would turn him on to a female or two. He obviously wasn't getting shit on his own.

When I arrived, I hit J up and asked if he was still down to meet. He gave me his location and told me to slide through before he left. I shook off the bullshit Drako was talking and mentally counted my money as I headed toward my potential regular. I made up my mind that I would pay Ceasar his money in a few hours. I wanted to get that monkey off my back as soon as possible.

With the bag in hand, I walked up J's driveway. He opened the door and greeted me with a smile. We exchanged bags, ensured everything was all good, and shook hands like men. It wasn't until I turned to leave that I realized there was a problem.

"One more thing," J said, causing me to turn around.

"Yeah, what's that?"

Niggas appeared out of nowhere, running toward me and tackling me to the ground. J held up a shiny badge, letting me know that I was fucked.

"You're under arrest."

14

JOIE

"I THINK something is wrong with me, Sev," I mentioned, curling up into a fetal position. I pulled the cover up to my neck and stared at the ceiling. I definitely didn't feel like myself.

"Why you say that?"

"I had a dream."

"Okay," she huffed. "People dream all the time. Why's that such a big deal?"

"It was about Drako," I whispered into the phone. Even though I was alone, I felt weird saying it out loud. It was crazy. Of all the people to dream about, why did I have to dream about him?

"Wait? What? Drako? Why are you dreaming about that nasty muthafucka?"

"Will you stop asking me so many questions? How the hell do I know?"

"Well, what happened?"

I was almost embarrassed to tell her. I mean, how could I tell my best friend that I was getting dicked down by a nigga that I didn't even like. Drako was all about himself. Each time we crossed paths, he acted as though I wasn't even there, but that last time…umm umm umm. That last time was everything. I wasn't so drunk that I didn't know what was going on. Some of the night's events were a blur, but not Drako. I remembered everything about that man, right down to the shoes he had on his feet. I felt his toned, sexy arms pick me up and carry me to the car. I laid my head against his tight chest and felt secure for the first time in what seemed like forever.

He smelled so damn good, too. His presence gave me a euphoric high. I wrapped my arms around his neck, and he stopped and stared at me...like he was looking into my soul or something. There was a faint twinkle in his eye that disappeared altogether...then it happened. Something clicked. I felt those same butterflies that had my stomach in knots the first day we met. Unlike my teenage days, my drunken state had me ready to act upon my feelings. The moment was intense; prompting me to pucker my lips in anticipation. I thought his mouth would connect with mine, but he broke the gaze and turned away.

"Promise me you won't think I'm crazy," I asked, lowering my voice.

"Too late! I know you're crazy. Anybody who thinks about Drako needs to be in a looney bin!"

"I'm serious, Sev! Will you stop with the jokes?"

"Fine. I'm listening."

"Hold on real quick." I laid the phone on the bed before Seven could object. For some reason, I felt the need to inspect the apartment. Norien was known to sneak in and out without being detected. I didn't want to risk him overhearing something that he shouldn't have. Satisfied that I was alone, I retrieved the phone again from the bed. "Okay, I'm back."

"Took you long enough," she barked. "What the hell were you doing?"

"Checking to see if Norien was here."

"Girl, you know that nigga ain't there. He's never there. Why would today be any different?"

I huffed in frustration. Why did Seven have to be so negative? This wasn't about Norien. It was about me.

"I'm not going there," I instructed. "Now, look here...if you only knew what that man did to me in my dream. Girl…it was so real. I could feel him touching me and everything."

"Okay, that's TMI. I think I'm about to throw up."

"Bye, Seven! I knew I shouldn't have called you. You play too much."

"You better not hang up on me!" Seven warned. "How are you gonna get mad at me? I can't have an opinion?"

"You can have whatever you want. I really don't care."

My attitude was evident in my voice. I wanted Seven to help me figure things out. Instead, she made me feel stupid for even thinking about Drako in the first place. I didn't understand it myself. I needed clarification, and Seven wasn't helping me find it.

"What's with the attitude?" Seven spat. "This is Drako we're talking about…Drako! He doesn't care about anyone but himself. Unless you know something I don't, it doesn't make sense, Joie."

"He wasn't always like that," I attempted to stress. "Back in the day, he was much different. He always had this cockiness about him, but he was…you know, normal."

"I'll take your word for it, Joie. You know him much better than I do. All I know is the nigga he is now. Believe me, he's nothing to be dreaming about."

Silence took over our conversation. I had nothing else to say. Every time I opened my mouth to voice my opinion, Seven shot me back down. She must have felt my apprehension. Changing her tone, she offered me a bit of advice.

"For some reason I'll never understand, you got a thing for Drako." Before I could respond, she quickly continued. "You don't have to admit it. I know it's true. There's no other explanation why you'd be thinking about him."

"Sounds to me like you're the crazy one."

Staring at the clock, I noted the time. Norien still wasn't home, nor had he called to check in. Realizing that I had been played for a fool yet again toyed with my emotions. Why was I so stupid? I should have known something was up when he told me we would ride out when he got back. Knowing him, he wouldn't be back for a while, which technically meant he didn't do anything wrong. He never gave me a specific time, but I managed to fix a late breakfast, take a bath, watch television, prepare lunch, lay down for a few hours, and run my mouth on the phone without him returning. It was going on six hours that he had been gone. He at least could have called.

Not only was I alone, but I was stuck at the apartment. That's what I hated the most. I had become so dependent on Norien that without him, I had nothing. I had no license, no car, not even a fucking bike. I relied on my feet or other people to get around town. When they didn't come through, the reality of my pitiful life became clear. I needed my own shit.

"I'm not crazy," Seven spoke up. "I know you better than you know yourself. I'll even prove it to you."

"How are you gonna do that?"

"Don't worry about it. I'm on my way. Just be ready when I get there."

"But—"

She hung up, leaving me wondering what she had up her sleeve. How could she prove me wrong? I knew what I knew. I didn't have a thing for Drako.

An hour later, Seven was calling me to come outside. I was still an afterthought in Norien's mind, which allowed me to throw the strap to my purse over my shoulder, lock both locks on the door, and scurry down the steps guilt-free. She was all smiles when I practically fell into her passenger's seat. With her foot on the gas pedal, she peeled off before I was able to pull my door closed.

"Damn," I complained. "Can I at least close the door?"

"Sorry, girl. Ceas is on my ass. I was supposed to meet up with him thirty minutes ago."

I began to fidget in my seat. "What do you mean? Where are we going?"

"Somewhere. Just sit back and relax."

That 'somewhere' turned out to be a massive estate in Mountain Brook. An older brick home sat on what looked to be about three or four acres. Small, green bushes lined the well-manicured lawn. It took us a while to drive up the gravel driveway, but once we did, I was even more impressed.

"Who lives here?" I questioned, slowly surveying the property.

"I don't know. I think one of Ceas' friends. I've been here a couple times, but there's always a house full of niggas. I can't tell who lives here and who doesn't. Come on. Let's go."

Seven took her phone out her purse as we exited the car. Before we reached the front door, it swung open, revealing Ceasar on the other side. He smiled with a half-full beer bottle in his hand.

"It took your ass long enough."

"My bad. I had to go pick up Joie."

Smiling, he greeted me. "What's up, girl?"

Ceasar glanced in my direction before softly kissing Seven on the cheek. I offered a weak smile, but didn't really pay them any mind. I don't know why they were trying to keep up their 'secret' relationship. I already knew they were fucking. Everybody else probably did, too. Seven giggled and acted as if Ceasar was the first man to ever show her some attention. Their chemistry was undeniable. I knew my girl well enough to know that she was in love. It was obvious.

"Y'all follow me," Ceasar urged, leading the way into a large room.

The sound of music serenaded us, getting louder with every step we took. Ceasar bopped his head to the music and stopped abruptly to bust a few moves. It caught me off guard, but watching Ceasar act a fool reminded me of just how silly he used to be. I joined Seven as Ceasar's hype man, pumping him up like he was really doing something. He was actually a good dancer, but at that particular moment, he was just playing around.

The space Ceasar and I were in was…complicated. We knew each other, and well. At one time, I considered us to be close. If you saw Kyan, you saw me. Because of that bond, I was around Ceasar just as much as his own blood. He confided in me things that you wouldn't tell a random acquaintance. He trusted me in a sense. I trusted him as well. That all changed when I left town. In my mind, I didn't think distance would be a factor. Slowly, the communication became more and more infrequent before eventually ceasing all together. When I came back, it didn't make sense for me to reach out. Ceasar and Kyan's silence over the years made it perfectly clear. They weren't rocking with me anymore. That was cool and all, but now that Seven was doing whatever she was doing with Ceasar, it made the situation awkward. Ceasar was far from a stranger, but our brief interactions made it seem as though we barely knew each other.

"Y'all ain't ready," Ceasar chuckled, wiping his forehead with his hand. "That's all y'all get for now."

"Boy, please," Seven began, sucking her teeth. Rolling her eyes, she cocked her head to the side. "You know you tired. Look at you... sweating and shit."

"That's cuz it's hot."

"Nah baby, you done had one too many beers," Seven joked. "It ain't even hot."

"Yeah it is. Ain't it, Joie?"

I heard Ceasar speak, but my mouth wouldn't move. In the back of the room, there were people laughing, dancing, and having a good time. A game of Spades was overshadowed by a tall man standing up and slamming a single domino onto the table. "Twenty-five, bitches!" he yelled in satisfaction, but even that didn't hold my attention. All that commotion was nothing compared to the paralyzing effect of Drako's firm stare. He rubbed his goatee while sitting on the edge of a couch. His dreads were pulled back into a neat bun while a white tee and gold chain covered his chest and neck. The way the light bounced off his pinky ring almost blinded me, but I was stuck. I couldn't turn away.

"Joie?" Seven repeated, grabbing my forearm and shaking it. "Are you okay?"

"Yeah," I managed to say.

Seven traced my gaze and giggled when she saw my target. "You staring kinda hard at Drako. Want me to call him over?"

"No!" I asserted, finally finding my voice. That was the wrong time for my girl to call me out. "I don't have nothing to say to him."

The sly smirk on Ceasar's face had me fuming inside. I was embarrassed, but I tried hard not to let it show.

"Why not?" Ceasar asked, taking a sip of his beer. "Drako's a good dude. You know that."

"Only thing I know is that I'll be waiting in the car."

Taking a deep breath, I turned on my heels and took a few steps toward the door. Seven jumped in front of me and blocked my path.

"Move," I demanded.

"Girl, what's wrong with you? Why are you leaving?"

"Because. You didn't have to say that shit in front of Ceasar."

"Chill the fuck out. It's not even that serious. You're the only one trippin'. Look, you're already out the house. You might as well chill and have a good time. What else is there to do? Sit around and wait for Norien not to show up?"

"He'll be there," I added.

"Yeah…tomorrow. But right now, you're chilling with me. I saw Kyan sitting over there and you know that bitch don't like me. I don't wanna be here alone." Grabbing my hand, she led me further into the room. "And if you think about leaving to go back to the car, I'll just send Drako out there. You'll be back in here in no time."

"You wouldn't," I challenged.

"Try me."

Seven joined Ceasar next to two adjacent couches. Kyan and her female friend sat on one couch with Drako occupying the arm. Three men sat on the other couch, but I had never met them before. Seven spoke, but only the men acknowledged her. Kyan didn't so much as look our way. Her friend didn't either. Her eyes stayed on Kyan's hands as she carefully rolled a blunt.

"Hey everybody," I greeted, following Seven's lead. The men said their 'heys' and 'what's ups', but Drako had to be difficult.

"What are you doing here?" he spat, seductively chewing on the end of a toothpick.

"I was invited," I shot back.

"By who?"

"By me," Seven interjected. "Is that a problem?"

"Sure is," Kyan answered, using her tongue and lips to close the blunt. "You weren't invited either. Why are you here?"

"A'ight, calm that noise down," Ceasar warned. "We're all here, and we're all about to have a good time. Now, I see a lot of empty glasses and bottles sitting around. All that liquor wasn't free. Drink that shit."

"Come on, Nova." Kyan nudged her girl, and they got up and walked off.

Ceasar grabbed the blunt Kyan left behind and examined it before popping the smallest end in his mouth. "Somebody gimme a light."

He took the lighter being extended in his direction. Taking a deep pull on the blunt, his eyes fell on me. "Do you know these niggas?" he asked, pointing to the men on the couch.

I shook my head 'No'.

"Damn, why we gotta be niggas?" one of the men huffed.

"Cuz you are. Joie, that's Tommy. He ain't shit. And neither are the two muthafuckas sittin' beside him."

"Fuck you, nigga," the man in the middle spoke. "Don't listen to that dude. I'm Monty. Nice to meet you."

The last man was identified as Rod. No one in the trio was interesting to look at and when Ceasar offered to introduce me to the other occupants of the room, I quickly accepted. Drako had me feeling uncomfortable under his gaze. He spoke as though he didn't want me there, but he never took his eyes off me.

I loosened up after being introduced to everyone in the room. Apparently, they all worked together, although no one mentioned their place of employment. Ceas explained that every now and then, they all linked up and chilled. There were over twenty people in that room alone. It didn't count the people Ceasar claimed were outside.

By the time we returned to where Drako sat, Kyan and her friend were back. Kyan rolled her eyes at Ceasar as she put the finishing touches on another blunt. He called her out on her attitude, just as my phone started ringing in my purse. The number wasn't familiar, but I answered the call anyway.

"Hello?"

"Joie?"

"Yeah, it's me." I recognized Norien's voice immediately. "Who's number is this?"

"It's a long story. I'm...over some bullshit. I need...like yesterday."

"What?" Static filled the line. I closed off my free ear with my finger in an effort to hear him better. "Huh?"

"I said...tonight...hopefully..."

"Norien, I can't understand you. Say it again." The static had taken over the line. It was hard to make out what was being said. I took a few steps away from the group and the buzzing sound disappeared. "That's better. I can hear you. Now, what's going on."

When he yelled into my ear and repeated himself, I almost dropped the phone.

"Jail? What the fuck? Why? How?"

He attempted to explain his drug deal gone bad in a code that I didn't understand. Picking up on an occasional keyword, I tried to make sense of his gibberish. I was lost.

"What's going on?" Seven questioned, placing her hand on my shoulder. "Is everything okay?"

That's when I noticed that I had everyone's attention. My conversation became the topic of the moment, and inquiring eyes waited for my reply.

"Norien's in jail," I advised.

"What the fuck do you mean that nigga's in jail?" Ceasar huffed. He looked at Drako, who rose to his feet.

Exhaling loudly, Drako poked Ceasar in the chest with his index finger and spoke through gritted teeth. "You vouched for that muthafucka."

I didn't understand what was going on. Who vouched for who, and why? I had Norien in one ear and Drako and Ceasar in another. I just wanted it all to make sense. When Ceasar stepped forward and snatched the phone out of my hand, I was even more confused.

"Nigga, you better start talkin'."

15

DRAKO

Dumb ass nigga.

I grilled Ceas with an exceptional amount of anger and disappointment. He tried to be 'Mr. Muthafuckin' Nice Guy' and got us screwed over. From the jump, I knew Norien would be a fuckin' problem, but with Ceas being my boy, I trusted his judgment. He vouched for that nigga, only for him to fuck up and get caught slipping, like I knew he would.

"Everybody get the fuck out!" I barked. I didn't have to repeat myself. Everyone there knew how I was when I was pissed and didn't want to be on my bad side. Within seconds, the place was empty. Ceas, Seven, Joie, and Kyan all stayed behind. Even Nova dipped because she knew shit was about to get real.

I paced the floor as I waited for Ceas to hang up on that nigga. Fuck talking over the phone, we needed to see his bitch ass in person. Licking my lips, I swaggered over to Ceas, snatched the phone, and hung it up. He turned around with his chest poked out, walking up on me. Ceas was a little taller than me, but on everything, that nigga didn't put no fear in my cold heart.

"Say what the fuck you gotta say, nigga. Walkin' up on me like you gon' do somethin'," I challenged, shoving him back with one hand.

"You ain't got shit to say because YOU trusted that muthafucka, Ceas. Now, look what the fuck happened. I knew we shouldn't have fronted his ass a got damn thing! On everythin', I'm bodyin' that nigga."

"Body? Oh, no. You can't kill him," Joie spoke up with a frightful expression. "Can someone explain to me what happened?" she asked, never taking her eyes off me.

With a menacing stare, I bluntly stated, "We're about to take you to go say goodbye to yo' nigga. Contact his family about funeral arrangements. Let's fuckin' go, Ceas. Kyan, let Seven and Joie ride with you."

"Nah, I'm good. They can go the way they got here, Drako," Kyan brushed me off and walked out. Shaking my head, I followed behind her and hopped in my ride while I waited for Ceas. I mugged his ass as he jogged to the passenger side and climbed in. I peeled off with Kyan and Seven right behind us.

"I should fuck yo' ass up, man. What that nigga say?"

"His ass was speakin' in riddles. He was avoidin' my questions, so we gon' find out at the same time what's goin' on," Ceas answered. Just like me, Ceas was hot. I could tell by the way his nostrils flared that he was ready to fuck some shit up.

I made a call to our lawyer, Christine, on the way. I needed her to look into the specifics of the situation. She was already in the area and agreed to meet us at the jail. Ceas and I passed some gas back and forth on the drive over. No conversation was needed. He knew he fucked up, so I didn't have to tell him again. Norien was *his* fuckin' problem that *I* was about to solve.

Throwing my car in park, we hopped out. Christine met us at the door. She explained Norien had gotten set up to sell to an undercover. He was being transported from his cell to one of the interrogation rooms. When she told us the amount of drugs that had been confiscated, I wanted to set the entire precinct on fire and burn that nigga alive. It was the exact amount he needed Ceas to front him. That dirty muthafucka was supplying for other niggas. He was trying to sell that shit behind our backs. The idea of it all took my anger to a different level. Mugging Ceas, I brushed past Christine and walked inside the precinct.

"Sir, may I help you?" a woman asked from behind a desk.

Ignoring her, I walked through the swinging doors to the back where they had the interrogation rooms. Christine was yelling for me to stop while Kyan warned her to watch how she talked to me. I walked by every room until I saw Norien sitting at a table with his head down. Calmly, I swaggered inside, picked him up by his shirt, and slammed him into the wall. Then, I fucked his ass up. I was sending blows all over his body while he tried his hardest to use his hands as a shield. I didn't stop until Ceas pulled me off him and pushed me toward a wall.

"Calm the fuck down, Drako. We need this nigga alive to know what the fuck happened," Ceas roared.

Two guards rushed in and started toward me. Ceas stepped in front of them and said, "I advise y'all to get the fuck out and not fuck with him. Neither of us are in the mood."

"It's our job t—"

"I don't give a fuck what yo' job is. Get the fuck out before you get put the fuck out," I threatened. My patience was very thin, and I was liable to snap somebody's neck.

The two guards exchanged glances and looked at Norien before leaving. I waved Christine away and picked up one of the chairs to sit in. I sat down, observing my knuckles. Norien was laid out on the floor, causing me to chuckle in amusement.

"Get yo' pussy ass up and talk. You costin' us too much damn time and money."

Ceas took a seat next to me. We watched Norien struggle to get up and sit down. His face was fucked up and I knew he probably had a few broken ribs. That was light work. His life depended on what he said next. If he was smart, he'd say some clever shit.

"What happened?" Ceas questioned once Norien was seated.

"I... uh... I..."

"It's funny how you seem to have developed a stutterin' problem. Do I need to knock that shit out, too?"

"I fucked up," Norien replied.

"Stop beatin' around the bush before I let Drako finish what he started. I ain't gon' stop him this time."

"Just say the word, Ceas. I been itchin' to kill that nigga with my bare hands," I encouraged, staring Norien in the eyes. "Bitch."

Looking away, Norien lowered his head and began to explain what happened. To keep from jumping across the table and killing him, I laughed out loud like he'd said the funniest shit ever. He cocked his head to the side, and I challenged him to say some shit I didn't like. I blinked and Ceas had his hands wrapped around Norien's throat. His strong ass picked him up with one hand while going in on him about being stupid. The shit didn't have anything to do with me, so I sat back and watched in amusement. If Ceas fucked around and killed him, then oh fuckin' well. He deserved it. I was disappointed when Ceas dropped him and he fell to the ground, gasping for air.

"How you gon' fix this shit? You owe us money and product with a whole lot of interest," Ceas spoke coolly, sitting back down.

"Y'all gon' get me out?" Norien coughed.

"The fuck we look like helpin' you out when you tried to screw us over? You on yo' own with this shit. You got less than twenty-four-hours to get us the money and product you owe us."

"That's... that's not enough time. I'm still locked up. How y'all expect me to do that from the inside?"

"Figure it out, dummy. If we don't have it, you'll be responsible for all the loved ones you lose. Like I said before, nigga, I'll go after all yo' blood to get what the fuck belongs to us. I'm tired of lookin' at yo' dumb ass. You better have something figured out when we come back tomorrow," I warned, getting up and walking out.

I meant every word I said. It didn't faze me to kill anyone. It was a cold world, and I was even colder. That was the only way to survive.

Leaving him sitting there, I walked toward the front of the building. I didn't say a word when I noticed Seven and Joie sitting in the waiting area. Joie stood when she saw me, but I continued out the door. I ignored Kyan as she called out to me. I even left Ceas behind. He could catch a ride with one of the women. The way I felt, I didn't feel like dealing with anyone. My head wasn't in the right space, so I left and headed straight to Nek's house. I needed to relieve some built up pressure, and she was the perfect person to help me with that.

Twelve minutes later, I pulled up to her house and noticed an unfamiliar car in the driveway. I waltzed right inside like I owned the place, waving my gun at the nigga sitting on the couch next to her. He got the message quick, grabbing his shit and rushing out. Nek started in with her attitude, but I shut her up by sticking my dick in her mouth.

"Suck my dick until my balls are dry. And get nasty wit it. You know how I like it."

Obediently, Nek slithered her tongue down my shaft before deep throating my shit. Her jaws locked around it as my head repeatedly hit the back of her throat. She sucked like her life depended on it. I leaned my head back when she eased my balls up my dick to where she was sucking and licking simultaneously. Nek was the muthafuckin' head master, and that was the only reason I kept her around.

Roughly, I rolled her long weave into my hand and placed it on the back of her head. I moved my dick in and out of her mouth at a nice, steady pace until I felt my nut rising.

"Take this shit," I growled lowly, picking up my speed. Nek was gagging and soon, my seeds coated her throat. "Toot that ass up," I demanded.

Nek happily lifted her nightgown and turned over with a sly grin. Rolling a condom down my shaft, I licked my lips when her ass looked back at me. She arched her back perfectly, giving me easy access to tap her spot. Biting my lower lip, I went in, smacking her ass as the ripples went through each cheek like waves. When Nek reached her hand back and placed it on my stomach, I knew it was becoming too much.

"Move yo' fuckin' hand, Nek. Take this dick, girl."

"Ooohhh, Drakooo! Slo…slow down!"

"I feel that pussy tightenin'. Let that shit go, Nek."

I ran a marathon in her pussy. She moaned in delight as each stroke outdid the last. I gave her three more long, deep strokes before pulling out and releasing into the condom. Nek's body fell to the floor and she gasped for air. I smacked her ass and walked off to go wash up. She was right behind me, smiling for no damn reason. For the first time that night, I smiled. I did the damn thing. Nek had no complaints.

My crib was on the other side of town and I was tired as fuck. I went to Nek's bedroom and got comfortable. I set an alarm to get up at the crack of dawn to go home and wash my ass. I planned on being at the precinct before visiting hours. If Norien didn't have the answers I wanted, shit would get real again.

The next morning, I threw a few bills on Nek's table before I left. I was able to get another hour of sleep after I made it home. By eight, I was heading out the door to pick up Ceas. He was waiting for me by his mailbox when I pulled up.

"Where you go last night? I rode by yo' crib, but you wasn't there," Ceas explained.

"Mindin' my damn business."

"Shit was crazy. I thought Kyan was about to whoop Seven's ass."

"For what?"

"Ky thought Seven wasn't gon' snap back at her for sayin' slick shit. Ky tried to square up when she did. I had to break that shit up."

"You know Kyan ain't wrapped too tight," I chuckled, shaking my head.

"None of us are."

"You damn right. Let's go see what this nigga got to say today. I hope he slept on that shit."

We stepped inside the precinct and went straight to the back. Norien was in the same room from last night, and he looked like shit. A smile turned up my lips as I observed his appearance. One of his eyes was swollen shut, his nose was crooked, and his lips were busted. With his good eye, he grilled me with pure hatred. Just for that, I sat directly in front of him and smirked.

"You figure shit out yet? You had all night to think about it," I said, getting straight to the point.

"Yeah, I did," he answered, looking at Ceas. "I know someone who can work in my place. She can work off my debt until I'm released, and I'll handle it from there."

Ceas and I looked at one another, then back at Norien.

"She?" Ceas asked, rubbing his chin.

"Yeah. A chick I know named April. She's a very submissive bitch. Whatever you need her to do, she'll do it. And I do mean whatever."

"Nigga, we ain't lookin' for a piece of pussy. It's pussy walkin' all around us," I spat. "I don't know that bitch. She ain't workin' for us."

"What?"

"You heard what the fuck I said. She could be like yo' dumb ass and try some slick shit and end up dead. Besides, I didn't say shit about givin' you more time. Pay day is today. Come up with another plan."

"I ain't gonna have it today."

"Cool," I stood, interlocking my fingers and pressing outward. "You ready to die now? Or do you wanna wait until your twenty-four hours is officially over."

"Man, I ain't tryna die at all," he whined. "You gotta give me more time."

"I ain't gotta do shit but stay black and die."

"What would you gain from killin' me?" Norien challenged. "You still won't have your money. I'm tellin' you now…none of my family got shit. Only thing you're gonna have is a few more bodies under your belt with nothing else hittin' your pockets. At least if somebody works in my place, you'll get your money back."

I thought about it for a minute. The grimy mothafucka was right. Even though I wanted him dead, I wanted my money back even more. "I'm listenin'."

Before Norien could continue, Ceas beat him to it. "Actually, that's not a bad idea."

"What the fuck are you sayin'?" I asked curiously.

"I want my money," he stated firmly. "If a bitch can get it back for us, I'm all for it, but it can't be a random. It gotta be somebody who won't fuck us over."

"Anybody associated with that mothafucka can't be trusted," I told him. "Birds of a feather, my nigga."

"Not if it's Joie," Ceas suggested. Norien's eyes grew wide, and he swiftly shook his head.

"Joie? Nah, man. Joie ain't built for that."

"Apparently, you ain't either, nigga," I spat. "You think we can trust her?" I asked my boy.

"Yeah, I think so."

Turning back to Norien, I gave him an ultimatum. "It's either Joie or death, nigga. You choose."

"A'ight, a'ight," Norien caved, lowering his head. "Don't go too hard on her. Joie is a good girl. I'm not feelin' exposin' her to this life."

"Should have thought about that before makin' stupid, impulsive decisions. Be thankful you don't have a bullet splittin' yo' skull. You still might get one, though."

We figured shit out, so I was done. There was no need to be in his presence any longer. I pushed the table against his body and left with Ceas in tow. He was talking, and I was hardly listening. My mind was on Joie and how we could make her essential to our operation. I thought about her pretty ass and smirked. She was about to see what it was like to fuck with a real nigga.

16

KYAN

"Aw, hell no, Ceas! We're not letting that bitch work with us!" I fumed. "Y'all didn't feel the need to speak with me about it first?"

Ceas gave me a 'the fuck?' glare, and I knew he was about to be on some shit I wasn't feeling.

"Yo' head gettin' too big, Ky. Drako and I run this shit. You work alongside us, but that doesn't give you the right to try and dictate shit. You ain't got no say in the matter, so you gon' have to deal with it," Ceas explained, shaking his head. "What happened between y'all anyway? Why you don't like her now?"

"Does it matter? The two of you are responsible for how I act toward her. If the bitch leaves here cryin' every day, it's on y'all."

"I ain't got shit to do with whatever female drama y'all got goin' on," Drako spoke. "Leave me out of it. Fuck you and her."

"No, nigga. Fuck you!"

These niggas knew how to get my blood boiling. I was ready to steal off on them both, but I knew the consequences wouldn't be good. At times, I hated being the youngest and only girl. It had its advantages and disadvantages. At the moment, I was at a disadvantage. I was outnumbered and my complaint didn't mean shit. Rolling my eyes, I kissed my teeth and mugged Ceas. He knew what I was thinking.

"You're too spoiled, Ky," Ceasar began. "You better chill with that shit. How you gon' be mad because you don't like how I'm movin'? It's business...that's all. You can take that attitude somewhere else."

"You're really goin' to make me deal with her, Ceas? What about Nova? She ain't gonna like that shit either."

"Don't nobody give a fuck about Nova's opinion. Shove that shit up her pussy. Sit on her face or whatever the fuck y'all do. Bump pussies or something," Drako said, and Ceas doubled over in laughter. I didn't find that shit funny at all.

Not able to handle them anymore, I grabbed my keys and left, making sure to slam the door behind me. I hopped in my ride with no destination in mind.

Joie was a sensitive subject for me. Once upon a time, she was the sister I never had and I loved her to death. I would do anything for her and vice versa. We met our seventh grade year, immediately clicking when I snapped on a bully for picking on her. She was shy, but no one messed with her because they knew she was my best friend and I would go to war for her.

When Joie and I hit high school, our main goal was to have fun. I giggled to myself as I thought of our daily activities. We were something else, and if Ceas or Drako knew of half the things we did, I would probably still be on lockdown for it.

Our bond was solid, until Joie moved our eleventh grade year. It was the first heartbreak I experienced. I took her moving hard. There were many nights I cried myself to sleep because I missed her so much. The one sister I had left me, and that triggered the resentment I held for her. She left me alone, and not once did she try to reach out to me. That's the same shit my momma did. After Ceas and I were put in the system, she went about her life as if she didn't have any kids. I knew Joie had been back for a few years. I waited to see if she would reach out and let me know she was home, but she didn't. She continued on with life like I never existed. I decided to do the same.

Working with Joie would be a struggle for me. I had no desire to be in her presence whatsoever. There were questions I wanted to ask her, but didn't want to know the answers to. The only reason I didn't was because if she fucked around and said the wrong thing, the city would be working on her missing persons case forever. I wasn't the same young Kyan she once knew, and I was positive she figured that out after our little encounter at the store. A bitch was a different breed.

Another thing I wasn't feeling was the fact Joie was close to that hoe, Seven. I already had to deal with the fact that she was sucking and fucking on my brother. I never liked her. There was something about Seven that rubbed me the wrong way. To me, I felt she wasn't genuine with shit. The bitch was scandalous. Everyone around the block had heard about Seven, including Ceas. I didn't understand how Ceas could look past that shit, but I wasn't the one eating her pussy.

To blow off some steam, I decided to hit up my favorite stores and spend a couple of bands. It was the perfect therapy. I started at Nordstrom and ended my two-hour shopping spree with some *Big Spoon Creamery* ice cream. It was the best ice cream around and I had been craving it for weeks, but I was too lazy to get it. Nova would be pissed if I got some and didn't get her any, so I ordered her favorite.

The door opening caught my attention, and so did the person walking inside. I didn't mean to, but I did a double take. Whoever she was, she was beautiful. She was about five foot nine, a little on the taller side like myself. Her skin was smooth and chocolate like a Hershey's bar. She was thin, but had a slightly curvy frame, natural hair, plump, glossy lips, and slanted eyes. Everyone stopped to stare at her. She was that damn stunning.

The worker clearing her throat knocked me out of the trance the mystery woman had me in. Grabbing our ice cream, I went to grab more napkins. I discreetly listened to the woman order and raised a brow when she recited Nova's favorite, a Cookies and Cream Sammie with extra cookies. It was a popular item, so I was sure it was just a coincidence.

Taking a bite of my Sammie, I blasted Dej Loaf's EP on the drive home. I was in the middle of rapping along to *Big Shit Talker* when my ringtone interrupted my flow. My eyes immediately rolled as Jake's name popped up on the screen. I didn't feel like being bothered by him or any other nigga for that matter. For a second, I contemplated answering, but when I thought about how Ceas basically called me 'the help,' I sent him to voicemail. I silenced his alerts, along with Drako and Ceas'. All I wanted to do was lay under Nova and watch Netflix movies.

"Babeeee!" I called out. "I'm home. You'll never believe what the fuck Ceas and Drako decided to do."

"I'm in the room! Come in here and tell me!" Nova yelled back.

"Hold on."

I went to the kitchen to put our Sammies in the freezer before going to the car and getting my shopping bags. In total, I took three trips and chastised myself for spending so much money. I did some crazy shit when I was mad. Oh well, at least everything I bought was cute.

When I walked back inside, Nova was standing there shaking her head at all the bags. I knew what she was thinking, so I ignored her 'really?' facial expression. My attention was on something else.

"Why the fuck you got clothes on?"

Nova was a free spirit. If it wasn't frowned upon, she would be naked all the time. Whenever we were home alone, she was either naked or hardly wearing any clothes. It was unusual seeing her fully clothed in the comfort of our home, so I knew that meant one of two things; she was about to leave or someone was coming over.

"I forgot to tell you. I ran into an old friend the other day and I invited her over," Nova informed me. Rolling my eyes, I groaned. I hated surprise visits, especially from muthafuckas I didn't know. "She used to be my best friend in high school."

"Oh, speakin' of old friends, I need to tell you about Ceas and Drako first. When is your friend comin'?"

"In about fifteen minutes, I think."

"Cool. That gives me plenty of time to rant, and…" I paused and flashed her a smile. "And for you to help me put everything up."

"Wait a minute! No one told you to go grabbing all this shit, Kyan. You should have thought about it before you did."

"Come on, babe. You know I picked you out a few things too. Besides, I didn't have to go all the way across town and get you a Cookies and Cream Sammie, but I did."

Gripping her wrist, I pulled her into me. Reaching my hand under her shirt, I bypassed her bra and fondled with her erect nipples. Nova closed her eyes and I smirked. I lifted her shirt more to get a better view, but she slapped my hand away and pulled her shirt down.

"Don't be tryin' to butter me up. We don't have time for that. You asked for my help, didn't you? Well…come on. Thanks for my Sammie, though. I can't wait to eat it." She spun around to pick up a few bags. I slapped her ass a few times before grabbing a few myself.

As we put everything away, I explained to her what happened earlier with Ceas. Thinking and talking about it had me pissed all over again. Low-key, my feelings were hurt too, but I wouldn't dare let Ceas know. They had me feeling as if I wasn't shit. I'd gotten them out of so much shit, and to hear that my opinion didn't matter hurt me to the core. If that was how my brothers felt, then so be it. I just knew where I stood.

"I'm sorry, babe. I know how you feel about Joie. I hate that they're being assholes and makin' you work with her. It'll all work out though. Maybe working with her will give you the closure you need. It might actually be a good thing."

"Fuck that. You know how I am."

"I know, and that's exactly why I'm sayin' it, Ky. You can be a bit harsh at times, especially to someone who's hurt you. Hear her out. This might be a good thing."

Nova was right, but I didn't want to agree with her. I honestly didn't give a fuck, to be all the way real. I was me without a doubt, so whoever didn't like it could kiss my ass.

The doorbell sounded, and Nova's excitement grew. She grabbed my hand and led me into the living room. My eyebrows rose in astonishment when I laid eyes on the brown beauty from the creamery. Nova squealed and embraced the woman tightly.

What a fuckin' coincidence!

"Oh my gosh, Sadee! I'm so glad you came!" Nova exclaimed. "Come in."

Who I now knew as Sadee switched inside with her eyes trained on me. The way she gazed at me had me feeling some type of way. Her eyes glowed with curiosity the longer she stared. My inner Drako came out and before I knew it, I was popping off at the mouth. "Why the fuck you keep starin'?"

"Ky!" Nova shouted. "Don't start actin' like yo' rude ass brother. She's a guest. If it's a problem, you can go in the other room while I talk to Sadee."

Nova's attention was on me, so she didn't peep how Sadee continued to stare at me with a mischievous smirk tugging at those pretty lips of hers.

"Nov, it's fine. Pretty women like her are always the rude ones, but you know I can handle my own," Sadee spoke confidently. "It's nice to meet you. Ky is it?"

"Kyan to you," I advised.

"Okay, Kyan. It's nice to meet you...and that smart mouth of yours," Sadee teased.

"Let me go in the back before I fuck yo' friend up, Nova. She don't know me."

I turned to walk away, and I could have sworn I heard Sadee mumble, 'I would let you'.

My ears were probably deceiving me, but I had a feeling they weren't. Sadee was beautiful, but something about her was off. I had a feeling she was going to be a problem and my gut never steered me wrong. I wasn't about to let her be a problem in my relationship. At least, that was what I told myself. I was definitely going to keep an eye on her.

17

CEASAR

"What are you doin' here?" I questioned, surprised to see Seven walking alongside Joie. I hadn't called or told her what was going on. I wanted to keep her as far away from everything as I could.

"I think I have a right to be here," she responded, sucking her teeth. Crossing her arms in front of her chest, she shifted her weight to one foot and rolled her eyes. "So, what's really going on, Ceas? Why are you calling my girl to meet up with you? You tryin' to be on some sneaky shit? Huh? What's the deal?"

Her accusations caused me to laugh in her face. She was getting all worked up and bent out of shape for nothing. Joie was cute and all, but Drako was my nigga. Any bitch he ever showed interest in was off limits to me. Besides, I knew Joie before her evolution; when she was flat-chested and had bad skin. Just like she wasn't my type then, she wasn't my type now. Seven was bugging.

"First of all, lower your tone when you talk to me." I ignored the mumbling she did up under her breath and continued. "Whatever craziness you thought up in your mind, forget that shit. Believe me, it ain't like that."

"Well, what is it then?" she challenged.

"We'll talk later. Right now, I need to rap with Joie."

"Fuck that!" she huffed, allowing her arms to flail around wildly. "I wanna know now."

"And people in hell want ice water…do they get it?"

"You are so full of shit, Ceas! I thought we were better than this. What's with all the secrets? If it's not what I think, clear this shit up now. What's going on?"

"You're starting to piss me off," I warned. "Listen to me…right now ain't the time, okay? Let it go."

"Make it the time," she challenged. "I ain't leaving until you tell me something."

"I told you what it was. Either you can accept it or just stand there and be mad. I ain't gonna keep going back and forth with you." Turning to Joie, I let my frustration get the best of me. "Get in the fuckin' car."

"Where are we going?" Joie asked, turning up her face in confusion. She quickly glanced in Seven's direction before turning back to me. "Can *I* at least know what's going on. You didn't say anything about us leaving."

"Why do y'all gotta be so difficult? Damn! Y'all act like I'ma do somethin'."

"Well," Joie began. "Are you?"

"Man, get the fuck outta here. I thought you knew me better than that. If I wanted to do somethin', I would have done it by now. I certainly wouldn't have called you over. That's bitch shit. I would have went straight to your door and knocked on that muthafucka. Don't insult me like that."

Things weren't turning out like I planned. I was supposed to be halfway to Drako by now. He wanted to personally give Joie the rundown of how she would be paying us back our money. Just in case Norien ran his mouth and told Joie about how Drako fucked him up, he thought it would be best if I brought her to him.

That's all I was trying to do. I could have easily found out where she laid her head, but I wasn't trying to cause any problems. I felt that it would be easier to meet in a public place, discuss the plan, and roll out. The reason I didn't go to her house was the same reason Seven had an attitude. I didn't want it to look like I was trying to push up on the girl. Besides, Seven knew good and damn well that Joie was gonna run her damn mouth anyway. I cared for Seven and all, but I refused to tell her anything about our operation. Technically, we were just fucking. She had to work her way up for that information.

Realizing I wasn't giving up any information, she turned her back to me. As bad as I wanted to say something, I kept my mouth closed. My ringing phone captured my attention. It was Drako. Stepping toward my car, I answered his call.

"What's up?"

"Nigga, you tell me? What's takin' so damn long?"

"I'm tryin'...shit. Seven's here askin' questions and Joie—"

Before I could finish what I wanted to say, Drako cut me off. "I'm on my way. Where are you?"

"I got it," I reassured, glancing over my shoulder at the girls. "Just gimme a minute. We'll be there."

"When? Next year? Anytime Seven is around, you lose your fuckin' mind. You already know I don't like to wait. That includes right now. I'ma ask you again. Where are you? You know it'll only take me a few minutes to find out anyway."

Knowing he was right, I gave up our location. After hanging up with him, I walked back over to the girls and tried one last time to get them to cooperate. Drako didn't have a filter. If he had to come to us, he was sure to have an attitude. I wanted to prevent that from happening. Drako was my boy and all, but he could be an asshole when he wanted to be.

"Are y'all done flappin' y'alls gums yet?" I questioned in irritation. "I ain't tryna be out here all night."

"Will you tell me what this is about?" Joie asked. "Why can't I know what's going on?"

Exhaling loudly, I rested my hands on top of my head. That's exactly what I was trying to do. Why didn't she understand that? She was too busy trying to figure things out on her own when I was willing to tell her myself. All she had to do was follow directions and do what the fuck I said. We could have been on our way to Drako and she wouldn't be staring back at me with that stupid ass look on her face.

"You know what. Fuck it!" I exclaimed, throwing my hands up in the air. "I tried. You can deal with his ass yourself."

"Who?" Seven asked, raising a hand to her hip.

She hadn't learned yet. I wasn't telling her shit. The way she was acting, I wasn't calling her ass either. I hated when bitches didn't listen. Grilling me like a nigga on the street, that's exactly what I thought of her at that moment.

Leave it to Drako to make an entrance. He showed up right on time...rounding the corner while pushing the brakes. The smell of burnt rubber was heavy in the air, and the noise from the tires screeching hurt my ears. He hopped out his ride, adjusted the jacket and pants of his track suit, and walked over to us like he wasn't fazed at all.

"Nigga, you still out here choppin' it up with these females? Didn't I tell you we got shit to do? What's the problem?"

"Man," I began, exhaling loudly. "She's asking all these muthafuckin' questions. I told her to come on, but she's stubborn."

"Don't talk about my friend like she ain't standing here," Seven interjected. "We're not going anywhere until y'all tell us what this is all about."

"Handle that," Drako warned, turning toward me. "If I do, I ain't showin' no mercy."

"Is that a threat?" Seven challenged. "Cuz I don't know who you think—"

"Yo...Seven, chill. Damn." With Drako watching me intently, I stepped in her direction and pulled her to the side. As soon as we were out of earshot, I tried my best to calm her down. "What the fuck is wrong with you, girl? What did I tell you?"

"Nothing! That's the problem." Rolling her eyes, she walked past me as if my words didn't mean shit. Rejoining Joie's side, she dismissed everything I said. "This shit's for the birds. Girl, you ready?"

"Nah, she ain't ready," Drako hissed. "But don't let that stop you. You can take your ass on. I'll get her home."

"I ain't leaving my girl with you. You 'bout as crazy as your friend. I don't know you like that, and I sure as hell don't trust you."

I shrugged and threw my hands up when Drako's eyes darted in my direction. What could I say? Seven didn't bite her tongue. The girl was bold and had more heart than some of the niggas I knew. She didn't back down when it came to her friend. That was a quality I couldn't help but respect. Loyalty went a long way in my book.

"Ceas," Drako mumbled through gritted teeth. "I'ma hurt this broad's feelings if she keeps on. I know you fuckin' her and all, but if you don't get her ass together, I will."

As crazy as it sounds, Drako was being nice. If Seven and I weren't messing around, he would have got in her ass without a second thought. The fact that he respected me saved her from his verbal assault. That didn't mean he wouldn't snap. Drako would cuss his own momma out if she stepped to him wrong. He was cold-hearted. Anybody could get it.

The way the muscles in his jaw flexed repeatedly told me that he had a lot more he wanted to say. Seven just kept on. She wasn't used to a muthafucka with no filter. His attitude was ten times worse than hers. Sucking her teeth, she started rolling that damn neck of hers. *Here we go*, I thought.

"You ain't gonna do shit!" she announced, turning up her nose. "Ceas…you're really just gonna stand there and let him talk to me like that?"

Now she wanted to talk to me? What kind of shit was that? When I wanted to talk, she downplayed everything I said. What made her words more important than mine?

"I told you to leave a long time ago. You should've listened."

"Everybody, calm down!" Joie stated, finding her way into the center of the madness. "This whole situation is going left, and quick. Drako, I don't know what you have to do with all this, but you coming at my girl like that ain't cool. All she's trying to do is figure out what's going on, just like I am. Ceasar never calls me, now out of the blue, he wants to meet up. You'd be skeptical too if the tables were turned. Don't get mad at her for doing the exact same thing you would."

Before me or Drako could get a word in, Seven spoke up. "It's all good, Joie. You ain't gotta defend me. I see how it is. I'm out. Are you coming with me or staying?"

"I'm—" Joie began.

"Staying," Drako finished for her. "Do you ever listen? I told you that already."

When Joie didn't move, Seven got the picture. "Fine. I'll catch up with you later, girl. Call me if you need me." Turning up her nose at Drako, she added, "She better make it home too. Or else!"

Even I laughed at that. Drako's face softened as he smiled widely. Her mouth may have been big, but her small, petite frame wasn't. She didn't scare nobody. In fact, her choice of words issued a challenge that Drako had every intention of accepting.

"Or else what? What the fuck are you gonna do? You shouldn't have said that shit. Now she ain't comin' home at all. I can guarantee that."

"A'ight, a'ight…chill." Stepping in to intervene, I pulled Seven to the side once again. The back and forth was getting on my nerves. It was a waste of both time and energy. "She'll get home, I promise. I'ma run this shit down to her, then let Drako take over. It won't take long. I'll drop her off and then swing by. Is that cool?"

"Nope. You ain't chilling nowhere with me, nigga. You got me fucked up."

Flipping the colorful tips of her wig off her shoulder, Seven spun on her heels. Finally, she was leaving, although a part of me wanted her to stay. I enjoyed having her around, but mixing business with pleasure was something I didn't do. Seven wasn't about that lifestyle. I had no intention of bringing her into it. She could be mad for now but eventually, she would come around. If she didn't, well then, I guess she wasn't the woman for me.

When I returned to Drako, he had pulled Joie off to the side. He stood in front of her, partially blocking her from my view. Speaking with his hands, he was blunt with his words.

"Fuck all that! What you don't know, you'll learn. That's what Kyan's for. She's gonna teach you what you need to know."

Judging from her facial expression, he had already revealed her new role in our organization. When Drako mentioned Kyan, Joie quickly glanced in my direction, but returned her eyes to my boy. If I wasn't in earshot, she probably would have said something about my sister. Good thing for her, she bit her tongue. Everybody knew I didn't play when it came to Kyan.

"I'm not working for you," Joie responded defiantly. "I'm not putting my life or my freedom in jeopardy for you, Ceas, or anybody else. What's wrong with you?" Turning to me, she asked, "Ceas, is this really what you called me here for? For this? We barely talk as it is. What makes you think I would just agree to something like this."

"You ain't got no choice, Joie," I stated, trying to sound as compassionate as I could. I felt for the girl. This wasn't the lifestyle she was used to; however, she chose to mess with a fuck nigga. That was her choice. Now, she was a pawn in his bullshit. "Norien owes us a lot of money."

"But that has nothing to do with me. That's between y'all. Keep me out of it." Shaking her head, she let out a loud sigh. "Just wait until I talk to him. He's gonna be pissed that y'all even propositioned me in the first place."

"He's gonna be pissed?" I repeated with a smirk. "Let's see."

Pulling out my phone, I dialed my contact at the precinct. I requested to speak with Norien and was placed on hold while he was retrieved from his dorm.

"How do y'all know each other anyway?" Joie asked, breaking the silence. "Norien never mentioned anything about working for y'all."

"There's a lot he don't mention," Drako countered. "Take that shit up with him."

"What's that supposed to mean?"

"Exactly what the fuck I said. Ask that nigga how he knows me. I don't gotta explain shit to you. You ain't my bitch."

"Thank God for that!" Crossing her arms, Joie gave Drako the death stare. "Did he answer yet?" she asked me, still looking Drako's way.

"Nope," I responded.

"When he does, I want to talk to him first."

"That nigga don't give a fuck about you," Drako spat. "I don't either. All I want is my money. We ain't negotiating here, Joie. Ceas didn't bring you here to ask your opinion. Do you think I care about how you feel? Feelings don't put money in my pocket…and neither did your sorry ass nigga. That's why we're here. If you want somebody to be mad at, be mad at him. You can tell him any muthafuckin' thing you want. I'm still puttin' that ass to work."

"Hello? Hello?" I repeated, hearing a faint response on the other end. "Norien?"

"Yeah, it's me. I'm here. Who's this? Ceasar?"

I put the phone on speaker for all to hear. "The one and only. I got Drako here with me. Joie too. She ain't feelin' this arrangement we worked out."

"Let me talk to her. I can get her to agree. That's the only way I'm gettin' up outta here."

Joie stared stone-faced at the screen. I attempted to pass her the phone, but she never reached for it. Maybe she thought Norien wouldn't agree to the terms. After hearing him speak in his own words, she now knew that wasn't true.

"Go on," Drako urged, forcing the phone into Joie's hands. "You wanted to talk to that nigga so bad… he's on the line."

"Hello," Joie spoke, repositioning the phone in her palm. "Norien?"

"Yeah, baby…it's me. I need you to—"

Taking the phone, Drako hung it up. "What did you do that for?!" Joie roared.

"Fuck him." Drako tossed the phone back to me. "Your priorities are fucked up. Time is money and you got a lot to make. Get in the car."

Drako gave me a pound and I climbed back in my car. I decided not to follow them to my sister's crib. Nah, I needed to clear things up with Seven first. The way she looked when she walked off told me it wouldn't be easy, but I was still going to try. Hopefully everything ended well. If not, there wasn't much I could do.

SEVEN

I WAS FUMING. Ceas had me fucked all the way up, and so did Drako. I was pissed at myself for the way the tears streamed down my cheeks. Swiftly, I wiped them away and turned up my music as I drove with no particular destination in mind. I wasn't going home because I knew Ceas. He would be coming over to try and make shit better, but I was cool on him. He should have had that energy when I was in his presence.

"How could you be so stupid to fall for a nigga like him, Seven?" I spoke to myself, slapping my hand against the steering wheel. "It's apparent he doesn't care for you like you do him, or he wouldn't have been so secretive about shit with *my* best friend."

My thoughts were running wild as I thought of what Ceas and Drako could possibly want with Joie. She was genuinely confused, and they weren't trying to say shit in front of me. Joie would tell me, though. I would wait for her to call or come see me before bombarding her with questions. It was the principle about the whole thing. Why couldn't Ceas just tell me himself? If I called Drako and asked to meet up with him, Ceas would be hot. I wouldn't do that, though. I respected Ceas too much. I just wanted him to give me the same respect that I would give him.

I ended up at my parents' house. Deuce wasn't supposed to come home until later that day, but I needed to see my baby to cheer me up. My mood was shitty, and he was the only person who could change it. Parking behind my father's truck, I hit the locks on my car and jogged up to the front door. I could hear Deuce yelling in the backyard, so I let myself in the house and went straight to the kitchen. Anytime Deuce was there, my momma cooked big meals. I helped myself to a plate of lemon pepper baked chicken, pilaf rice, green beans, red potatoes, and a roll. Grabbing a bottle of water from the fridge, I went out back to join them.

"Mommyyyy!" Deuce yelled, jumping off my father's back and running toward me. He attacked my legs and squeezed. "I missed you!"

"I missed you too, buddy. So much so, that I had to come get you early."

"Awww! But I was play fighting with Papa."

"You can keep playing. I'll be here for a while. I gotta eat my food first."

That was all he needed to hear. With a huge smile plastered on his handsome, chocolate face, Deuce hugged me tighter before running off to join my father again. I sat at the table and watched their interaction while stuffing my face. I adored the relationship my parents had with Deuce. They truly loved him, and I couldn't help but wish they would have treated me the same way growing up. My father wasn't around back then, but that's a different story. For my mother, it was all about making sure I stayed on the straight and narrow path. In a way, she was like a drill sergeant, demanding that I do whatever she said when she said it. It was what caused me to be rebellious in the first place. Even with her strict rules and demeaning behavior, I still found a way to be successful.

Once I was halfway finished with my plate, my mother, Dorie, walked outside and joined me.

"I didn't know you were here, Seven. Why didn't you come find me?" she questioned, taking a seat next to me.

"I smelled the food and had to eat. I haven't eaten all day."

"That's not how I raised you. You know better than to come to someone's house and not speak first. That's rude."

"Sorry, Ma," I replied dryly. I wasn't in the mood to hear her shit or have an argument for that matter. The way I felt, I was liable to let anything come out my mouth.

"I hope you're not here to pick up Deuce. I was going to call and see if we could keep him another night or two. There's this play your father and I want to take him to after he gets out of school tomorrow."

I contemplated my options in my head. Being home by myself was lonely, especially since I wasn't allowing Ceasar to come over. Then again, the break was much needed. Deuce had been with my parents all weekend, but I would leave it up to him if he wanted to stay or not. If he was ready to come home, then I was going to pack him up and leave. It didn't matter what my mother had to say.

"Does he have enough clothes?" I asked. "Let me ask him if he's ready to come home."

"Oh, stop it, Seven. You know he loves staying with us. I already asked him, and he wants to go to the play."

Ignoring my mother's statement, I called Deuce over and asked him. He looked back and forth between my mother and I before saying he wanted to come home. My mother's demeanor changed, and I could tell her feelings were hurt. Oh well. Deuce loved being with his mother, too.

"Well, I guess we'll have to go see the play some other time," Mom sighed.

"If you want, y'all can come get him and take him. I'm sure he'll enjoy that."

"How about the both of you come? You never do family outings with us anymore, Seven. It would be nice if you joined us for once." Before I knew it, I rolled my eyes hard as hell. My mother saw me and scoffed, shaking her head. "I don't know what your problem is with your father and me, but you need to fix that attitude. We're your parents, and we're not getting any younger. You need to call and come around more, and not just when it pertains to Deuce."

"Ma, I don't want to have this conversation. I love you and Daddy, but you know why our relationship is strained, and it damn sure isn't because of me."

"Oh, so you're saying this is all *my* fault?"

"That's exactly what I'm saying."

"What have I ever done to you? All I've ever done was love, cherish, and nurture you."

"Is that what you call it?" I sarcastically quizzed, kissing my teeth. "I don't remember it being like that."

"Well, how do you remember it, Seven? I remember you being a little spoiled, unappreciative brat who rebelled against me about everything. You were so defiant. You don't know how thankful I am that Deuce didn't inherit your ways. You're lucky! If Deuce was half the child you were, you'd be ready to pull your hair out."

Despite our rocky relationship, my parents were the only people I held my tongue for. At the end of the day, they were my parents and I had to respect them.

Standing up, I yelled for Deuce to come on and walked away with my mother calling my name. I went inside, sat my plate in the sink, and gathered Deuce's things. I could hear my mother instructing my father to come talk to me, but I wasn't in the mood to speak with either one of them. All my father would do was side with my mother, and I couldn't handle them ganging up on me. Grabbing Deuce's hand, I yelled over my shoulder that I loved them and left.

This must be piss Seven off day, I thought.

"Mommy, can we go get some ice cream?" Deuce pleaded from the backseat.

I glanced in my rearview mirror to see him with his hands clasped together and bottom lip poked out. There was no way I could resist that sweet face, even knowing my parents had probably fed him every sweet thing he asked for. Nodding, I took him to *Big Spoon Creamery* and decided to sit inside to eat. During our one-on-one time, my phone continuously vibrated in my purse. I checked it once and rolled my eyes when I saw it was Ceas. He'd called and texted numerous times, but he wasn't getting an answer. I didn't have shit to say to him.

Deuce fell asleep on the way home, like I expected him to. Long weekends and car rides always got to him. The only thing I dreaded was picking his heavy butt up and carrying him inside the house. He needed a bath, and I would fight with him on that. He was so cranky when he was sleepy, but he wasn't getting in his bed dirty.

"This muthafucka," I mumbled, blowing out an exaggerated sigh.

Parked in my driveway, Ceas sat on the trunk of his car with a sexy, deep scowl on his face. Despite the anger and disappointment I felt toward him, I couldn't deny how got damn fine he was. Chocolate was my weakness, and Ceas was covered in it. I felt a tingle between my legs and the urge to lick all over him. Instead, I shook those thoughts away and got out without acknowledging him. I opened the back door to get Deuce out when I felt Ceas walk up behind me. Rolling my eyes, I carried on as if he wasn't there.

"Move," he demanded, pushing me to the side. When he grabbed my son in his arms, Deuce slightly opened his eyes and smiled when he saw Ceas.

"Uncle Ceas...I missed you," Deuce mumbled, laying his head on his shoulder. As soon as the last word left his lips, he was drifting back to sleep.

"I missed you, too."

Ceas grilled me before brushing past me to the door. He let himself inside using his key. Taking Deuce straight to the bathroom, Ceas ran Deuce's bath water. If I wasn't so tired, I would have objected to his help. I didn't want or need him doing shit for me. While Ceas handled Deuce, I went to the bathroom in my room, making sure to lock the door behind me. I showered quickly, wondering what Ceas wanted. When I was finished, I stepped back into the room to see Ceas sitting on my bed with his muscular arms folded across his chest. I attempted to walk past him, but he caught me by my towel, ripping it off in the process.

"You can see yourself out, Carl. I don't have shit to say to you," I huffed, going to my dresser to pick out what lotion I wanted to put on. Knowing my Peach Mango scent was his favorite, I rubbed it all over my body as he watched me intently. I parted my lips to speak when Ceas found his way over to me and gripped my face. My eyes darted everywhere to avoid looking at him, but the longer he held me, I failed. Tears welled in my eyes, and I silently cursed myself for allowing him to see me weak – weak for him.

"Get. The fuck. Out."

"Why the fuck you been ignorin' my calls and shit, Sev?" he replied, matching the malice in my tone.

"It doesn't matter. Since you like keepin' secrets, I can too."

"I see you want to be petty and act childish. What happened didn't have anything to do with you, so I didn't have to tell you shit. I called Joie, not you."

"Well, you can go call her or any other bitch you're fuckin' with, Carl. It's obvious you're up to some sneaky, snake ass shit that I want no parts of. You think I'm supposed to be cool with you hittin' up my best friend without informin' me? Why?"

Ceas shrugged and stated, "Yeah. You're not my girl, so I don't have to explain everything to you."

That…that was a muthafuckin' blow to my heart. I felt that shit all the way down to my knees, and from the expression on Ceas' face, he knew it too. His handsome face softened, but it was too late. He'd already spoken his words into the atmosphere. He words confirmed my worst fear. Sadly, he didn't feel the same way.

"Oh, I see," I expressed, nodding my head before shaking it. I closed my eyes tightly to stop the fresh, salty water droplets threatening to spill out. "You can leave me the fuck alone then, Ceas."

"Seven, let me explain."

"There's not a damn thing to explain. You said all you needed to say when you said that. You made things perfectly clear on where we stand and what we are."

"I didn't mean it like that. You know I fucks with you heavy, girl. At the end of the day, we're not together."

"Exactly. So, get the fuck out. You're right. You *fuck* with me. That's it. Period. I'm sure I'm not the only female you 'fuck with', so nothing else needs to be said. Just go."

My breathing increased, and it took everything in me not to lash out. The only reason I didn't was because I was hurt beyond words could express, and that pain only deepened when Ceas kissed my forehead and walked out. The second I heard my front door close, I laid on my bed and released the tears I'd been fighting to keep inside.

Honestly, I didn't want Ceas to leave. I wanted him to stay and confess his love for me, letting me know he felt the same way I did. That wouldn't happen though. Ceas made his true feelings known.

"I knew shit was too good to be true," I told myself.

Climbing under my thick comforter, I laid there and cried myself to sleep, praying I would wake up and learn that this was all a dream.

19

NORIEN

I HIT the wall in frustration. Ceasar and Drako were on the 'outside', but I could still feel their presence within the four walls holding me hostage. Every move I made somehow got back to them. For more than I week, I had been trying to get in touch with Joie. Drako told me to leave her alone, but I needed to make sure she was okay. Drugs weren't Joie's thing. I didn't want the situation to become too much for her. If it did, I knew my days were numbered. My sanity...my survival...my freedom, all rested on Joie's shoulder. Because of that, I ignored Drako's warning. At the end of the day, she was my bitch. I could contact her if I wanted to.

Well, that's what I thought. I called a couple times, but she didn't answer. It wasn't like her, but I wasn't really pressed. I figured Joie would see that I called and make sure she was available the next time I dialed her line. Nope, that didn't happen. Within the hour, the door to my single dorm was opened and two big, cock diesel muthafuckas entered. I held my own as best as I could, but I took an 'L' big time. It wasn't until the taller of the two men delivered his last blow that I was able to figure out what was going on.

"Next time, fuckin' listen," he barked. "Don't call the girl again."

It didn't take long for me to figure out who he was referring to. I had been banned from reaching out to my own girlfriend. The men were sent by Drako to prove a point. They could have easily ended my life, but for some reason, Drako wanted to keep me alive. Maybe it was to remind me just how much pull he had. My movements were being watched and reported back to both him and Ceasar. I didn't like it, but there wasn't a damn thing I could do. I was in a fucked up position. Unless Joie came through for me, it wasn't going to get any better.

"Smith," the CO called out, hitting my window with his fist. "Get up. You got a visitor."

Not again, I thought, slowly sitting up on the hard metal bed. Each time I had a visitor, I ended up getting my ass kicked. So far, the only people who had come to see me were Drako and Ceasar. As sore as my body was, I wasn't in the mood to dodge any more punches.

"I don't wanna see anybody," I advised, remaining seated on my bed.

"I don't care what you want," the CO shot back. "Get your ass up. I'm opening your door in two minutes."

With a sigh, I made my way to my feet. My body felt as if I had been hit by a truck, knocked down, forced back up, and hit again. The aches and pains radiating throughout my entire body had me hunched over like an old man, but I made my way to the door anyway. The CO was coming in whether I wanted him to or not. It was best just to follow directions and go with the flow.

When my door opened, I turned around, giving my back to the CO. A pair of handcuffs were placed around my wrists. I turned my nose up and grunted as the handcuffs were adjusted to cut off my circulation.

"Damn," I complained. "Do you really have to make these muthafuckas that tight?"

Being the asshole he was, the CO tightened the handcuffs even more. I gritted my teeth, almost convinced that the skin around my wrist was gone and the white meat was exposed.

If I ever see this nigga on the street, I thought to myself. Before I could get too deep in my feelings, I was pulled out of the small space I temporarily called home and led to a room I'd never been in before. A man in a too big suit flipped through the contents of a manila folder. He was leaned up against the large table with one of his feet resting comfortably in a plastic chair. He briefly glanced in my direction when I entered the room, but returned his focus to the papers in the folder.

My handcuffs were removed, and I was ordered to sit in a chair directly across from him. Not knowing who the man was or why he was meeting up with me, I cautiously obliged with my guard up.

"Mr. Smith, so glad you could make it," the man said, tossing the folder on the table.

With a smile, he extended his hand for me to shake. I looked at the ashy, rough paw reaching toward me and turned my head. "Who the fuck are you?"

"Hopefully, the man that's gonna get you out of here. Unless, of course, you want to stay locked up in this cage."

"Hell nah! If you can get my black ass outta here, I'll owe you one. Anything you want."

"Good try," he began, easing down into his seat, "But the state of Alabama won't allow me to take bribes. Excuse me, Officer." He turned toward the CO standing protectively by the door. "I'd like to speak to my client in private. I'll let you know when I'm done."

With an attitude, the CO snarled before departing. Even with him gone, I wasn't convinced that our conversation wouldn't be heard. Paranoid, I studied every corner, crack, and crevice of the room. If Drako or Ceasar popped up out of even the smallest space, I wanted to be prepared.

"Are you okay, Mr. Smith?" the man asked, alarmed by my quick change in demeanor.

Rubbing the side of his face, dead skin flaked off and fell down in front of him. He appeared oblivious to the pile forming in front of him. That shit was gross and made me sick to my stomach.

"Yeah, I'm fine. Just makin' sure there's no one else here?"

"O-kay." With furrowed brows, the man opened the folder once again and began rummaging through the paperwork. "I didn't see anything about mental health in here. Maybe we can use that to get you off."

"I may be a lot of things," I barked in irritation, "But I ain't crazy! You don't know what the fuck I've been through. This shit's hard, man."

"As it's supposed to be," he replied dryly. "Jail isn't all fun and games. You should know that. This isn't your first time here."

And? What the fuck was he trying to say? "That shit don't matter. I'm here on some bullshit. I was set up. They got the wrong guy."

"Well, if that's true, I'm going to do everything in my power to make sure you're proven innocent." Reaching in his blazer pocket, he passed me a card. "My name is Melvin Barnes. I've been assigned to your case."

"What happened to Christine?"

"Who?"

"You know what," I started, shaking my head. Leaning back in my chair I figured things out on my own. Christine was on Drako and Ceasar's payroll. Since they weren't helping me, she wouldn't be offering her time and assistance either. "It don't even matter. That broad ain't gonna help me."

"Okay. Well...Do you have any questions before we begin?"

Snatching up the business card, I studied his credentials. "A public pretender?! Nigga, you gotta be kiddin' me. Yeah, I got a question...a serious one. How the fuck can you help me? You ain't even a real lawyer. I'd be better off representin' myself."

"I'm more than qualified to assist you, Mr. Smith."

"Will you quit sayin' that 'Mr. Smith' shit? Nigga, just call me Norien. Damn."

"Okay then...Norien."

"What?"

He looked at me as if he had seen a ghost. Furrowing his eyebrows, he cleared his throat. "You just told me to call you Norien."

"Yeah...when you want something. Who says a person's name just because?" Shaking my head, I placed both elbows on the table and rested my chin in my cupped palms. "Are you sure *you* ain't sufferin' from mental health? Is that why you can't get a job as a *real* lawyer?"

"Norien, I'm not here to be insulted. If you don't want—"

"You went to one of those online schools, didn't you? Yep, that's exactly what happened. They'll give anybody a degree."

Standing, he stuffed the papers back into the folder and tucked it under his arm. "Good luck with your case. You have a nice day."

What did I say that was so bad? I simply called it like it was. Melvin Barnes didn't have to get an attitude. His antics were bitch made. Real lawyers had tough skin. Melvin did too, but not in the same sense. He *literally* had tough skin. It was dark, blotchy, and rough-looking…like an alligator or one of those funny looking lizards. I'm not sure what the name of his condition was, but he definitely had something wrong with him. The fact that his ugly ass had the audacity to walk away from me rubbed me the wrong way.

"Where you think you goin'? You better sit your ass on down. We ain't done."

"If you're going to continue insulting my intelligence, then yes we are. I can have someone else assigned to your case."

"Are they gonna have that same shit on their face and hands you got? What is that anyway?" I couldn't help myself. Staring at the ashy blotches had me scratching my arms. Was that nigga contagious?

"Bye, Norien."

"Wait! I'm serious. Do I need to get a check-up?"

"You need something," he shot back, mugging me. "Maybe a few boxing lessons. That's a nice shiner you got. I see that mouth of yours has gotten you into trouble already." Stuffing the folder under the other arm, he continued. "You know what, let me help you out. My sister teaches self-defense. It's geared toward women, but you can learn a few moves. If you ever get out, look her up."

"Man, fuck you!" Aggressively, I stood, forcing the chair I was sitting in to fall backward.

"Whoa!" He held his hands up in defense. "Hold up now. I don't swing that way, but if you do…I see why you don't want my help. You ain't trying to get out. You want to stay."

The CO had perfect timing. Maybe he noticed me standing through the small glass window. Maybe he had a hunch that something was wrong. Regardless of the reason, he opened the door and made his presence known.

"Is everything okay in here?"

"Nothing I can't handle," Melvin stated firmly. "Is there something you need?"

"Yeah…gotta follow protocol. Unless you two are done in here, he needs to be seated at all times. If not, I have to handcuff him again."

"Are we done?" Melvin asked with a smirk.

Easing back down in my seat, I crossed my arms over my chest and pouted. "Nope. We haven't even got started yet. Sit yo' ass down," I instructed Melvin. Grilling the CO, I added, "What are you still standin' there for? Go on. Go on back to pretending like you're workin'."

Once Melvin and I were left alone again, he sat down and got down to business. He read me off the list of charges I had accumulated. "I'm assuming you want to fight these charges."

"Damn right! I'm trying to get out. I don't want to serve any time."

"I don't know if I can pull that off, but I'll sure try. These are some serious charges."

"They're bullshit."

Melvin mumbled under his breath while jotting some notes down on a steno pad. "I'll get in touch with the prosecutor and see what we can do. It would be great if I can at least get some of these charges reduced. I might be able to get these minor charges thrown out. Even with that, you're still looking at some serious time."

"Man…" I growled. "I gotta get out of here! When am I gonna see a judge? How much is my bond?"

"You haven't seen the judge yet?" he asked, turning up his nose. "That's odd." He flipped through the paperwork again. "You know what, I don't see any information about a bond either. You've been here over a week. This ain't adding up. Let me look into this for you."

After promising to visit me again within the next few days, Melvin made his way to the door. I didn't have any faith in him or anyone else for that matter. It was obvious that I was being fucked around. Ceasar and Drako probably had the judge on their payroll and I was getting the short end of the stick.

"Just wait until I get out of here," I spoke under my breath.

"What did you say?"

"Nothing."

"Alright then. In the meantime, is there anything I can do for you?"

The bells went off in my head. I could use the crusty muthafucka after all. Since he liked running his mouth so much, he could be my messenger. "Hell yeah, there's something you can do. My girlfriend... her name is Joie. I need to see her ASAP! Here's her number..."

20

JOIE

"Will you fuckin' relax?" Kyan spat, shaking her head in my direction. "You're gonna give us up."

"Sorry," I mumbled.

"Yeah…you're gonna be. Chill, a'ight?"

Sweat coated my palms as I gripped the steering wheel. Glancing in the rearview mirror, the red and blue flashing lights obstructed my view. Relaxing was easier said than done. I was behind the wheel of someone's car, with no license, and enough drugs in the trunk to put me away for a long time. Closing my eyes, I took a page from my mother's book and called on help from the Great Man above.

"Lord, please," I began feeling tears well up in my eyes. "Please don't let me go to jail. I can't do it, Lord. I won't make it."

Kyan's harsh words broke up my prayer. "If you don't shut the fuck up. You wasn't prayin' when you laid down with that nothin' ass nigga! Don't start prayin' now. Get yourself together. Here he comes."

I glanced toward my window just as a set of knuckles tapped against it. The brightness of a flashlight blinded me as I struggled to lower the window.

"Do you know why I stopped you?" a deep voice asked.

I looked up into the eyes of the man speaking to me. The darkened sky made it hard to see his facial features, but I noted he was tall, dark, and had a midwestern accent. Staying as cool as I could, I shook my head 'No'.

"Three things, actually. You failed to make a complete stop at the stop sign. You were going forty-eight in a thirty-five mile zone. Not to mention, you have a taillight out. I need to see your license, registration, and proof of insurance."

I turned toward Kyan for help. She simply shrugged and dismissed me by examining her nails. Inwardly, I panicked, but fought like hell to keep it from showing. With a nervous smile, I returned my attention to the officer.

"Umm...I don't have any of that."

"You do know your license is supposed to be on your person at all times, right?"

I nodded. "Yes, I know."

"That's a problem," he stated. "And you're positive you don't have your registration or insurance information either? Most people keep those documents in their glovebox. Do you want to at least look?"

Kyan slapped my hand when I reached across her. "It's not in there. I already checked."

You didn't check shit, I thought to myself. Her firm stare dared me to question her further. I took heed to her warning and accepted what she said as truth. "She looked in there while we were waiting for you. I'm sorry, Officer. I didn't bring that information with me."

Pointing the flashlight inside the car, he visually examined the front and back seats. With little to go on, he stuffed the flashlight in one pocket and retrieved a small pen and notepad from the other.

"What's your name?" he asked.

"Joie," I responded.

"Joie what?"

"Sutherland."

"Dummy," Kyan mumbled, loud enough to hear.

The officer heard her, too. He lowered his head to get a better view inside. "What did you say?" When Kyan didn't respond, he continued. "And what's your name, ma'am?"

"Did I do something wrong?" she huffed, addressing him with an attitude.

"No, but—"

"Well, there's your answer," she finished for him. "You don't need to know my name. I'm a passenger minding my own damn business."

"I see you got a mouth on you. I could get you for not wearing your seatbelt," he threatened.

"The car's not moving...therefore, I don't have to wear a seatbelt. But, if you wanna be an asshole, go ahead. It's not on me. It's on her."

I froze when Kyan pointed to me. How could she tell me to be cool when she was so quick to pop off at the mouth? She was the one who was going to get us caught. I didn't want to give the officer any reason to search the vehicle. Kyan, on the other hand, made it obvious that she didn't care. I would be the one fucked. I was driving.

"Fine, I will," the officer shot back. Returning his attention to me, he continued, "You may want to tell your friend to watch her mouth. She's only making it harder for you. Let's see here." He glanced at his notepad again. "Is this vehicle registered in your name?"

"No."

"Who is the registered owner?"

I didn't have an answer to that question. That day was the first day I had ever laid eyes on that car. After Kyan refused to let me drive hers, one of Drako's boys tossed me a set of keys. I knew the dude by face only. Mostly everyone in Ceasar and Drako's operation went by some sort of nickname. I didn't even know that.

"I'm sorry, Officer..."

"James," he huffed. "Now, answer the question."

"Officer James...I got this car from a friend. I don't know who the registered owner is, but he does. If you just let me go, I'll take the car right back to him. I'll make sure he fixes the tail light."

I don't know what I said that was so funny, but something tickled Kyan to no end. She laughed as if I had said the funniest things she ever heard. "You 'bout the stupidest bitch I've ever seen."

My face turned beet red. What the fuck was her problem? I was trying to come up with a solution to my problem and she was making it worse. What did I say to make her call me out my name? *Just wait until we get out of this*, I thought. She had me fucked up. At that moment, I realized that Kyan and I would never be friends again.

"Step out of the car, please," Officer James instructed.

Nervously, I obliged. Stepping out the car, I closed the door behind me. "Is there a problem, Officer?"

"You tell me," he stated firmly. "Something about all this doesn't sit well with me. My gut never lies. Is Joie Sutherland your real name?"

"Yeah. Why would I lie?"

"You'd be surprised. Tell me this…when I call your name in, am I gonna find any warrants, suspended license?"

"Nope," I shook my head with conviction. "You won't find any of that."

Technically, I told the truth. My license wasn't suspended. I was never issued one. Although I knew how to drive, I was always someone's passenger. I had also never been arrested or even approached by an officer. That day was a first. I hoped my honesty would work in my favor.

"Okay. What about the car? Is it stolen?"

"No, it's not. I told you the truth."

"I hope you're right. Give me a moment. You can get back in the car." He unclipped his walkie-talkie from his side. Before he pressed the button to speak, he called out to me as I eased back into my seat. "One more thing. Is there anything in the car that I should be concerned about?"

I froze. Why did he have to ask me that question? As honest as I had been up until that point, disclosing what was in the trunk would have had me in a cell not far from Norien.

"N-n-no," I stuttered. "There's nothing in there."

"You don't sound too convincing. Why don't I take a look?"

When he opened the back door, Kyan snapped. "What the fuck do you think you're doing? You don't have probable cause to search this vehicle."

"I can do anything I want. Keep talking and you'll be under arrest."

"For what?" she barked.

"Anything I say," he smirked. "Now, shut up and let me do my job."

Climbing pack in the car, I panicked. The officer turned into an asshole right before my eyes. He thoroughly searched the backseat for something that didn't exist. Frustrated, he ordered us both to get out of the car. I was out the car in seconds. Kyan defiantly stayed put.

"I said get out the car," he instructed again.

"Unless I'm under arrest, I'm not moving."

"Look, there's nothing in there," I stated, stepping in to intervene. "If you're gonna give me a ticket, fine. I'll take it. All this other stuff is a waste of time. Please, can we just be on our way?"

The officer looked me up and down. His stare was intense and rubbed the wrong way. I felt uneasy when he sucked his bottom lip into his mouth and grunted. His eyes remained on me as he rubbed one of his hands over his crotch. I stood there...speechless. What the fuck was he doing?

Licking his lips, he reverted back to asshole mode. Walking toward the back of the car, he pounded his fist on the trunk. "Open it."

"I told you," I pleaded. "There's nothing in there."

"Either you open it, or I'll do it myself."

"Please, Officer James," I whined, stepping closer to him. "None of this is necessary. We're not doing anything wrong."

"My gut tells me otherwise. There's something in here you don't want me to see. I'm gonna find out one way or another." Lowering his voice, he licked his lips. "Unless, of course, you give me a reason not to open the trunk."

I knew what he was insinuating when he grabbed his crotch again. His bottom lip found its way back into his mouth. How could the city of Birmingham employ such a sick pervert?

I cursed myself for not following Kyan's advice. She told me there was an easier way to get to my destination, but no...I chose to do things on my own. I let my phone's GPS guide me right into a newer development. Empty lots and half-built homes surrounded us. Besides Kyan, there was no one else in the vicinity to witness what was taking place. I swallowed hard, not knowing what to do or say. Kyan was no help. She hadn't as much as turned around to check on me. I was on my own. Not willing to go to jail, I nodded and agreed to his request.

His baby dick was out his pants in seconds. My dinner threatened to reappear when I spotted the extra skin hiding the head. He wasn't even circumcised. A cynical smile spread across his face when I dropped to my knees and took a deep breath. I stared at the nappy hairs hiding most of his shaft. I couldn't do it. My pride wouldn't let me.

"Come on," he urged, pushing his semi-erect dick toward me. "Hurry up. Stop wasting time." When I didn't move, he viciously grabbed the back of my head and pushed it into his crotch. "I said hurry up."

I snapped. Fighting against his resistance, I opened my mouth and bit down as hard as I could.

"Fuck!" he cried out, doubling over in pain. "You bitch!"

Releasing my grip, I jumped to my feet. I couldn't fight, but I squared up and swung on him anyway. I got the best of him, using my fists, knees, and feet to get him onto the ground. Even then, I didn't let up. That muthafucka tried to get me to suck his dick. That shit wasn't cool. I made sure that when I was done, he would think twice about trying that shit with someone else.

I stopped when the blood spilling from his nose and mouth had my stomach turning. The realization of what I had done had me scared out of my mind. I assaulted a police officer. If I wasn't going to jail before, I was definitely going now. What was I going to do?

Seeking Kyan's input, I rushed toward her door. When I opened it, her arm extended in my direction. My eyes widened when I realized I was being handed a gun.

"Handle that," she said nonchalantly.

"What? You want me to kill him?"

"Damn right! And hurry up. You got a delivery to make…and we're late."

I had never shot a gun before in my life, but I took the pistol and walked back over to my target. He knew my name. Sparing his life guaranteed that I'd spend the rest of mine behind bars. I couldn't let that happen. Thinking about the vile act Officer James attempted to force me to do, I aimed the gun toward his head, closed my eyes, and pulled the trigger.

Before getting back in the car, I searched the ground for the notepad with my name on it. Once it was spotted, I stuffed it in my pocket and climbed back into the driver's seat. Kyan was finishing a call when I started the engine and pulled off.

"Good job," she acknowledged. "The crew is on their way to clean this shit up."

"Crew? What crew?"

"The clean-up crew. Do you know anything?"

"You act like I do this for a living," I huffed in irritation. "I don't know nothing about this life."

"Well, you do now," she laughed. "Just wait until I tell Drako. He ain't gonna believe this shit."

It pissed me off that Kyan found humor in what I went through. She didn't have a nasty dick in her face. That shit wasn't funny. She just sat there and made me fend for myself.

I drove the rest of the way with the radio turned up to the max. I didn't want to hear anything Kyan had to say at that point. I was heated, but still cautious enough to follow the laws of the road. While Kyan stayed in the car, I got out, made the exchange, and reentered the car with a bag full of money. On the way back to Drako, Kyan turned the music off and cleared her throat.

"Let me give you a bit of advice," she softly spoke. "At the rate you're going, it'll take you forever to work off this debt."

"You think I don't know that?" I spat, mad that I was in the situation to begin with. "You think I don't want this shit to be over and done with? Well, I do!"

"Stop being so gullible and boss the hell up then. You only knocked ten grand off that nigga's debt today. Ten grand. That's chump change. You could have gotten way more than that."

"How?"

I listened to Kyan's explanation. In order to pay off Norien's debt, I was making deals and delivering the product myself. Drako told me his price, and anything extra I received went toward what Norien owed. I didn't know shit about how much the drugs cost. I just knew I had to make a profit. Each brick I delivered, I quoted five thousand more than what Drako quoted me. According to Kyan, I was busting my own head.

"Drako's giving you one hell of a deal," she disclosed. "I don't know why, but that's none of my business. He's charging you less than he would charge a nigga on the street. Use that shit to your advantage. Up that muthafuckin' price! The quality speaks for itself. These niggas will pay it."

"So, how much should I charge?" I questioned, running numbers in my head.

"I said a *bit* of advice," she countered, slowly turning the music back up. "I'm sure you'll figure it out."

21

DRAKO

Joie and Kyan arrived, and from the pleased smirk on Kyan's face, I figured some shit went down. Joie held a black bag in her hand with a distant look in her eyes. She didn't acknowledge me as she walked inside and sat it down. Plopping her small frame on the couch, she palmed her face with both hands and screamed.

"Aye, chill the fuck out with that shit. Ain't nobody tryna hear all that. Fuck wrong with you?"

"Caught her first body, so I'm sure 'Little Miss Innocent' is traumatized," Kyan answered, opening one of the bags and adjusting the money counter on the table. "She got pulled over and the officer tried making her a deal to suck his little dick. That was *after* she damn near got us fuckin' caught."

"Nah, that shit would have been yo' fault, Ky. You were supposed to be showin' her shit. You knew product was in the back like she did. You know she's new to this."

"Whatever," she mumbled, smacking her lips while rolling her eyes. "She gotta learn somehow. I was tryin' to teach her ass how to be smart. I guess her scary ass is smarter than I thought."

"*You* be fuckin' smarter next time. Which officer was it?"

"He wasn't on payroll, but clean-up is handlin' him. I already took care of it."

"Good lookin' out."

Glancing over at Joie, I saw how fucked up she was and decided to leave her alone for the moment. I let her get through her little breakdown while Ky and I counted the money. We were halfway finished when Joie started mumbling.

"I can't believe I killed him. I can't believe I killed him."

"You gon' take yo' ass in the back if you about to be havin' mental breakdowns and shit. I need peace and quiet while I count this paper," I stated, side-eyeing Joie.

"This wasn't part of the deal! I'm only supposed to be making deliveries, not taking lives! I'm not a killer!" she exclaimed.

"You are now, so deal with it," Kyan responded in an annoyed tone. "Would you rather be sittin' here with us right now, or down at the precinct waiting to be booked? You did what you had to do to not only save yourself, but my ass too. Think of it like that and keep it pushin'. The dirty muthafucka tried to make you suck his lil' gummy worm. Don't feel bad for takin' care of yourself."

Kyan's words caused Joie to sit up and wipe her face. Tear continuously fell, but she remained silent. We were able to finish counting the money and it was all on point. Without warning, Kyan slipped out the door while I was in the back putting everything up in the safe. I strutted back to the front to see Joie sitting there alone, staring off into the distance. Sighing heavily and running my hand over my beard, I walked to the back to call Kyan.

"Where the fuck did you go? You forgot somethin'," I growled the second she answered. Hearing her giggle, I knew she was on some extra bullshit.

"Where you think I went, Drake? I'm takin' my ass home to my girl. I'm done dealin' with that bitch for the day. I wasn't about to listen to her whine and cry. You can handle that. You know you want to."

"It ain't my job to train her, Ky. That's *yo'* job. Tryna go eat Nova's pussy and shit. How you know I ain't have shit to do?"

It was taking a lot for me to keep my cool. Joie was too damn emotional for me to be dealing with at that moment, and I didn't have the patience for it. The shit that came out my mouth would have her deeper in her feelings. Kyan's ass owed me...big time!

"Because you don't. If you did, I would know about it, so don't front. I've been dealin' with her all fuckin' day. The least you can do is drop her off at home."

"You don't know everything I gotta do. Don't be surprised if you see her standin' on yo' front porch. I'm not playin' either."

I hung up and blew out a frustrated sigh. Feeling someone's presence, I peered up to see Joie standing against the doorframe. She looked distraught, and it kind of fucked with me. I felt soft for allowing her to get to me, so I shook that shit off. I tried, but failed when I saw tears resting on the rim of her eyes. It reminded me of the young girl I was crushing on once upon a time. I could lie to everybody else, but I couldn't lie to myself. I still had feelings when I wanted to remain heartless. I didn't want to allow myself to ever get close to another woman, but Joie's light bright ass was doing something to a nigga. Having her around was only going to make shit harder.

Truth be told, I'd been checking for Joie all along. Whenever I thought about rapping to her, Willow invaded my thoughts. I could vividly see that bitch fuckin' another nigga with her mouth. It would be crazy to ever trust another woman like that. Joie could be a good fuck, but that was as far as I'd allow shit to go.

"I can find my own way home, asshole," Joie spoke, sniffling. "I'll call an Uber."

"Man, bring yo' ass on. You don't know where the fuck you at. It wouldn't be smart to wait for an Uber unless you want to be a trendin' on tomorrow's news," I chuckled, licking my lips and brushing past her. I smirked when I felt her right on my heels.

I made sure the house and everything in it was secure before leading Joie to my car. She trailed behind me, so I stopped to allow her to get in front of me, but then she stopped too. Gently, I tugged her arm and pulled her next to me. Instructing her to keep walking, she stopped fighting me and followed directions. I opened the passenger door for her before jogging around to the opposite side to climb in the driver's seat.

Sensing Joie was uncomfortable, I asked her if she was straight. She glared at me like I had two heads, but remained quiet.

"I asked you a damn question, Joie. Answer when I speak to you, or I won't ever say shit to you again and you can walk home."

"You're so damn rude. Why would I want to talk to you?"

"Because I'm Drako. Self-explanatory. On some real shit, speak yo' mind. You need to be strong and have a voice dealin' with this life."

"I can't believe y'all have me doin' this," she mumbled, but I clearly heard her.

"We don't have yo' ass doin' shit. That's on that nigga you call yo' man. You wouldn't be in this predicament if it wasn't for that fuck boy. This should teach you a lesson."

"What lesson?"

"How to tell the difference between a real nigga and fuck nigga, ma."

"So, let me guess, you're the real one?"

"Realest you gon' ever meet, besides Ceas," I answered, stopping at a light and glancing over at her. Despite it being dark, I could see she was blushing. She turned her head away and exhaled.

"Why can't I see or communicate with Norien?"

"That's not how this shit works. That's all you need to know. Have you spoken to him?" She shook her head. "Keep it that way and shit will continue to run smoothly. Until then, you need some extra trainin'. What happened today won't be the last time it happens, so since Kyan abandoned you, you're stuck workin' with me for the rest of the day."

"Woohoo," she sarcastically said, waving her hands up. She glanced over at me and a cute smirk tugged at her lips.

Minutes later, we pulled up at a range. It was an old, fucked up building that was used as a disguise for the illegal business. The owners also sold illegal machinery underground, using the range as a legal cover up. Ceas and I had our men train there. We paid a monthly fee for them to have access to it at all times, along with whatever machinery was needed.

With her face scrunched up, Joie questioned our whereabouts. I told her to follow me and she would find out. We stepped inside and her hands immediately went to her ears. I grabbed us both a pair of new earbuds, helping her put them in. She gave me a 'what the hell?' look, and I raised a brow at her. Leaning over, I spoke in her ear.

"Practice makes perfect."

I nodded my head for her to follow behind me. There were a few people there, so I took her to the far end of the place and chose the targets I wanted her to practice on. Joie was visibly uncomfortable, but it was a task she needed to get used to. I went and rented a small Ruger for her to practice with.

Taking my time, I showed her three times how to break it down and put it together before watching her do it. I was impressed. She successfully did it exactly as I showed her. She was a quick learner, which made shit a lot easier for me. It took us a good hour to get her precise with one target on command. By the end, Joie had become comfortable with the feel of a gun.

"Good job," I complimented her. "I need you poppin' niggas like that always. If a nigga fucks with you, you know what to do."

"I'm more comfortable with shooting a gun, but not killing people. I'm not sure that's something any normal person could get used to."

"Nobody in this world is normal, ma. Every muthafucka walkin' this Earth is fucked up in some type of way. Some hide it better than others."

"Do you truly believe that?"

"Yep," I paused, wetting my lower lip and focused my gaze on her. "I know that for a fact. Open yo' eyes, and you'll see one day."

She nodded in response, and I could see the wheels turning in her head. I noted the fact that Joie took in what I said instead of immediately speaking or displaying some type of reaction. It meant she was a thinker; a good, but dangerous quality.

Since we were out and my stomach was talking to me, I decided we could stop somewhere to grab a bite to eat. Joie didn't protest either, but it wasn't like she had a choice. I was going to eat if she wanted to or not.

I craved *Pappadeaux*, so that was where we went. It was packed, taking forty-five minutes for us to be seated. By then, I was grumpy and rude as fuck. I informed the waiter they had twenty minutes tops to have our food ready or they would be shutting down early. We got out food in fifteen minutes with everything being fresh. The waiter got a nice tip, and everyone was still alive.

On the way to take Joie home, I noticed we were close to the address Kyan sent me on Willow. I hadn't got around to paying her a visit. It probably wasn't the right time with Joie in the car, but as my heartbeat quickened, I reacted on impulse. My trigger finger was itching something terrible. My fantasies about killing Willow had me making an illegal U-turn and heading in her direction. Joie questioned me on where we were going, but my mind was elsewhere. I wouldn't feel totally complete until I killed the one person who took my heart and played with that muthafucka.

An eerie feeling crept over me as I cruised down the street. I could see the house where Willow was supposed to live, but my gut told me to stop. Always listening to my first instinct, I stopped two houses down, and that was when I saw it. A blacked out old Honda slowly crept down the street. Two men sat together on a porch nearby. They didn't notice the car at first, but when they did, all hell broke loose.

Joie screamed at the rhythmic sound of a machine gun going off. I demanded that she duck down. Throwing the car in reverse, I pushed the gas. Another Honda pulled up behind us, letting off more shots. A few bounced off my car, and that sent Joie over the edge. She cried hysterically, calling upon God to keep her alive.

I allowed the Honda to pass before spinning the car around. Headed in the opposite direction, I looked over at Joie crying uncontrollably. I felt bad as hell. In my quest for revenge, I had Joie scared out of her mind.

Glancing in my rearview mirror, my eyes darkened and I hit the brakes. I thought my eyes were deceiving me, but they weren't. It was Willow. She was hopping in a parked car with some nigga. Everything around me stopped, and the only thing that brought me from my trance was Joie's pleas. She lifted her head and cocked it to the side in confusion while yelling for me to go. Knowing she'd already been through enough, I spared Willow's life. Stepping on the gas, I continued on toward Joie's place. Silence filled the air the entire drive. I pulled up to the curb next to her spot, and Joie just sat there staring at me.

"Fuck you starin' for?"

"Uh…I'm scared," she whispered.

"Scared of what?"

"I don't know. So much has happened today, and I'm scared to be by myself."

"That sounds like a personal problem, Joie. Take yo' ass in the house, so I can leave."

Huffing, Joie hopped out the car and slammed the door. I watched as she stomped to her door, fumbling with her keys to unlock it. She was giving me that feeling again, and I was convinced something was wrong with me. After seeing Willow, my mind should have been focused on cruising the city and finding her; not on if I was going to cater to Joie's feelings. Raking my hand over my face, I turned my car off, and hopped out. I hit the locks and followed Joie inside.

All she wanted me to do was sit in the living room until she fell asleep, but I found myself there all night. As crazy as it sounds, it wasn't so bad. It made her feel better. I guess that was all that mattered.

Looking toward the ceiling, I let out a loud sigh. What was Joie doing to me?

22

KYAN

It was a chill day for me and I expected to spend all day cuddled up under Nova, but she had other plans. She planned a girls' day out with Sadee. I was cool with being home alone. It gave me time to think and clear my mind. Don't get me wrong, I could do the same when Nova was around, but there was something about having the peace of loneliness after feeling so overwhelmed.

The work I did consumed my life at times, and it became too much. I enjoyed being in the streets. I loved the rush of it. The fast money…The power… I enjoyed it all, but often, I thought about how it could all be taken away in the blink of an eye. Either by death, prison, or going legit. Nova had expressed her concerns to me before about how dangerous things could be. I promised her that whenever we got married, I would stop. She'd been waiting on me to propose, but since she gave me an ultimatum, she could wait until I was ready.

Lying in bed watching *Wentworth*, I thought about Drako. Ceas called and told me what happened the day I left Joie with him. Drako was fucked up over it because his attitude had been on ten. I knew it was because he allowed Willow to get away once again.

The reason he didn't blow her damn head off stood out to me. Joie had a nigga caught up. He put her feelings before his, and that spoke volumes. I knew my brother all too well. When we were younger, Drako was feeling Joie hard. I didn't expect those feelings to linger for so long, though. I mean, I thought he was over it. I guess not.

"How long are you goin' to be gone?" I asked Nova. I was laid across the bed watching her get dressed. She was so, so sexy.

Before she could respond, my hands were on her waist while my lips pecked circles around her belly button. Nova was everything to me, and I showed her just how much I loved her every chance I got. When my kisses traveled lower, she grabbed my head and pulled away.

"No ma'am, I don't have time to sneak in a quickie," she giggled, swatting at my reaching hands.

To tease me, Nova traveled a finger down to her clit and pleased herself for all of five seconds. It was long enough to have my kitty purring and my mouth watering.

With a mischievous smirk jerking the side of my mouth, I had Nova pinned against the wall by her throat. Her freaky ass giggled. I went to attack her pussy, but the loud knocks on the front door stopped me. Nova demanded that I go answer the door while she finished getting dressed. She pecked my lips and gripped my ass before saying, "I'll sit on your face later."

"Nah, I'm sittin' on yours," I corrected. The knocking started again, so I left Nova to go let Sadee in.

I swung the door open and came face-to-face with the mocha beauty. She smirked and cocked her head to the side while examining my body from head to toe. Sadee looked good enough to eat, and I meant that in a literal sense. The sexual thoughts I had of her as we silently stared each other down were wrong on so many levels. I should have only saw Nova when I had those fantasies, but I couldn't shake the image of Sadee lying spread-eagle on my bed out of my mind.

"Are you goin' to let me in, or are you goin' to continue eye fuckin' me? I'd much rather you do the *real* thing. Not with your eyes, though," Sadee spoke, breaking me from my thoughts. Her statement caught me off guard, and I couldn't hold back my low giggles.

I knew she would be a fuckin' problem, I thought. *Let me keep my distance. Fuck around and get me caught up.*

I stepped back to allow her to enter. Switching her thick hips, Sadee brushed against my breasts with hers. A teasing smile graced her plum painted lips and I had to glance away. I pushed her back by her shoulder and walked off.

Going back to my bedroom, I sat on the bed and watched Nova apply her makeup. I battled with my inner demons on whether I needed to tell her about my encounter with Sadee. Her words replayed in my head, and I couldn't get her pretty face out my mind. I laid back on the bed and sighed heavily. Deep down, I knew I needed to tell Nova, but I wasn't prepared to answer the questions I knew would come with it. Even though I technically didn't do anything wrong, guilt consumed me. I decided against telling Nova. Eventually I would…well, maybe.

"What's wrong, Ky?" Nova quizzed. Her soft touch on my leg caused me to jump. Cocking her head to the side, she gave me a concerned, bewildered glare. The bed beside me sank when she sat down and rubbed my arm. "Talk to me."

"Nothin', just all this shit with Joie. Plus, I'm worried about Drako. He ain't himself," I half-lied. Those things were bothering me too, but not like what happened with Sadee.

"Oh, baby. It's goin' to be okay. Don't stress about it. You know Drako will find and slaughter that bitch Willow, and as for Joie… it wouldn't hurt to rekindle an old friendship, especially with how close the two of you used to be. I mean, look at me and Sadee. We lost touch for a while, but look at us now. It's like no time has passed at all. I know you care about the girl, so don't front like you don't," she called me out. My lips broke into a smile, and I rolled my eyes. "Exactly. You know you can't hide who you are from me. Just think about it, Ky. You're stubborn when you want to be."

A knock at the door interrupted our conversation. The door slowly opened, and Sadee poked her head in. Her eyes were directly on me.

"I was hopin' I wouldn't be walkin' into anything," she spoke. "Are you ready? Our appointment at the spa is in thirty minutes, and you know how traffic can be around this time of day."

"Yeah, I am. Let me grab my purse."

Nova leaned down and pecked my lips. She got up, and I couldn't resist slapping her ass in the process. Giggling, she looked back at me and winked.

I felt the intensity of Sadee's gaze, but I fought hard not to look her way. When I couldn't resist temptation any longer, my eyes met hers and it was over. Nova was so caught up with her chirping phone that she didn't notice her friend. Sadee's eyes scanned my body until her focus shifted to my pussy. She licked her lips seductively and moaned softly. I didn't know what the fuck she was trying to do to me. Her homegirl was right in the same room, but something about that gesture was so damn sexy to me. *I love my girl*, I repeated over and over in my head. *I love my girl.*

Nova insisted that I walk them to the door. I followed behind her while Sadee switched ahead. Kissing Nova, I demanded she call and let me know when she was on her way home. I watched them back out the driveway before retiring back inside to eat and take a quick nap.

Two hours later, my work phone woke me up. I groaned in annoyance when I saw it was Jake calling.

"What?" I answered.

"Were you sleep? My bad."

"I'm up now. What do you want?"

"I can't get in touch with Ceas or Drak—. Hol' up, this Drako callin' now. My bad, Ky," he replied before hanging up in my ear. I wanted to go fuck his snowflake ass up for disturbing my peace for nothing. I attempted to go back to sleep, but it was no use.

Hours had gone by and Nova hadn't made it home, nor was she answering any of my calls. I had sent her numerous texts and saw that she was all on social media, which only pissed me off. It was cool. I had something for her ass.

Throwing my hair in a messy bun, I kicked my feet in my Gucci slides and grabbed my phone, purse, keys, and gun. Nova must have forgotten I could have her location pulled up at the snap of my fingers. Since she didn't want to answer, she was gon' 'see' me.

I swung the door open and immediately raised my gun, pressing it into someone's head. It took a second for me to register who it was.

"April, girl. You can't be doin' no shit like that. Poppin' up unannounced ain't cool," I griped, tossing my gun in my purse. "Why are you here?"

"Well, hello to you, too. I needed my friend, so I decided to pull up on you. I didn't know it would be a problem."

"It's only a problem because you didn't call or text before comin'. You know how I am about that. Come in."

I led April and Damien into the living room before going into the kitchen to get us something to drink. April was on the phone crying when I walked back in, so I played with Damien until she finished her conversation. From what she was saying, I knew it had to be Norien. *Fuck boy.*

When I first found out about Joie and Norien, I figured he was messing with her on the low since I'd only known him to be with April. Now, I saw things for what they truly were and couldn't believe April would settle to be the side piece.

"He gets on my damn nerves!" April exclaimed, wiping her tears away.

"Norien?"

"You know it's not anybody else. It's been so hard since he's been gone, Ky. He didn't have much, but he helped out the best he could. It made a difference, that's for sure," she explained. "Since he's been gone, his attitude is on a different level. He never comes through on any of his promises. I hate answerin' the phone sometimes."

"So, why do you? You wouldn't be sittin' here cryin' if you didn't."

"Damien is the only reason I'm putting up with all this shit. If he didn't need his father, I would say fuck Norien."

"Wait, what? Norien is Damien's father?" I questioned with wide eyes.

"Girl, yeah. He looks just like him. Can't you tell?"

I was that friend who wasn't all up in everybody's business. I didn't ask a lot of questions. If my friend wanted me to know, then she would have told me. April never disclosed who Damien's father was, and I never asked. It wasn't my business.

Studying Damien, I could see strong features of Norien. I didn't know why I never noticed before. Maybe because I never looked at Norien like that to put two and two together. Plus, when April got pregnant, Norien wasn't the only person she was sleeping with. I assumed it could be anyone's baby. No shade, just facts.

April stayed and talked for a while. Nova still hadn't returned my calls or texts by the time April left. Instead of popping up on her, she would be blowing me up asking why I changed the locks. She knew better than to play with me. Games were for kids and I was a grown muthafuckin' woman.

23

CEASAR

"Hey! Ceas!"

Staring out the tinted window, I searched for the female voice screaming my name. It had to be someone who knew me well. I wasn't in any of the cars I typically cruised the streets in. Instead, I busted out my tricked out Denali reserved for meetings on the go. I was being chauffeured around town by my driver, Tango, while I sat comfortably in the back seat.

"Ceas!"

I heard the voice again. This time, it was closer. I scanned the crowded street until I noticed Nova running toward my ride. A taller chick trailed far behind her, but it was obvious that they were together. I contemplated instructing Tango to keep it moving without stopping to see what she wanted. I scratched that notion real quick. What if it had something to do with my sister?

Rolling my partially cracked window down the remainder of the way, I waited until Nova was close enough to open the door before I spoke.

"What's up, girl? What you doin' around here?"

We were in a modest section of town, filled with lots of stores and boutiques for shopping. Although it wasn't unheard of for Nova to venture off on her own, unless she was with Ky, she usually stayed in the house. Ky dropped her and picked her up for both school and work. Nova being without my sister struck me as odd.

"We're stranded," she stated, stopping to catch her breath. "I would have called Ky, but my phone's dead. Do you think you can give us a ride?"

"Us?"

"Yeah, I got my girl Sadee with me. Sadee!" she yelled, waving the girl over. "Come here. Don't be shy."

I got a good look at the chick I saw following her. She was a sight to see. Her tall, thin frame didn't do much for me, but her face...damn! She had an exotic look that captured my attention and forced me to stare. Her smooth dark skin, slanted eyes, and full lips twisted into a shy smile had me wondering her sexual preference. Was she nibbling on pussy or swallowing dick?

"What's up?" I acknowledged, studying her intently.

"Hi. Nice to meet you."

"Likewise."

"So, Ceas...are you gonna help us out?" Nova asked. "I want to get home before Ky gets worried."

The mention of my sister's name caused Sadee's smile to widen. I peeped that shit, but didn't call her out on it.

"What does that have to do with me?" I asked, chuckling in the process. "That's your problem. What...your friend ain't got no phone?"

"It's dead too," Nova stated softly. "We're fucked up right now, Ceas. Can you help us?"

"Damn...you're right. You are fucked up."

Rolling the window back up, I instructed Tango to pull off.

"Are you sure?" he questioned, glancing in the rearview mirror. "You want me to just leave them?"

Hell yeah, was what I wanted to say, but I kept my mouth closed instead. Watching Nova beat on my window with her fist was almost comical. She looked like a damn fool trying to gain access to a ride that wasn't hers. Her sidekick wasn't much better. Sadee made her way to the other side of the SUV and attempted to open the door. The silly bitch didn't realize the doors were locked. I wasn't that careless.

When Nova gave up her quest and kicked my ride, I cracked the window.

"Kick my shit again, hear?" I threatened. "I'ma forget you're lickin' my sister's pussy and treat you like a nigga on the street. Don't play with me, Nova."

"No…you're the one playing!" she countered.

"Why are you being so difficult? You act like it's gonna hurt you to give us a ride. That's bullshit."

"You don't need *nothing* from me, remember? You said that."

I tried to act like Nova choosing Kyan over me wasn't a big deal, but it was. Although she was just a jumpoff, my pride wanted an explanation. That's when she fucked up my ego and told me that she was happy and didn't need me or my dick.

"Really? You're gonna bring up something that happened years ago? Will you let that shit go, Ceas? I have. You should, too."

Sucking my teeth, I played it cool. She was right. That was the past and I had moved on. She was good for what she was at the time, but my taste was much different now. On her best day, she wasn't half the woman Seven was. Unlocking the doors, I allowed both women to enter.

"Where's your car?" I asked, turning my attention to Sadee. She conveniently took a seat next to me and threw her designer bag in between us.

"On the next block. We walked over here to see if we could use a phone or something. That's when Nova saw you." Blushing, she added, "I'm glad she did. You're a lifesaver."

"I wouldn't say all that." I chuckled, realizing she was trying to flirt. If only she knew, she was wasting her time. "I ain't did shit yet."

I let my gaze fall back to Nova. She sat across from me, snuggled against the door. It was obvious that she was avoiding eye contact at all costs. Even when I called her name, she didn't look in my direction.

"Yeah," she answered.

"Chill with that attitude, you hear me?"

"I don't have an attitude," she countered, crossing her arms over her chest.

"So what's all that, then?" I questioned with a smile. She was in her feelings for no reason at all. Not only did I take the time out of my day to stop in the first place, I let her in. I didn't have to do either. "I could've left your ass standing out there."

"Whatever, Ceas. You know good and damn well Kyan would be in your ass if you didn't pick me up. Stop playin'."

"Is that what you think?" I challenged.

"Yep. It's what I know."

Sadee giggled next to me before smoothing a large section of her straight hair behind her ear. "You must be the little brother, huh?"

"Ain't nothin' lil' about me, girl. Believe that."

"I'll take your word for it," she blushed. "So, what are we doing? It's obvious you two got something going on, but that's on y'all. I'm just trying to get my car together and go home."

I could have easily called someone to assist. My connections were strong. I could have had a tow truck on the scene within minutes. I would have done that if Nova's attitude wasn't so foul. She acted like telling Kyan would faze me. That bitch had problems. Fuck what Kyan thought. I didn't bite my tongue for nobody.

"Aye, Tango," I called out. The tinted partition that was half-way down lowered the remainder of the way.

"Yeah, boss."

"Drive this bitch."

"Anywhere in particular?"

"Nope. Just go."

I passed Sadee my phone. She dug into her purse and retrieved a small card. Examining the numbers, she carefully tapped away at the screen. I watched her carefully as I lit the blunt I was saving for later. I didn't trust any woman around my phone. That's how muthafuckas got caught up. When Sadee lifted the phone to her ear and began talking, I removed my focus from her and watched the scenery pass me by.

Tango drove the speed limit, which made me feel as if things were moving in slow motion. I drove with a heavy foot, making me used to a faster pace. The slowness was cool, though. It allowed me to think while the loud I smoked calmed me down.

Seven came to mind. As much as I tried to dismiss my feelings for her, they returned even stronger than before. No woman had ever affected me the way she did. I hated the way things ended between us, but I had a point to prove. She didn't control me or my actions. Business was separate. What I had to talk to Joie about was business – nothing else. She should have known that I wasn't trying to push up on her friend. Seven was so insecure that it was frustrating at times. Just because there wasn't a label on our relationship didn't mean that I was on some fuck shit. While it was true that in the beginning, I fucked around with other women, she probably did the same. We didn't question that kind of shit. She was free to move as she pleased, and I was too. Actually, she still could—if she wanted that nigga to catch a hot one straight to the dome.

Never in my wildest dreams did I think Seven would be the one, but somehow, she found a place in my heart. She had a reputation back in the day, but so did I. Who was I to judge? I probably fucked triple the amount of people she did. I couldn't fault her for the same shit I did myself. Even if I crossed paths with any of the niggas she laid down with, none of them could say they fucked her better than me. It was impossible. I had her pussy trained to come on command. It was mine and mine alone. At that moment, deep inside her pussy was where I wanted to be.

I vaguely heard my name being called before a tug of my arm knocked me back into reality.

"Here," Sadee stated, passing me my phone. "Thank you."

"Yep."

After ashing the tip of the blunt in my hand, I took a hard pull. A thin cloud of smoke filled the confined space. Nova turned up her nose and attempted to fan the smoke away. Opening my mouth, I blew a steady stream in her face.

"Why would you do that?" she huffed. "That shit stinks."

"That's how you know it's good," I countered, blowing more smoke in her direction.

"Stop! Damn. You're such an asshole."

"Nah, that's Drako."

"Well, it's rubbing off on you. I'm not trying to go home smelling like I work in a dispensary."

"Why not? It smells better than that shit you got on."

"You're crazy. Ky only buys me the best and you know it."

"The best from where? Target? Ain't that where you work?"

"Ain't nothing wrong with Target."

"You must've used your employee discount. Was that shit on clearance?" Watching her face redden in frustration, I laughed in response. "Yeah, I'm right, ain't I? They couldn't get nobody to buy that shit, so they practically gave it to you for free."

"Fuck you, Ceas."

"You already did, remember? A few times."

"What?!" Sadee exclaimed. "Nova, you fucked your girl's brother? Ain't that some shit. Where's my cup so I can sip this tea?"

"Don't pay him no mind. That was in the past...before I even met Ky."

"Still," Sadee added. "That's crazy. You've been with the sister *and* the brother. That's really keeping it in the family!"

Laughing, I blew more smoke in Nova's face. The fact that she was getting mad only made it that much more funny. She waved it off while grilling me like I was the grimiest nigga alive. There she was, talking all that shit and she couldn't take it being thrown back at her. She could lie and try to downplay what we had, but if I didn't mean shit, she wouldn't have been sitting across from me pouting.

"Aww...Nova," Sadee said, easing forward in her seat. "I know you're not mad. I was just playing with you, friend. Don't be like that."

"Don't apologize to that broad. Let her sit there and have her fuckin' attitude. She ain't stoppin' shit." Turning to Sadee, I asked, "You smoke?"

"I do now."

She took the blunt from my fingers and sucked hard. The tip lit bright orange just as she began to choke. Breaking out in a coughing spell, she handed the blunt back to me.

"Take it easy. This ain't no regular shit."

"I...Know," she coughed, choking after each word. "I...Ain't... New...To...This."

"Girl, you ain't no damn smoker. Stop playin'."

I'd seen Nova enjoy a hit or two with Kyan before, but I damn sure wasn't offering her nothing I had. She tried to act like the medicine keeping me sane was bothering her to no end. If Kyan was in the SUV with us, Nova wouldn't have said shit. Because it was me, she had a problem. Fuck her!

It took a few minutes for Sadee to get her breathing under control. I sat back in my seat and enjoyed the euphoric high that had come over me. When I glanced at Sadee, her eyes were low and bloodshot red. She might not have been new to getting high, but she was definitely new to the quality I kept. The way she stared off into space told me her mind was somewhere else. *That's that good shit*, I thought, taking another hit to the head.

"Uh...are you done riding around the city?" Nova barked. "We weren't trying to go on no damn tour. I already told you Kyan is probably worried."

"I heard you the first time," I responded.

"Well, what's up? Are you gonna take us home?"

"Yeah, when I'm done. You're on my time. You might as well get comfortable. I ain't goin' back that way no time soon."

"You play too damn much, Ceas! I wouldn't have got in the car if I knew you would be on this bullshit. Take me home...now!"

Who the fuck did she think she was talking to? Certainly not me. I didn't give a fuck what she had going on.

"She's right," Sadee added, giggling for no damn reason. "I gotta get somewhere and charge my phone. Allstate is supposed to be sending someone to me in about an hour. I'll just go home with Nova." Glancing in Nova's direction, Sadee continued, "Do you think Kyan will take me to my car?"

Nova nodded, but my attention was on something else. Hearing

Sadee mention Allstate had me thinking about actor Dennis Haysbert reciting his famous line, 'Are you in good hands?' Before I knew it, I was palming my phone, sending my sister a text.

Me: Is your bitch in good hands?

Kyan: What, nigga?

I let some time pass without responding. Kyan blew my phone up with question marks. When I still didn't respond, she hit my line – twice. Each time, I sent her to voicemail before finally giving in and acknowledging her text.

Me: Where's Nova?

Kyan: Idk. She obviously wants problems. She shoulda BEEN home.

Me: I just scooped her nasty ass up. The bitch got an attitude.

Kyan: She ain't seen an attitude yet. Just wait until I see her. I got something for her.

Me: She's right here. Wanna talk to her?

Kyan: Nope. She ain't gonna like what I gotta say.

Me: You gettin in that ass, sis?

Kyan: Deep in that shit.

Me: I'm OMW. I wanna see that shit.

"Tango...change of plans," I called out. "Take this broad home."

"Broad?! Nigga, you got the wrong one. Just wait until I tell Kyan."

We'll see, I thought with a smirk. If only she knew how much shit she was in. Kyan was like a Pitbull, protective of everything she claimed. That included Nova. She liked to know her movements at all times. In a way, she was controlling, but it was for Nova's own good. In our line of work, retaliation was common. If someone couldn't get you, they wouldn't hesitate going for someone you loved. Because of that, Kyan kept Nova on a tight leash.

The ride to Kyan's condo was silent. Nova kept her attitude and I let her be mad. She was only hurting herself. For me, it had been and still was a good day. Nova's antics did nothing to dim my shine. At the end of the day, I was still Ceasar...one-half of the powerhouse running the streets of Birmingham. Nova, well...she was simply a 'kept' bitch. If I were in her shoes, I'd probably be mad too.

Kyan met us outside. Her hair was pulled back and a pair of fresh kicks were laced up on her feet. When the SUV came to a complete stop, she uncrossed her arms and opened my car door with enough force to take it off the hinges.

"Hey, Ceas," she spoke. "Nova, you already know…bring your ass on."

"Kyan, I—"

"I don't wanna hear shit," Kyan cut her off.

After Nova scooted out the door, I followed behind. I had a feeling World War III was about to go down and I wanted a front row seat.

"What are you getting mad at me for?" Nova huffed. "It's his fault!" She pointed to me like I was the culprit. "I would have been here if Ceas hadn't taken the fuckin' scenic route."

"Hold on now," I interrupted, hating how I had been thrown in the mix. "Don't blame that shit on me. You ran up to my car, remember?"

"My car broke down," Sadee announced, causing everyone to look in her direction. "It's my fault. Please, don't take it out on Nova."

"It's nobody's fault," Nova continued. "I'm late…sorry. It's no big deal. It ain't like I have a curfew."

"What the fuck is that supposed to mean?" Kyan grilled her, cocking her head to the side. "So, you think it's cool to stroll in whenever you want? Huh? Is that what we're doin' now?"

"My phon—" Sadee began, but Kyan rudely cut her off.

"I ain't fuckin' talkin' to you!"

"Don't talk to her like that," Nova defended. "She didn't do anything."

"Just like you didn't, right? This ain't no fuckin' game, Nova. When I tell you somethin', you're supposed to listen. You're gonna fuck around and not be allowed to go nowhere at all."

"This is bullshit! I'm not a child, Ky!"

"You're actin' like one."

Proving Kyan's point, Nova stomped off toward the front door. The action I thought I was going to see didn't happen. Sadee and Kyan entered into an awkward staring match, and I felt like the third wheel. Bored, I told my sister I would catch up with her later and climbed back into my ride. I don't know what, or if, the two of them said anything to each other, but they were still standing in the same spot when Tango pulled off.

"Where to now?" he quizzed, opening the partition.

I thought about it for a minute before advising him to take me home. We got halfway to my spot when thoughts of Seven flooded my mind. I missed her. No matter how 'hard' I tried to be, something about her made me soft. I couldn't just walk away after all we had been through. My feelings didn't just stop with her. I bonded with her son. Deuce was my lil' nigga. He wasn't my flesh and blood, but I cared about him like he was.

"Tango," I called, clearing my throat.

"Yes, boss."

"I changed my mind. I wanna see Seven."

"Will do, boss. Am I dropping you off, or waiting out front?"

"I don't know yet. I'll see when I get there."

The answer to that question was up to Seven. I just hoped she was willing to hear what I had to say.

SEVEN

Deuce had fallen asleep on my lap and I dreaded picking his heavy butt up. For him to be five, he had some height and weight on him. He was both bigger and taller than the average five-year-old. I loved that he was a strong, healthy boy, but it was hard when I had to pick him up.

I'd been in my feelings since everything that went down with my parents and Ceas. All that was too much to deal with in one day, so I'd completely shut myself off from everybody. He was the only person in the world who could keep me from going into a depression over some bullshit. I needed him now more than ever.

Joie was there when she could be. She made herself available whenever she had the chance. I was grateful for my friend, but things with her had been off. It raised suspicion in my heart. Since Ceas and Drako's rude asses had a secret meeting with her, Joie's actions were different. I noticed off jump. I didn't want my other problems to cloud my judgment and make me paranoid, so I brushed it off. That only caused the issue to bother me more. I wanted to know what was going on.

My parents reached out to speak to Deuce, but avoided discussing *our* problems. As usual, the same cycle repeated itself. We'd have an altercation and not discuss how we felt. We'd simply let time pass by until we thought things were better. It was unhealthy, but it was the way we handled things. Deep down, I knew we needed to find a resolution. Not only was it unhealthy for us, but it was also unhealthy for Deuce. At the end of the day, his well-being was all I cared about.

Carl was still heavily on my mind. He didn't even deserve to be called by his nickname. My situation with him hurt me the worst. My heart broke when those damaging words escaped his lips. All throughout the day, those same words replayed in my head. I felt my heart tearing more each time. Not only was I pissed with him, but I was pissed with myself too. That's because I knew Carl was right. He spoke nothing but the truth. I knew we hadn't put a label on anything we did. I allowed myself to fall in love, when I shouldn't have.

I laid my head back on the couch and closed my eyes. I freely let the tears seep from the corners of my eyes while I rubbed Deuce's head. *Fuck!* I was so damn tired of crying over Carl. Every day, it was the same cycle and I was tired of wasting my tears on him. It was obvious he didn't give a fuck, so why did I?

Leaning over and swiping a few tissues from the box, I cleaned my face and nose. I placed my attention on watching the rest of *Hotel Transylvania 3*. Deuce loved all three movies, so I was surprised he fell asleep. My baby must have had a long day at school.

Once the movie was over, I tried to wake Deuce up to go use the bathroom, but he was so out of it. Chuckling to myself, I fixed my arms to pick him up when I heard the doorknob jiggle. I froze in place, holding my breath as I listened intently. I heard the sound again, and fear immediately crippled my body. I immediately went into protection' mode. Deuce was everything to me and I couldn't let anything happen to him. Even if I got hurt in the process, I'd give my life to protect his. Carl bought me a small Ruger some time ago, but it was in my bedroom. It didn't do me any good in there.

The front door creaked open. I grabbed the closest thing to me, which happened to be a lamp. Heavy footsteps sounded off the walls, and I knew exactly who it was. The only other person who had a key to my house. The person who broke my heart just a few short days ago.

What the fuck is he doin' here? I questioned myself.

Carl strolled around the corner, led by his enticing cologne and heavy smell of weed. His dark tinted eyes were low and glossy. My body tingled in excitement, and I wanted to jump all over him. I missed him so much, but I refused to give him the satisfaction of knowing. I broke our intense, silent, staring match and attempted to pick Deuce up, but Carl stopped me by swatting my hand away. He took my son in his arms and carried him out of view. Rolling my eyes, I plopped down on the couch and carefully listened as Carl took Deuce to the bathroom before tucking him in his bed.

Seconds later, he walked back in the living room and stared at me. I kept my focus on Netflix, flipping through to see what I wanted to watch before I fell asleep. It wasn't long before Carl snatched the remote out my hand and turned the TV off.

"What the fuck, Carl?!" I griped, sucking my teeth. "Why are you here? You can see your way out."

"I ain't goin' no fuckin' where, Seven. You don't control what I do. I came here to talk, and that's exactly what we're goin' to do," he stated sternly.

A loud, dramatic laugh slipped through my lips and I waved him off.

"I don't have to do shit. I'm my own person, my nigga. I'm not tied down to anyone, so what makes you think you have the right to barge up in here and tell me what you want me to do?"

Carl wet his lower lip with his tongue and sighed. I was getting under his skin, but oh fuckin' well! He clearly established what we were, so I didn't see the problem.

"Watch yo' mouth, Sev. You don't gotta talk, but you *will* listen to what I need to say."

"I don't care what you have to say. You've said enough."

Easing down onto the coffee table across from me, Carl leaned forward and took my hands in his. I tried jerking them away, but he tightened his grip. He demanded that I look at him. I couldn't. I wouldn't. I refused to allow him the satisfaction of seeing how he truly affected me. Just from his touch, I wanted to break down and cry again. I tried to fight my feelings, but eventually I gave in. When he grabbed my chin and forced me to look into his eyes, I cursed myself. My cheeks were stained by my salty tears. Gazing at the man I loved so deeply was harder than I thought. The feelings I had for him weren't mutual. Our relationship had been one-sided. Should I have expected more after keeping things on the low for so long with no title?

"Let me go, please," I whispered, feeling weak.

"No. You're about to hear me out," he instructed, pausing to make sure I was listening.

"What I said was a mistake, Seven. I meant what I said, but it's not how I want things to be. I want you to be my girl. I want us to be exclusive and have a title; whatever y'all females be sayin'."

A lump formed in my throat hearing the sincerity in his tone. I searched his eyes and found truth in his words. It was the first time I'd seen him so vulnerable and outspoken with his feelings. From his actions, it was obvious he had to care about Deuce and I, but when he spazzed out and practically told me I wasn't shit to him, I began to think that I had been reading too much into things. I had to admit, he did do more than the average man would do, but that didn't change the words I heard fall from his lips. I wasn't good enough to claim before. Why did he want things to change now?

"Oh, really? That's not what you were sayin' before, Carl. You blatantly informed me that I was good enough to fuck, but that was it. Why the change of heart?"

"Because, I love yo' stubborn ass, girl. You and Deuce."

Ceas didn't give me time to process his words before crashing his soft, pouty lips into mine. I moaned at the taste of mint gum and weed on his tongue; a flavor I become familiar with. A flavor I craved. He kissed me with intense emotion and passion. I felt all his emotions through that kiss, and I knew he felt mine. His words rang over and over in my ears. I needed to hear him say it again. I needed to know he wasn't playing with my heart. That was something I couldn't handle.

I pulled away from Ceas and gazed at him intently. He looked me up and down before placing a light peck against my lips.

"Do you mean that? Do you truly love me and my son? I..." I paused to get myself together. I was becoming emotional once again. "I can't take another heartbreak, Ceas. The other day, you broke my heart into a million pieces. What you said was true...there was no title, but I felt so much more. I've been in love with you for as long as I can remember. You came in and took on not just me, but my son, too. You did things I never thought a man would do for us. You fucked me up when you blew me off like you did."

Leaning over, he kissed my lips again before answering.

"You answered your own question, Sev. You know me better than any fuckin' body besides Drako and Kyan. Do you think if I didn't love y'all, I would do the things I've done? Exactly. I wouldn't. I look at Deuce as my own. Our bond is on a different level and no matter what, I'm always goin' to be the father he knows. As for yo' hardheaded, stubborn ass, I love yo' dirty ass drawers," he joked, pinching my cheeks. "I ain't never felt this way about any female. I don't know what type of voodoo shit you got over me, but it has me hooked. I apologize for hurtin' yo' feelings, Seven. That was never my intention. I can admit I was bein' a pussy for not admittin' my true feelings from the jump. You pissed me off that day. Still, it's not an excuse."

"And, you don't think I wasn't pissed, Ceas? Matter-of-fact, are you ever goin' to tell me what that lil' meetin' was about?"

"Business, baby. That's all I can say. You ain't spoke to Joie? I thought she would have said somethin' by now."

"No, she hasn't. What do you mean business? Why can't I know, Carl?"

"You gon' get enough of that Carl shit. I don't give a fuck how mad you are. It's Ceas or 'Daddy' when addressin' me," he explained with a deep, sexy scowl. "And, like I said. It's business. You're smart, baby. Use that brain to think about it."

"Whatever."

"You can't be like that. Everything I do is to protect you and Deuce. The less you know, the better. Trust me."

Nodding, I couldn't do anything but take his word for it. I would be picking Joie's brain for information, though. If Ceas was trying to protect me, then I needed to know he was doing the same for my best friend.

"You ain't answer my question. You gon' be my girl, Seven?"

"Of course, Ceas. I wouldn't want it any other way."

We confirmed our commitment with a long, passionate kiss that led to Ceas having me climbing the walls. I moaned as he pleasured my body. Our sex was different. It was the first time Ceas made love to me and had me on cloud nine. He gave me a high I didn't think I'd ever come down from.

After years of messing around on the low, I was finally Ceas' girlfriend. Life couldn't get any better than that.

25

NORIEN

I WAS TIRED of seeing niggas and manly bitches all day. Being locked up like a caged animal was taking its toll. I was in a one-man cell, but still managed to get my ass kicked on the regular. Drako had niggas and COs riding for him to the fullest. My door would conveniently be left unlocked for a random muthafucka to enter. One-on-one, I could usually hold my own, but when niggas were supplied with weapons, I didn't stand a chance.

The last beating I took was the worst. After refusing my dinner tray, my door was opened anyway and two niggas as big as gorillas entered. My body was still sore from my previous encounters, but I fought like hell anyway. I threw a few punches that seemed like taps against their massive frames. One of the niggas paused and glanced at the spot where my fist connected.

"Nigga, what the fuck was that? You hit like a bitch."

Everything was a blur after that. I woke up in medical with two stab wounds to the chest, a dislocated jaw, and enough bruises to have people wondering if I was half Dalmatian. The staff held me hostage on a small stretcher while I recuperated, but my injuries required serious medical attention. The only reason I was sent to the hospital was thanks to an impromptu visit from my public defender, Melvin.

One look at my battered body, and he threatened to implicate the entire staff in a lawsuit. That got everyone's attention. I was escorted to the emergency room and kept overnight.

My injuries weren't life-threatening, but they did require an examination by a medical professional. My dislocated jaw was manipulated back into place while my wounds were cleaned and sutured up. By the morning, my elevated blood pressure had returned to normal and I was sent back to the place I called hell. The only thing that got me through the next couple of days was the pain medicine I was prescribed. I wasn't a pill head on the street, but the way those Percs had me floating in the sky made me want to be one when I got out. I didn't have a care in the world, until the medicine started to wear off and I was reminded of my circumstances. That's when I would call for the nurse and advise her that my pain had reached an unbearable level. I was at that point when I was advised that I had a visitor. Although I wanted my legal high, I wanted to see my two visitors more.

April was a pleasant surprise. Being around niggas and manly COs made me appreciate seeing any woman's face. She sat at a small circular table, holding my sleeping son in her arms. The smile on her face when I appeared in the doorway faded with each step I took. By the time I reached the table, her face was all the way turned up.

"What the hell happened to you?!" she asked, visually examining me from head to toe.

"Jail politics, ma. It's all good. Stand up. Gimme a hug."

"No contact," the CO warned, reminding me that I had been escorted into the room.

For some reason, I was viewed as a threat, limiting the amount of contact I had with others. I was the only muthafucka in the room handcuffed to the damn table, but instead of complaining, I just went with it.

"Is all that necessary?" April challenged, shooting daggers at the CO with her eyes. "Where can he go?"

"If you want to continue your visit, I would advise you to be quiet," the CO spat. He checked to make sure the handcuffs were secure before walking toward the other side of the room.

"It's all good," I stated, smiling as best I could. The pain in my jaw was intense, but I refused to let it interfere with my visit.

"No, it's not. Look at you. You look like shit."

I wasn't the only one. Dark, heavy bags occupied the space under April's eyes. Worry lines formed in the middle of her forehead. Her glossy, reddened eyes told me she had been crying. But why?

"Talk to me," I advised, glancing down at my son sleeping peacefully against his mother's breast. "How you holdin' up?"

"How do you think?" she challenged, fighting back tears. "It's hard out here, Norien. Really hard. I can't even afford Damien's Pull-ups. He got on underwear right now and I pray to God he doesn't pee on me. They wouldn't let me bring in an extra pair of clothes."

"Yeah, they're strict about that shit," I mentioned. "It'll be a'ight. I'ma find a way to get out of this shit. Just watch. Everything's gon' be straight."

"How can you be so sure?"

"Trust me. I just know."

"Well, knowing doesn't pay the bills. How the hell am I supposed to get by? I'm broke, Norien. I don't have anybody to turn to. You should see the stack of mail waiting for me...nothing but bills." Sniffling, she continued. "I had to keep Damien home from daycare this week. They said I didn't pay last week and in order to bring him back, I have to catch up both weeks, plus two additional. That's a whole fuckin' month!"

"It won't hurt him to sit out a few days," I told her, raising my voice to emphasize my point. "You ain't doin' nothin'. You can watch yo' son."

"*Our* son," she corrected. "He's just as much yours as he is mine."

I shoulda waited on my pills, I thought, sighing loudly. I knew Damien was mine. That wasn't the issue. I was trying to get her to understand that with me being locked up, daycare was an unnecessary expense.

"I know he's mine," I growled. "That's not what I'm sayin'."

"Well, what are you sayin'? Because right now, I'm hearin' a whole lot of nothin'!"

If my hands weren't chained to the table, I would have went upside her head. Even without money, she was in a better predicament than me. Hell, I was broke too! Just as quick as the money came in, I was spending it. Thousands of dollars were thrown away on bullshit. I didn't even have nothing to show for the amount of money that passed through my fingers. On top of that, I was missing out on money and had to watch my back at every turn. She wasn't the one who had to pee and shit in the same room she laid her head. No, she got to lay on a firm mattress big enough for her to roll around. I was tired of hearing her complaining. We were both fucked up, but I had it ten times worse.

"Look!" I belted out in frustration. Seeing heads turned my way caused me to lower my voice to just above a whisper. "I'm workin' on some shit, a'ight. Gimme a few weeks. Everything's—"

"A few weeks!" This time, it was April raising her voice. Damien's eyes shot open as he glanced around in confusion. "It's okay, baby," April softly spoke. "Mommy's sorry."

Damien's eyes fell shut just as quickly as they opened. I waited until he was snoring softly before I continued.

"Right now, you ain't got a fuckin' choice," I stated sternly. "My back's against the fuckin' wall. I owe people. Until that debt is paid, I won't have shit." Licking my lips, I glanced around the room. Everyone seemed to be enjoying their visit but me. Why did April have to make things so difficult? Continuing, I leaned further into the table. "I got shit in motion as we speak. Joie's out there—"

"Joie? Really? Don't speak that bitch's name to me. Fuck Joie!"

The conviction in her voice surprised me. I knew she wanted to take Joie's place, but she had never spazzed out like that. "You can chill with that noise. You already know what it is."

"Like I said…fuck her! I'm over here struggling, and that bitch be eating good at *Pappadeaux*."

"What the fuck are you talkin' about?"

"Oh, you didn't know? That's your girl, right?" April smirked. "She was havin' a good ol' time. Her and some nigga was there."

"I don't believe that shit."

April's jealousy was at an all-time high. I never thought she would sit back and lie to my face. Joie would never entertain another nigga. She was loyal to the core. April was just hatin'.

"Believe what you want. I know what I saw. She was there with a dude. Trust me when I tell you that nigga looked like money. He had dreads...long dreads..."

My nostrils flared as a single name came to mind. *Drako.*

The single pill I took did nothing for me. I was supposed to be flying with the birds. Instead, I was stuck staring at the ceiling, wondering what the fuck was really going on. Thankfully, I wouldn't have to wait too long. While getting my medication, I conned the nurse into letting me use her cell phone. Turns out, she enjoyed Percs just as much as I did. In exchange for one of mine, I was able to call and talk to Joie. It turns out, she never got a call from Melvin. She agreed to come and see me. Two days later, she did.

Once again, I was handcuffed to the table. I didn't give Joie a chance to ask why I looked as bad as I did. I already knew she wasn't used to seeing me looking so rough. That wasn't the issue. I needed to know if she was holding up her end of the bargain.

"Everything cool?" I asked, trying to pick her brain for information.

"What do you think?" Leaning into the table, she continued. "I'm out here doing your dirty work. Of course, everything's not cool."

I examined her demeanor. She sat with her legs together and her arms crossed in front of her chest. She wore a pair of jeans that hugged her tightly. If she had more hips and ass, she would have been forced to change. Even though her natural beauty was evident to anyone with a pair of eyes, the scowl on her face told me she meant business.

"What's Ceasar been havin' you doin'?"

"Ceasar doesn't have me doing shit. It's Drako."

"Yeah, I figured that," I smirked. "From what I hear, he's havin' you doin' way more than what the job entails."

Offended, she turned up her nose. "And what's that supposed to mean?"

"Shit, you tell me. How was *Pappadeaux*?"

Guilt spread across her face. "How did you know about that?"

"I'm locked up, Joie. Not dead. I still have my ways of findin' shit out. Just know everything you do eventually gets back to me." Pausing briefly, I cleared my throat. "So, what's up? Anything you wanna tell me?"

"No."

"You sure about that? You fuckin' around on me Joie?"

"No! It was only dinner, damn. It wasn't like that. You're making a big deal out of nothing."

"That's all it better have been. I don't trust that nigga. I knew it was a reason he wanted you instead of Apr—"

"Who?"

"Nothing." Inwardly, I kicked myself for slipping. I needed to be more careful with my words.

"No, you were gonna say something. What was it?"

"You heard what I said, now drop it."

"I ain't dropping nothing."

Joie wasn't the confrontational type, but the way she rolled her neck and sucked her teeth told me she had more to say. That wasn't like her. She was turning into a different person right before my eyes.

"What's gotten into you? Huh? You been hangin' around that nigga too long? He got you forgettin' who the fuck you talkin' to?"

"Whatever, Norien. Is that all you wanted? I got shit to do."

Now, I was positive something was going on. Joie was feeling herself. Whatever she'd been doing in the streets gave her confidence that I had never seen before. I didn't like that shit at all.

"You're gonna sit here and listen to what I gotta say."

"A'ight, then…talk. Just remember, I got a job to do. Time is money and right now, my time is being wasted."

"You sound just like that nigga," I barked, leaning forward in my seat. "You really lettin' that nigga get in your ear? He prolly got you out there doin' all kind of shit."

"You got issues. I'm my own person. Nobody controls me."

"I control you!" I was hot. I didn't care that all eyes were on me. I had a point to prove. "You do what the fuck I say, and nobody else."

"Will you lower your voice?" she whispered. "You're making a scene."

"Man, fuck these niggas in here. I don't care. Your loyalty should be to me."

"So, you're saying I ain't loyal?" she asked, keeping her voice low. "Where's that coming from? If that were the case, I wouldn't be out here risking my life *and* freedom for you. You can go on somewhere with that bullshit. I know where my loyalty lies."

"Oh, yeah?" I challenged, nodding my head as an idea came to mind. "Prove it."

"How?"

"Find out where he keeps his shit. I want to know addresses, how many niggas hang around, everything. Knowing him, there's probably a few spots. I wanna know 'em all. Next time you come see me, I want a list."

"For what?"

"Just do what I said."

"But why?"

She was starting to get on my nerves. She asked too many damn questions when the answer should have been obvious. "Why do you think? I'm tryin' to get out this bitch."

"How's an address gonna help you do that?"

"Use your head, Joie. Think about it. You give me the location, and I'ma have that muthafucka robbed. It's that simple. I'll see you in a few days. Yo, guard! I'm ready."

"Wait!" she called out. "But…what if…"

"Time is money, remember? Right now, you're wastin' time."

CONNECT WITH DEEANN

Website: http://www.iamdeeann.com
Facebook Author Page: http://bit.ly/DeeAnnFacebook
Reading group: http://bit.ly/DeeAnnsReadersDen
Twitter: http://bit.ly/DeeAnnTwitter
Instagram: http://bit.ly/DeeAnnIG
Email: iam.authordeeann@gmail.com

CONNECT WITH KEISHA ELLE

Website: www.keishaelle.com
Facebook Author Page: www.facebook.com/AuthorKeishaElle
Facebook Reading Group: www.facebook.com/groups/kickinitwithkeisha
Twitter: www.twitter.com/keisha_elle
Instagram: www.instagram.com/keisha_writes
Email: keisha.elle@yahoo.com

COMING TOMORROW

CPSIA information can be obtained
at www.ICGtesting.com
Printed in the USA
LVHW052301070319
609866LV00003B/383/P

9 781797 732107